LEGACY WITCHES

Hello, lovely reader!

Thank you so much for picking up Legacy Witches, but before you proceed, I want you to know that this is a gritty story, very rated R. It deals with murder, gore, violence, old-fashioned beliefs, and characters who have a lot of growing to do. There is a diverse cast in this book and not all characters handle that well. There is parenting gone wrong and lots of self-defense in various forms. BUT, I want you to know there are many moments of goodness and laughter, there are lessons learned, and there is hope. I want every reader healthy and happy and if the grit is too much, I understand. If this warning hasn't scared you off, happy reading!

To my boisterous father, whose love and support have always been louder than my inner demons. Stay loud, Dad.

And to my stubborn husband, who believes in me more than I do. I love you.

LEGACY WITCHES

CASS KAY

I

Welcome Home

Leaves rustled in the tree where Grandma Susannah hung. The hem of her brown peasant dress swayed with her legs as she swung backward, then forward, making the branch bow before the tip of her pointed boot hit the trunk. *Rustle. Creak. Tap.*

Vianna Roots sat in her rusted Ford parked in the driveway, windows down from the pre-dawn drive, jaw clenched, focusing on her childhood home instead of the ghost of her twelfth-great-grandmother that swayed in her peripheral vision. Her gut tightened, and she rubbed her eyes. No one could escape their family forever. That was truer for her than most, since she was the only one in her family who could see the dead. A gift she'd give anything to give back. Thanks, but no thanks.

Ten years had passed since climbing out her bedroom window in the middle of the night, and although she was no longer a teenager, the dark two-story house hadn't changed. The family home had passed down through their line since the 1700s, the numerous add-ons highlighted by mismatched windows of various sizes and shapes.

The crack in her windshield kept her focus as she avoided the inevitable. Her mother was dead and her burial scheduled for tomorrow—technically today since the sun was rising—making Vianna the last legacy witch in the Roots line. Which meant this house of horrors was now hers. She rubbed her palms against her thighs to chase away the goosebumps.

"Ghosts can't hurt you." She was an adult now, one who faced her fears instead of jumping out of windows. She bounced her knee up and down.

Sleeping in her truck felt like a reasonable alternative to sleeping in the house. She could also just turn around and drive back to Boston, leave Salem in the past where it belonged and let whatever or whoever deal with the haunted property. The forty bucks in her pocket wasn't enough for a hotel room and food, but it was enough for gas.

Her eyes veered from the cracked windshield back to the monstrosity of memories shaped like a house. With a sprawling wraparound porch, large mullioned bay windows, charcoal shingles, and pointed steeples of various heights, it was impossible not to notice. If she cleaned the place up, she'd make a buck, and it'd become someone else's haunted problem.

The shadows of branches reached across the lawn like fingers as sunlight spilled over the horizon. The vivid apparition of Grandma no longer swayed in the branches, leaving only the scent of mothballs and apples on the breeze. Ghosts had a habit of coming and going as they pleased.

Despite how much Vianna would rather skip the ceremony, that wasn't an option, so she needed to get ready. Inside the house was her only hope for proper ceremonial robes worn at a legacy witch's burial. Time to go inside.

When she shoved the rusted truck door open, it squeaked loudly enough to announce her presence to the row of houses, each passed down through families of witches just like hers. This neighborhood was coven territory. Luckily, witches weren't known to be early risers, so gawking eyes wouldn't be watching from the windows. Not just yet, anyway.

The same web of cracks covered the pavement, and she reached into the truck bed for her worn duffel. As she did, a handle caught on the lip, and the nylon tore. Clothes spilled out in a heap, most of them managing to land in a sludge-filled crack in the driveway. She groaned and sighed at the moon.

She kicked the pile, and a T-shirt flew against her Ford. "Curse the goddess."

With a sigh of defeat, she bent to gather the meager pile that contained most of her belongings. A low rumble from behind made her freeze. There was no point in turning around because nothing would be there. As a child, she'd explained away the grumbles and moans as an old house shifting with age and weather, but planks of wood didn't growl. And they especially didn't lock doors or hide things when a child misbehaved. This time, however, she wasn't a child to be scolded.

"Hush," she grumbled back.

Piling her clothes into a heap on the ripped duffel, she used the ruined bag as a sling to carry the load and headed toward the front door. Stepping-stones led beneath a rusted archway covered in wisteria. The weeds that laced through the wrought iron fence were the size of bushes, and her fingertips twitched at the urge to pull them. Instead, she shoved her hands into the pockets of her jean shorts.

A soft morning breeze sent goosebumps up her legs as she bound up the porch stairs. She tucked the ball of clothes against her stomach and pulled a rusted skeleton key from her pocket. When she slid the key into the old lock and tried to turn it, expecting the familiar *click*, the key wouldn't budge.

She grimaced and stepped back, leaving the stuck key in the lock. "You're not going to let me in?"

The house spat the key onto the weathered porch, where it landed with a fat *thwack* and she clenched her fists. Dropping her belongings at her feet, she kicked at the door. "Yeah, well, I don't want you either, but I'm all you've got."

Somewhere along twelve generations of Roots witches, the family familiar and demon had melded with the house. Now, because of nothing more than her birthright, Vianna possessed the passed-down heirloom. He seemed as pleased about the arrangement as she was.

She took a few deep breaths and started pacing the porch, considering her options, when her flip-flop caught on splintered wood. She stumbled forward, flinging her hand to the banister and lodging a sliver into her palm. Straightening herself, she tried to pull the wooden prick out of her skin, but it just wedged deeper. More deep breaths.

The porch swing blocked the main windows that lined the front of the house, so she went to the far edge of the porch and smeared a spot of dirt away from the edge of the window to see inside. The sitting room soaked up the rising sun, highlighting the same old-as-balls antique furniture she remembered from her childhood.

If the front door wouldn't budge, fine. She'd climb in through the window. Wedging her fingers beneath the seam of the frame, she yanked upward. Three of her fingernails cracked backward, and she yelped, bouncing on the balls of her feet and flapping her hands as if the movement would ease the pain.

"Mother of Satan," she yelled at the house. Yellow birds chirped their taunts from the trees, and she glared at them before continuing her pacing.

"She'll be pissed if I show up at her funeral looking like this," she said to the family demon, motioning to her crumpled T-shirt with a coffee stain. The drive had been too early for dexterity. "You know if anyone can make you miserable from the grave, it's her." Familiars were demons, but Mother was Mother.

Her fingers caught in the tangles of her dark hair as she forced it into a knot on top of her head. There wasn't any time for games. She needed those ceremonial robes. She was getting inside. Now.

Something heavy smacked her between her shoulder blades, then plopped onto the wooden porch. She gave a sad little squeak and spun around, looking down at the black beady eyes of a dead blue-bird. With a deep breath, she turned back toward the house. "Kinda predictable, don't you think?"

The possessed house had a standard set of antics that clearly hadn't changed in her absence. The ammunition varied: a bird, a frog, or a mouse, and always spit from the rain gutters. With narrowed eyes, she stepped over the dead bird and marched toward the side gate. The back door had a latch problem, and since nothing else about the place had changed, she was counting on consistency. In a hurry to act before the house caught on, she darted down the stairs and around to the side gate. Grabbing hold of the handle, she ran face-first into wood.

The house had jammed the gate door.

"Funny," she growled.

With a strong hip bump, the gate relented, and she burst into the backyard. Thick piles of mulch from seasons of neglect piled against the fence, and rose bushes drooped in a lopsided slant with wilted, unpruned heads. Mother never had been much of a gardener, making it Vianna's childhood job. But she didn't mind, because it was one of the few places she found peace and solitude.

She felt a sharp pang in her chest at the sight of the garden. The feeling had nothing to do with personal attachment; this was business. Real estate was worth more with a healthy landscape. Grass crunched beneath her feet as she noticed the bare branches of the apple and cherry trees. Trumpet and creeper vines strangled the shed on the east side, patches of wilted sunflowers sprouted wherever they saw fit, and deep green berry vines overwhelmed the full west corner. Although unattended, life thrived.

A faint screech sounded only moments before a stream of water blasted her chest, then face, knocking her backward. She squealed and turned her back to the attack, knowing exactly where it was coming from. This wasn't her first impromptu outdoor shower from the hose cart that sat on the deck next to the faucet. She'd learned in her teens to tie a knot in the hose as a precaution.

"Really, no new tricks? This is the best you've got?"

Water pelted her back as she walked backward, making her way up the porch steps. The stream ratcheted up her T-shirt and sent a waterfall of hair over her face. When she was close enough, she reached around, grabbed the hose, and yanked. With her foot on the squirming rubber snake, she cinched a knot, and the water stopped.

Her sigh came out as a wet raspberry. She wanted to be mad, and she was, but there was also a comfort in familiarity—even if it came from a demon house—though she'd never encourage him by saying the words aloud. She brushed wet strands of hair off her face then pulled open the patio screen door. The hinges splintered from the frame. The screen fell toward her as she half threw, half kicked it to the side, and it slipped to the porch with a crash.

Straightening, and refusing to make an even louder show for the neighbors, she pulled the suctioned wet shirt from her skin. With both hands on the knob, she lifted up and out, then jiggled. When the lock didn't release, she bumped the door with her knee. *Click.* It slid open and a rank puff of air rolled out.

She waved her hand in front of her nose and choked back a cough.

"Your appearance mirrors horse dung." Grandma Susannah now stood in the kitchen with her arms folded over the cut noose that hung from her neck like a twisted fashion statement. A violet hue tinted her lips and matched the bruising around her neck.

Vianna wasn't sure how long her body had hung after they killed her, but she suspected overnight, and judging by the bluish-purple coloring, maybe during winter. "You're looking dead as ever, Grandmother."

"Your hair looks like an owl in an ivy bush," Grandma croaked, like the old toads that burrowed into the garden beds. "And you're just as mouthy as when you left."

"Probably more so."

Vianna took a deep breath and stepped through the ghost, not surprised by the chill that raced over her skin. The kitchen looked exactly the same as the day she left. A large wooden block island sat in the middle of the room, with a small table and four mismatched chairs in the corner. An iron tea kettle with the same scratch down the side still sat on the stove, and out of habit, she filled it in the sink and set it back on the burner.

"Retrieve your rubbish from the porch at once. I will not have you tarnishing the Roots family appearance for our neighbors to see. If you must be an ungrateful mess, do so in the privy of your own company," Grandma croaked from behind her.

Vianna went to the nearest window to let in some fresh air, but the paint-chipped frame behind the sink wouldn't budge. She smacked the edge with her fist, then gave it another good shove, and it cracked open. The gasp of cool air wasn't enough to clear the cobwebs of memories, but it helped with the smell.

She shuffled around in the junk drawer filled with its namesake, pushing aside sticks of charcoal, crumpled sticky notes, garden twine, and an old pin cushion until she found a pair of tweezers for the splinter in her palm. Grandma Susannah clicked her tongue from the archway, but a lifetime of practice made ignoring ghosts second nature for Vianna.

After tugging the splinter from her palm, she turned and, this time, stepped around her grandmother before striding into the sitting room. Dust covered the antique furniture, and the worn spots on the red oriental rugs were just as she remembered them. Mother'd had a thing for antiques, and she'd added a set of velvet wingback chairs and an ornate table by the bay windows. A large gold fainting couch stretched over the main rug, kitty-cornered to Mother's embroidery chair, butted up close to the hearth.

Rows of framed black-and-white photos of witches past lined the fireplace mantel. Growing up, she'd always felt like they were watching her, and that feeling hadn't faded. With deep breaths, she counted to five and let her heart calm. Time wasn't frozen. She was no longer a child trapped in a demon house. Her blood-witch mother wasn't watching her, tapping a whipping rod against her palm in an even tempo. Vianna was a grown-ass woman. She'd built a new life for herself in Boston. The house may not have changed, but she had.

A shower and fresh clothes for the funeral were next, and those were upstairs. First, she unbolted the front door and scooped up her wrinkled belongings, keeping half her body in the house just in case the demon tried anything again. She used her hip to close the door and headed upstairs, skipping over the third step out of habit because the creak always drew Mother's attention.

The hallway at the top of the stairs had four closed doors, but it was the porcelain doorknob at the end of the hall that stole her attention. As a child, she'd been forbidden from Mother's room, but rules died with their enforcer.

"You look daft when you gawk like that," Grandma said from beside her.

Vianna's legs felt like sacks of compost, and her sandals sunk into the thick threads of the narrow rug with every dragged step. She shifted the bundle of clothes into one arm, then wiped her free palm against her shorts. The porcelain knob twisted easily, and the door swung open. Hot garlic flooded her senses. She gagged as she stumbled backward and dropped her clothes to the floor.

"Rotting hell," she barked between coughs.

"Garlic heals ailments, you worthless waste of good blood," Grandma said.

"Guess it didn't work out so well." She pressed the back of her hand beneath her nose. Mother had died of a heart attack in her sleep, and no amount of garlic was going to prevent that.

For once, it wasn't fear of her mother that made her hesitate, because Vianna knew Mother's ghost wouldn't be in the room. The freshly dead lacked the awareness to move beyond their corpse. Eventually they moved on to replaying their last moments in what Vianna called death cycles. Ghosts caught in their own death cycles made up a large chunk of what she saw when it came to paranormal activity. The rare ghosts who were aware of the living, or could haunt a place or object, were decades old.

Since Mother was a fresh ghost, she was safely tucked into the graveyard—for now. Of all the ghosts that roamed the world, her mother following her around was the only one that made her break out into a cold sweat. Preventing that outcome was her number one goal in life and the only thing that could have dragged her back to Salem.

Vianna marched across the room and yanked open the window. A gentle breeze brushed against her face and rustled loose strands of still-wet hair. She needed more than a slight breeze if she wanted to kick the stench. The house was ancient and didn't have central air, so Mother kept fans tucked into every bedroom closet. Vianna wrestled past the shoes and fallen clothes that cluttered the floor of the walk-in closet, retrieved the fan, and plugged it in by the door so the blades would suck air from the hallway and blow the repulsive odor out the open window.

There wouldn't be a scrap of cloth in the house that wasn't garlic-saturated. Sack-shaped gray dresses hung in the closet alongside long, dark robes. There'd be dozens of covens and crowds of witches all in the same velvet folds, and suddenly the idea of pretending to be one of them made her insides shrivel. She'd never joined a coven for good reason. Coven rules, traditions, this house, and mostly her mother were things she'd promised herself to stay away from.

A garment stood out from the others, and her fingertips ran down the side seam of the red fabric. The dress was her size, sleeveless, high neck, and midcalf. A final farewell to her mother in something so inappropriate felt right. She was different from the other witches, and everyone knew it. There was no point in pretending otherwise.

This afternoon, she'd face the entire witch community, but it was her mother's coven—the one she'd denied when she disappeared in the middle of the night—that struck fear into all the others. The Original Blood Coven was the death squad, killers for hire. Would they want revenge for her defection? And if they didn't, would her mother's ghost? The dress crumpled in her fist as she pulled it from the hanger.

Blood red was the perfect color.

2

Unmarked Roads

The shower was warmish and did the job, but her muscles remained in knots. Old soap washed from her hair and down her back in mushed clumps. Almond oil was the principal ingredient, if the smell was any indicator, which was great for skin but stunted follicle growth. Details mattered, but Mom had bothered with beauty products as often as she did gardening. Not bringing her own supplies, as meager as they were, had been a mistake.

The freestanding claw-foot tub felt smaller than when she was a child, but the checkered black-and-white tiles provided the familiar blurred-out backdrop as she focused on compiling a mental list of things to get done. When she reached down to turn the water off, a man's plump, ruddy face stared up at her from around the edge of the shower curtain.

Vianna backpedaled, splashing water into her own eye. She plastered her calves against the tub and smacked her back against the cold tiles. The man's giant mouth fell open and his eyes widened before he pulled away. Her chest heaved as she stared at the clouded shower curtain. With a shaking hand, she reached out and dragged it to the side.

A hulking man in mud-crusted overalls held his arm up to fend off a blow before a cut sliced open the skin of his forearm. Blood splattered across the white sink and framed mirror on the wall. She didn't let go of the shower curtain, squeezing it tightly.

"Just a ghost," she whispered to herself.

He continued to relive his death, pushing away, stumbling backward, then another gash sliced across his shoulder. The extra skin that hung from his cheeks shook with his head, and his eyes were wide as something, someone, came at him. Vianna could only see the struggles of the dead, not their attackers. There was no warning for her of what was to come, no wind-up or swing. Suddenly, scissors protruded from his right eye socket. He slumped against the wall, slid to the floor—blood smeared down the wainscoting from his descent—and then went still.

They stood that way for a few minutes, the motionless ghost on the floor and Vianna gripping the shower curtain, until he finally faded into a fog that slipped into the floorboards. She reached out her trembling fingers and yanked the towel from the rack before the ghost reappeared. The fabric was stiff under her grip, and she dropped it with a scrunched nose. Crunchy garlic towels were a hard pass. Wrapping her arms around herself, she stepped out of the bathtub and jogged from the bathroom, dripping water as she went.

Grandma Susannah stood in the doorway to the bedroom, leering at Vianna as she grabbed a T-shirt from the hallway floor and dried off her hair, then grabbed another to pull over her head.

"You've gained pounds around the waist. You must further the line before you completely let yourself go."

Nothing got past Grandma. "What's with the new ghost in the bathroom? He has scissors in his eye socket."

That wasn't Mother's style. She preferred embroidery needles soaked in a variety of poisons, not a remake of some knife-wielding slasher movie.

"Earl? He's a pervert. All men are." Grandma only tolerated females. White ones. And only witches. Anything "other" was of the devil. "After you skittered off in the middle of the night, your mother hired him to help out, disposing of unwanted things and the like." Grandma shrugged. "He behaved inappropriately, peeking at things he had no business seeing."

Mother would have claimed she'd made the world a better place. Was it wrong to kill if it saved others? Vianna didn't know, but hexes, torture, and murder never settled well with her, regardless of whatever justification was used. She wasn't sure if she was born with some defective moral thread her ancestors lacked or if her aversion to killing was simply a fear of creating more ghosts that would inevitably haunt her.

She jogged downstairs to the laundry room beneath the stairs to switch the load she'd started before her shower. Halfway through emptying the washer, a water faucet turned on. She paused, tilting her ear to identify where the noise came from. The water stopped. She finished loading the dryer, then stepped into the hallway. To her right was a hallway with doors, but to her left was the kitchen archway and a powder room just beyond, both with faucets.

The floorboards were unnaturally cold against her bare feet as she walked. The kettle was on the stove and the chairs at the table, everything in its place. She almost expected her breath to come out in white clouds, but all was normal, and she moved on to the powder room. She pushed open the cracked door, slowly inching in, but all was still inside. No water turned on, just a simple washroom with a toilet and sink. She turned to go upstairs when a figure with blond hair flashed across the large mirror.

Vianna froze. With deep, steady breaths, her chest rose and fell.

A faint sound bounced between the walls, maybe crying. Her

shoulders tensed, and she looked around, but nothing more came. Silence settled, and the stillness returned.

The brief flash in the mirror was too fast to make out, or it should have been, but the figure *had* looked like someone she knew. It'd been a long time, but the petite features looked like Nancy's.

Vianna hadn't spoken to her childhood friend since she'd left Salem. The figure couldn't be Nancy, though, because she wasn't dead. Vianna had even missed a phone call from her a few months ago. Nancy was the only person from Salem who knew where Vianna was or how to get a hold of her. Vianna had meant to call her back, or she'd at least thought about it. But when the biggest update about her life was her promotion to lead shelf stocker at the Craft Barn, it didn't put Vianna in a boastful mood.

It might not be crazy glamorous, but the Craft Barn had great discounts for employees, so Vianna could slowly build her inventory for the candle and soap boutique she was going to open one day. As far as she was concerned, being a shelf stocker was better than being an assassin witch protégé. She was choosing her own path.

The mirror was void of the mystery figure. The only person looking back was Vianna's own wide eyes, rumpled clothes, and wet hair. Her memories of the past were merging with the ghosts she saw. Or maybe she just needed to get a good night's sleep.

Shaking her head brought a chill that ran over her skin, and she headed upstairs to sort out her sleeping situation. A peek in the guest room confirmed it was still barren from when Mother had burned the mattress in the backyard after discovering a bed-bug infestation from a visiting witch. No more mattress meant no more ability to house guests for the coven.

The door to her childhood bedroom would remain closed—that was a Pandora's box she wasn't ready for. So that left the garlic palace. As the dryer rumbled beneath the stairs, Vianna armed herself with a roll of trash bags. The smell wasn't coming out, and she wanted nothing of Mother's anyway, so she bagged the bedding, the clothes in the drawers, and the rugs.

An exorbitant number of garlic cloves and braided charms—that seemed excessive for just healing an ailment—were wedged into the doorframes and windowsills. The placement looked like a ward to deflect negative energies. Maybe it had been; Mother could have easily picked up a few unfriendly fans over the years. Vianna cleared everything out, certain that the biggest threat of negative energy was about to be buried in the cemetery.

With the drawers empty, she unpacked her meager belongings, only filling one drawer. She slipped chunks of soap between clothing to help with the lingering smell. After the funeral, she'd burn some palo santo in a good smudging to disperse the crawling discomfort she couldn't shake.

By the time she finished sorting through the house, it was almost time for the burial to begin. Her meager supplies of makeup were spread over Mother's vanity as she stared in the mirror. There was no secret spell to get rid of the bags that hung below her eyes, and eyeliner and lip color only shifted the focus.

"Are you trying to give the pickthanks a show? You look like a whore," Grandma huffed. She turned her back to Vianna from the doorway.

Living in the 1600s meant makeup in any form turned a woman into a call girl, but Vianna had learned long ago to ignore her complaints. She snapped her eyeshadow case shut and slipped on the dress she'd retrieved from the dryer.

"That color is not appropriate for your mother's funeral," Grandma screeched. "You will taint the family name."

"One can only hope." Vianna pulled the zipper up her back.

Grandma Susannah crossed her arms over her stain-ridden apron that layered her peasant dress. With a quick intake of breath, Vianna walked through her, then marched down the hall and stairs. She grabbed her keys and left the house before she had time to question her own sanity in facing a Legacy Cemetery filled with witches, both dead and alive.

Her red Ford grumbled to life with a turn of the key. It shouldn't matter what anyone in Salem thought, but a tinge of embarrassment slithered its way through her mind when she thought of the looks she'd get when pulling up to the cemetery. This coven, all the covens, these witches, their families—they all thought she wouldn't amount to anything, and arriving in a rusted-out truck wearing a hand-me-down cocktail dress wasn't exactly proving anyone wrong. After putting the truck in reverse, she backed out before she lost all nerve. She'd show up in a red dress and matching lipstick. Screw 'em.

Every streetlight, stop sign, and run-down gas station tucked between looming historic brick buildings was exactly as she remembered. The rattling, bumpy roads felt as historic as the town—or maybe that was just her old truck. As she drove further, large trees replaced the brick and mortar, and cracked asphalt morphed into an old dirt road. The Legacy Cemetery lay deep in the Salem Woods on the outskirts of town.

She passed the more common road that led to the main hiking path where her elementary class had gone for field trips to observe the birds and learn the names of the trees. She'd always snuck off with Nancy to forage seeds for the garden instead. With her window down, the wind blew in the cleansing scent of pine and damp moss, and it made her grin. As little girls, they'd made crowns from the moss-covered branches.

A stab of guilt over not calling her back hit Vianna. She'd look for her after the burial and they could catch up. She was still reminiscing over the trees when she took the turn around a patch of forest pines, and she didn't see the parked truck until it was too late.

She slammed on the brakes, but it didn't matter. Her back tires skid against the loose gravel, she fishtailed to a stop, and the front of her truck clipped the tailgate of a shiny blue Chevy, her head slamming into the steering wheel.

"Ugh," she groaned as she gingerly touched the swelling bump on her forehead.

Luckily, there were no other cars coming in either direction. Putting her Ford in reverse, she backed away from the blue Chevy and then pulled onto the side of the road and got out. The summer air was muggy against her skin as she approached the blue truck. It was empty, with only a few loose folders on the passenger seat and a baseball cap with SPD stitched into the fabric.

She had somewhere to be and didn't have time to search out the truck owner. She should probably leave a note, but she didn't have insurance, and the scratch on the tailgate was minimal—barely anything. Maybe they wouldn't even notice. Her Ford, however, was unscathed, or maybe it was just that the rusted dents masked any new additions. She couldn't quite tell.

"Everything all right?"

She twirled to see a clean-cut, well-built, Black man approach from the tree line a few yards from the road. He had a pack slung over broad shoulders and a strong stride. Everything about him said determined and confident—and hot. There went the possibility of avoiding swapping information. He stopped a couple feet from her, his brows dropping beneath his aviator glasses, and his head cocked to the side as he looked at what was clearly his truck.

"I'm Grayson." He didn't hold out his hand in greeting, but folded his arms over a dark T-shirt. "Looks like we need to exchange insurance information."

Of course he would be a rule follower, because her luck worked like that.

"It's barely a scratch." She gestured toward the bumper, but his scowl made it clear that her argument wouldn't work. "I don't have insurance, and I'd rather not get the cops involved."

Not involving the cops in any situation was rule number one for witches. They had a long history that went back to the witch trials, where several witches shared the same fate as Grandma Susannah.

Grayson reached around to his pack and pulled out a leather wallet. He flipped a detective badge at her, and she wanted to melt into the ground.

He walked past her to the truck and let down the tailgate to set his bag on it. "Let's just exchange numbers, then. I'll let you know what the bill is for the damage."

How she was going to pay for anything was a mystery, but she nodded and took the pen and paper he held out, writing down her name and number. He exchanged a card that had the same SPD as the hat, Salem Police Department.

"Vianna Roots?" Grayson took off his sunglasses, staring down at her. Some people had a sort of empty stare, where they looked, but she wasn't sure if they really saw. His eyes were the opposite, noticing every single detail. "Busy day for you."

That earned a scowl. She folded her arms and looked back toward the woods he'd emerged from. "What are you doing out here, anyway? Officer..." She looked down at his card. "Elliott."

There was an unspoken arrangement between police and witches that each would avoid certain areas of town. Cops didn't patrol legacy neighborhoods, just like they drove around the Salem Woods, not through them.

He zipped up his bag and tossed it into the truck. "Just enjoying some of the local hiking. It's a nice day for it." The sky was overcast, blocking out the midday heat from the sun. He latched the tailgate. "I won't hold you up. I'll give you a call when I get the estimate for the damage."

"Yeah, all right." She narrowed her eyes in suspicion, and he arched a brow in reply. Then she turned on her heel and went back to her Ford.

"And get that bump on your head checked out," he called out.

She waved a hand in acknowledgment, then slid into her truck. Figuring out how to pay for that little blooper was a problem for another day. Right now, she had bigger issues. Bigger issues that she was going to be late for.

3

Secret Lollipops

Vianna turned her old Ford onto the unmarked road nestled beneath ancient oaks with heavy-hanging branches. The truck's back tires slid against the dirt as she took the corner, making her slow down. The Legacy Cemetery wasn't located on any map, and true to its namesake, it took a founding last name for your remains to rest in its soil. Nothing was more important than bloodlines within Salem circles.

She felt her grip on the steering wheel tighten as she drove between the narrow opening of trees and into a dirt parking lot crowded with cars. She wedged her truck between a black BMW and a shiny white Tesla. The Ford hiccuped to a stop, and she nudged the rusty door open with a loud creak. Several hooded heads turned in her direction.

The witches gathered in clusters that mimicked the headstones spread out across the open field. Each legacy family owned a marked plot of land within the cemetery, and each organized their graves differently, some in lines, some in circles, and some in indiscernible shapes. They constructed flower beds over the stronger dead witches of their line, as their remains enriched the soil to grow ingredients for spells. A small, steepled stone building that looked like a forgotten church sat in the middle, where the groundskeepers kept their tools. Groundskeepers consisted of children from legacy families who weren't in line to receive the family mantle due to not being the firstborn or being male.

As she stepped down from her truck, her heel slipped on a rock in the gravel and her ankle wobbled, making her stumble a few steps before straightening herself. *Smooth.* She tugged down the hem of her dress and took a deep breath. She could do this. All she had to do was say a final farewell to her mother and bind her ghost to the grave so she couldn't haunt Vianna for the rest of her life. Simple enough.

There were no fancy marble steps or funeral director to greet her like a proper mortuary, but instead, crumbling stone steps and an arbor with overgrown poison ivy on its weather-worn columns. A wrought iron arch loomed above the arbor and drew her eyes upward, making her miss the screaming woman that flew at her face. Vianna stumbled backward and threw her hands up in defense, but the ghost vanished. She grumbled at her own jumpiness. *Rookie move.*

That wasn't the first time Helen had snuck up on her. The ghost always screamed, just like her blood-soaked dress always flowed behind her, even without a breath of wind. Helen Douglas, died 1813. Stabbed in the back by Vianna's fourth-great-grandmother Francis for allegedly stealing her cat. Vianna rubbed the goosebumps from her arms as she assessed the scene. Most of the figures had their hoods up, but she still looked for Nancy.

A hooded figure approached with cherry-red ringlets that billowed from her caped black dress. Two witches flanked the woman, and Vianna knew all too well who the trio was. They stopped in front of her and pulled back their hoods.

"Tiphonie," Vianna spoke in a flat tone to the red-haired leader of the group.

"Vianna," the woman replied with a curt nod. The botched nose job was new and too small for her face. "You'll have to change. You can't wear that."

Tiphonie's lackeys giggled. Things hadn't changed since high school. Wherever Tiphonie went, the Ramsey twins followed. They were golden in hair and skin color, plus their legacy blood had made them suitable followers since grade school.

Vianna gave a tight-lipped smile. "I'm aware."

There was no jurisdiction that required an explanation of her wardrobe—or anything else—to Tiphonie. Being the daughter of the coven mother was like being prom queen; it didn't matter much in the real world. Vianna ignored their scoffs and moved farther into the cemetery with her weight on the balls of her feet so her heels didn't sink into the grass. Wind picked up, whipping strands of her hair into her eyes. A crowd of black cloaks circled around the purple-robed figure she sought. The same cherry-red curls as Tiphonie's caught in the wind. Josephine, the coven mother of the Original Blood Coven, turned toward Vianna with narrowed eyes and a pinched scowl. Ten years had made the wrinkles around her eyes and mouth more prominent. She folded her hands in front of her, and her long sleeves hemmed with knotted ribbons draped down to the overgrown grass.

Vianna didn't bow or lower her head as protocol demanded. She wasn't coven-bound, so she kept her gaze steady and offered a greeting. "Blessed be, Coven Mother."

The enormous nose that Tiphonie once shared sat on her mother's face. "I am not *your* coven mother. What are you doing here?"

"The daughter of a coven witch is granted temporary rights until after mourning, when she accepts or declines her mother's position. But you know that." Reciting rules to the coven mother was like poking a bear with a dead fish.

"It's not the laws, which we all know, that I am questioning, *child*. I'm interested in why you're suddenly willing to be a part of it all."

She had a point, but the truth of why Vianna was there wouldn't go over well.

Thankfully, Tiphonie appeared at her mother's side and interrupted. "We don't want you."

That wasn't much of an insult, but per usual, Tiphonie missed the point of the situation. Tradition dictated legacy names be accepted into the coven, regardless of popularity votes or being wanted.

"Hush," Josephine said to her mini-me.

Tiphonie scowled at Vianna as if she'd been the one to hush her.

"Have you accepted Angeline's mantle?" Josephine asked.

Angeline. Sometimes, it was hard to remember her mother was a person with a name.

"I'm here to bury my mother's body. Nothing more." In truth, she wasn't sure how mantles were passed down or if there was a choice to accept one or not. Could it have already happened and she didn't know? She hoped not. The mantle of the infamous Roots legacy witches was not something she was interested in. The magic passed down through her family wasn't the sparkly unicorn kind, more like the swamp monster of death and darkness.

"She can't *wear* that!" Tiphonie jabbed a dark, manicured nail at Vianna's dress.

Josephine raised a palm at her daughter. "Leave."

Scarlet bloomed across Tiphonie's cheeks before she stomped off. Josephine looked over Vianna's wardrobe with an arched brow and clicked her tongue, just as Grandma always did. Then, surprisingly, the coven mother smirked.

"That was your mother's initiation dress. I remember it well, as will a majority of the witches here." Witches of the same initiation class all wore the same ceremonial dress. The lead witch picked it, and Josephine and Angeline had been in the same initiation class. The same dress undoubtedly hung in the coven mother's closet.

Vianna bit back a groan. Her bright red defiance had turned into a declaration to follow in her mother's footsteps. She seriously debated stripping naked.

Josephine motioned toward the grounds crew, who were digging a hole by the back gate. "The preparations are waiting. You're late, so the normal time frame is cut short. You'll have to make do."

Vianna nodded and walked away without a word. There was no room for excuses—car wrecks or otherwise—when dealing with the coven mother. Vianna needed to work fast.

Her mother's wrapped body lay on the grass a few feet from a freshly dug hole, awaiting burial markings. The tight muslin wrap emphasized every pudgy lump, and Vianna's stomach flip-flopped. Bile bubbled at the bottom of her throat. This wouldn't be her first time touching a dead body, but it didn't mean she liked it.

She slid to her knees, into the soft soil turned up beside the body. The groundskeepers had left a small wooden box the size of a thick book beside the plot. Burned into the lid was the death symbol made by a sigil wheel, and inside were the crystals, herbs, and charcoal needed for the marking ritual.

There were five points of power on the body, representing the five points of a pentagram. Vianna unwrapped her mother's forehead, both hands, and both of her feet in order to mark them with the appropriate symbols. Then she would re-wrap each with crystals and herbs that tethered the bond from past, present, and future, securing the legacy connection. Every tradition for every ceremony was ingrained in her. It didn't matter how much time had passed. Some things a person never forgot.

For the first time in her life, she wished for a sibling to share the burden. The sorrow that gripped her when she looked down at the monster who'd made her existence hell surprised her. Now, limp and silent, her reign of terror had ended. Vianna's hands shook as she reached for Mother's swollen remains. Clawed hands sprang from the body toward Vianna's face, and she squeaked with a jump that sent her scrambling backward.

A howl bellowed into the air from the graying lips of Mother's ghost. No one else could hear her. The horrors of the dead were Vianna's alone to endure. With her eyes closed, she counted to ten, then faced reality. The ghost remained, but Vianna's nerves had calmed enough to block Mother out. It took time for a ghost to gather enough energy to leave the body, even just to slip into their death cycle. Mother scratched at the dirt around the corpse, her ghost hands looking more real than her discolored dead limbs. Soon, she'd be able to relive her death cycle at home in bed. Vianna was now more determined than ever; binding her mother was the only option she could live with.

She scooted closer to the body, clenching her teeth against the swiping claws of the ghost. With focused effort, her breathing evened, and her hands steadied. Her movements slowed, her precision juxtaposed with the frantic thrashing of Mother's ghost. Focusing on her own movements always helped when ghosts converged on her.

Mother's cheeks and neck sagged more dramatically than she remembered, but the deeply etched scowl was the same. Their shared mole on the cheek was larger on her mother and had sprouted hair. Shades of ash blushed the edges of her eyes and lips, giving her a striking resemblance to Grandma Susannah.

Wetness from the grass seeped through Vianna's dress as she sifted through the variety of crystals in the wooden box: amethyst, carnelian, kyanite, and various agates and quartz. She marked Mother's forehead and both hands with blood charcoal, then added different crystals, copal buds, frankincense, and mugwort before redressing. She paused at the last step. The markings on the feet unbound the soul from the body, untethering the bonds so it could unite with its ancestors and strengthen the mantle.

Her heart pounded as she pressed the edge of her charcoal across the top of Mother's foot, drawing a triple set of rectangles that overlapped one another. Once it was complete, she slashed a line through the center, ruining the marking. She then pressed a chunk of fire agate on the connecting line and wrapped it tight.

Each legacy line had their own markings, private traditions passed down. Giving privacy for such a ritual was traditional, and not a single coven member glanced in her direction. Only the groundskeeper five feet away saw her crime. Her stomach dropped. *Wait.* Where in Hades had the groundskeeper come from? She wore a purple bandanna wrapped around the hairline of her dark curly hair, pulled into a sloppy bun. With a wide grin, she leaned against her shovel, pink rain boots crossed at the ankles.

If anyone checked the body, they'd know she'd bound the ghost. The lines were blurry on binding a soul. There'd been instances of it done to enemies, but never a daughter to her mother, and certainly not to a legacy witch. If the groundskeeper made a show of the situation and announced Vianna's deed, things could go very badly. Still, there was no official rule on the matter, and Josephine wasn't likely to let a groundskeeper interrupt a ceremony—that would make her look bad. The coven mother would never listen to someone so beneath her station. Regardless, Vianna didn't need the attention.

With her head down, she quickly gathered the supplies back into the wooden box as her mother's ghost worked into a frenzy, fritzing in and out as she screeched in her efforts to break her bound feet.

When she turned around, the tips of pink rain boots peeked out from beneath the uniform coveralls only a few feet away, and

Vianna froze. The last sunrays slipped beneath the treetops as the groundskeeper knelt down, holding out a purple-wrapped lollipop.

Vianna looked up in surprise, then to the candy, and back to the woman. There were rules against attacks during the day of a burial. Unless the groundskeeper had a death wish, the candy wouldn't be poisoned; witches were sticklers for their rules. Was the candy code for something? It seemed best to find out, so Vianna accepted. The woman popped another lollipop into her mouth as she walked off, her boots squeaking with each step. Vianna tore off the wrapper as she watched the woman walk away without a word.

She crumpled the wrapper into a ball, then tucked it into Mother's wrappings. "Cheers, Mother."

The trees beyond the gates swayed as more witches from different covens arrived, all filing in through the large entry arbor. The coven hosting the funeral always arrived earlier for preparations. Many of the faces she recognized. Small towns worked like that. The Original Blood Coven was one of the four oldest covens in Salem. More sprouted throughout the years, and some stuck, but most fell away. Google witches, the ones who learned the craft from what they found online, came and went with the most frequency. The traditions and rules of this world weren't on a screen—those kinds of secrets passed from mother to daughter. Grimoires, family spell books, contained the only written words of legacy witches, and it was only legacy lines who were welcomed within these grounds.

Josephine met her halfway across the field. "It's time. Is her preparation to your satisfaction?"

Vianna nodded. There was no time to worry about being snitched on. She just needed to get through the ceremony, and then she could say goodbye to her mother forever. "Let's do this."

4

Lend A Hand

Groundskeepers in dark overalls with downcast eyes lowered Mother's body into the grave, but none of them wore pink rain boots. Vianna stood on one side of the grave, the crowds of witches on the other, like a captive audience waiting for her to perform. Once the groundskeepers had the body settled into the grave, they stepped away and made themselves scarce. Mother clawed at the dirt walls of her prison, trying to scratch out any inch of freedom. Vianna didn't look away. She would face the consequences of her actions.

The sun hid behind stretched strands of cloud puffs, and a dingy gray cast over the cemetery. Large balefires roared to life on each side of the grave with thick flames, and the spindles of smoke were laced with herbs. Every second was burned into her memory, jumbling with the past and creating a creeping fear of the future. Wind battered at her in an aggressive persistence, slicing at her exposed arms and whipping locks of hair across her face. Through it all, Vianna stood alone in her red dress.

Beneath the blur of dark silken hoods, Mother continued to thrash, demanding all of Vianna's attention, even in death. Nightmares were like that. With clenched fists, Vianna forced herself to look away in order to keep a wary eye on the living.

Covens clumped together with family members mingled among them. Very few occasions allowed non-coven members, but funerals were one of them, and so husbands, brothers, secondborns, and even thirdborns were all permitted. Births were the only other exception. The life of a legacy was best understood at birth and death for those looking in.

Josephine was front and center with the Original Blood Coven flanking her, Tiphonie to the right of her mother, and another coven member, Rose Barton, to the left, where Angeline Roots had once stood. Rose was the opposite of Mother in every way. Pink cheeks matched her name, and her heart-shaped lips rested in a smile instead of a grimace. The witches behind them took turns, stepping forward to toss offerings into the grave as dirt was shoveled over the body. Some of the younger witches threw cloth sacks filled with oil-soaked herbs, crystals, or vials of blood, while the older witches tossed dead rats, snakes, and birds.

After the crowds finished and the grave was filled, Josephine stepped forward with Tiphonie behind her, holding a black leash clipped to the collar of a goat with a red silken blindfold. The animal was well cared for; his small horns polished to the same sheen as Tiphonie's manicure. His fur was cleaned and fluffy, and his white-spotted ear looked velvet soft. The scrap of red silk kept the animal calm so it wouldn't disrupt the ceremony with his resistance, instead offering blind obedience. Was it easier to close your eyes and just do what those before you had done? Maybe it was for others, but the possibility of being a goat led to the slaughter terrified Vianna.

Josephine's purple robe fluttered out as her knees sank into the upturned soil at the edge of the grave. Tiphonie tugged the goat closer. Josephine untied a knot from her sleeve hem, and a petite athame slid into her palm. With the blade in hand, the coven mother locked eyes with Vianna. In one quick slash, the blade sliced through the tender skin of the goat's neck. No resistance came from the sacrifice, not even a whimper, as his furry legs wobbled and he slipped to his knees in the dirt. He toppled sideways, and blood seeped into the soil.

Movement flickered within the crowd, drawing her attention up, and Vianna narrowed her eyes as she tracked a tall woman in a heavy black dress, her dark hair twisted into a tight bun. The figure wove through the crowd with the ease of someone unhindered by uneven terrain or people in her way—she glided with the ease of a ghost. Stepping away from the crowd, the ghost approached the grave, trails of beetles scampering behind her, following her. She raised her chin, looking down at the grave, and recognition seized Vianna. The ghost was identical to the photo on the mantel at the house of Vianna's distant grandmother, Clarice.

The air went still, and the temperature turned frigid as more faces from photos on the mantel threaded through the crowd. Each ghost ended at the edge of the grave opposite Vianna. One wore a blue dress with blood splattered down her chin and chest, another had a short bob and wore a red flapper dress, one was a small child with ringlets whose giggle sent a ripple of goosebumps over Vianna's skin, but all of them watched with the same emerald eyes that had watched her as a child from their spots on the mantel. Generations of Roots witches stood before her, staring and assessing.

Before this moment, Grandma Susannah was the only Roots witch ghost Vianna had seen. If they planned to herald her into something greater, some new club of magic and murder, she had a massive wrench to throw into their plans. She had no intention of following in her ancestors' footsteps, bug-filled or otherwise.

The ghost of Mother's hand thrust out from the ground. Vianna's eyes bulged, but she didn't jump. The binding had worked; Mother couldn't escape. She was sure of it, mostly, despite the increased thud of her heart. The Roots witches of the past didn't offer a single glance toward the hand. They had no interest in the dead. They were there for Vianna.

The ghost at the far end of the line—with frizzy hair and a peasant dress similar to Grandma Susannah's—reached her hand to the shoulder of the ghost beside her, wearing a similar dress but with a corset lacing and a bonnet holding back dark strands. Each ghost reached to the next until a woman in a knee-length gingham dress stepped around the grave toward Vianna.

Vianna's instinct in her moment of panic was to freeze; she'd always been that way since she was a child. Luckily, not acknowledging the ghosts encouraged them to return the favor. Gingham Dress didn't seem to understand proper living and dead communication protocol and placed a hand on Vianna's shoulder. A jolt of static energy like she'd never felt sliced through her core, and she gasped for air as searing pain exploded across her collarbone. Clenching every muscle, she endured the power coursing through her body, feeling saturated by layer upon layer of pressure on her chest and lungs. When the sensation eased, she opened her eyes, and only the living stared back.

Focusing on deep, steady breaths, she counted the hollow gazes of the witches around her. When she reached a count of twenty, her nerves settled, and a tired numbness washed through her limbs. With a deep breath, she stopped counting and focused back on Josephine, who still knelt at the grave, soaked in blood. A tingle raced through Vianna's veins, either from whatever her ancestors had done or from the eagerness to have this whole thing over with.

The coven mother finished the ornate hexagram drawn in blood over the grave and sat up, straight and stiff. The crowds bustled as witches pulled small pouches that they dipped their fingertips in, coating them with a variety of crushed herbs and dried blood flakes. Josephine raised the blade into the air, and the witches raised their hands in unison. When the coven mother slammed the blade into the center of the hexagram, every witch snapped their fingers, and a cloud of cedar, cypress, garlic, and varying aromas exploded in the air.

Josephine pushed to her feet, flicking flecks of dirt from her cloak onto the goat. Not giving a glance to Vianna, she turned and led the way as groups of witches furled behind her. Vianna wrapped her arms around herself. The funeral was over. It was done.

The tender flesh on her collarbone bristled against the stiff fabric of her dress, and she pulled at the neckline, trying to get a peek. She could only see red, swollen flesh. With a grimace, she pulled on the dress to cover the injury. She wouldn't properly be able to see it without a mirror. Maybe it would fade.

"Vianna." A familiar face broke away from the descending crowd. Charlie was taller, with broader shoulders than she remembered in high school, but he had the same creamy complexion and golden hair. The wind colored his cheeks the same shade as his mother's. Once upon a time, Vianna had fantasized about going to the initiation ball with Charlie Barton, but Mother wouldn't hear of it.

He stopped in front of her. "It's good to see you, been a long time."

"Charles, darling!" Tiphonie squealed from somewhere behind Vianna.

Charlie's smile faltered for the briefest moment before he recovered with dimple-clad charm.

"I assume all of this drama was why I haven't heard from you since our date." Tiphonie looped her arm with his.

Vianna wrinkled her nose at the tackiness in calling someone's death a distraction to her dating life. She didn't need an excuse to walk away, so she nodded at them both and left.

"See you around, Vianna," Charlie called after her.

She didn't reply but kept walking toward the parking lot, weaving through the clusters of lingering witches. The older witches glared unflinchingly in her direction, but the younger witches avoided eye contact altogether, giving her a turned shoulder or developing a sudden fascination with patches of dandelions. Every coven-bound witch in Salem was at the cemetery, everyone but Nancy. Vianna slowed her step as she walked, scanning the faces, searching for Nancy's delicate features and arched brows, but she wasn't there. A knot of worry was growing inside of her gut. She'd give her a call later tonight.

There was no reason to linger and no one to catch up with or make plans with, so Vianna climbed into her Ford and headed out. The drive home was uneventful. Vianna resisted groaning as she pulled into the driveway, eyeing the front door and dreading more escapades. Maybe the trick was to act like everything was fine, a "fake it till you make it" type of deal. She breezed up the porch stairs and to the front door without hesitation, and to her surprise, the door swung open with a loud creak. It worked.

"We'll add oiling those joints to the fix-it list."

Tea wasn't strong enough to chase away the heebie-jeebies of the funeral, but she'd seen rows of mason jars filled with a dark amber liquid in the pantry and headed in that direction. "Let's investigate Mother's new hobby."

The lowest shelf of the walk-in pantry bowed from the weight of dozens of jars, and she grabbed the one closest to the edge. She ran it under the faucet to wash off the residue that made her fingers stick to the glass, twisted open the lid and took a whiff. The brown liquid was moonshine all right, and it smelled like lighter fluid. After the day she'd had, that was proof enough for her, and she took a deep swig. Liquid fire blazed down her throat, sending her into a coughing fit. It was the world's worst moonshine. She laughed out loud. Everything about this place was shit.

"Your drink-making is crap, Ma," Vianna spoke into the void and took another swig that ripped through her gut.

"Drinking is unladylike behavior. You are just like your mother." Grandma's voice came from the kitchen archway behind her.

Unwilling to acknowledge the insult of comparing her to her mother, she turned and rested her hip against the counter. "What else has changed in this house of horrors?"

"Learn for yourself, *solitary witch*." Grandma's ghost faded away.

If she'd known asking for help chased Grandma away, she would've started a decade ago. Witches who didn't pledge to a coven were deemed "solitary" and treated like the plague. It wasn't much of an insult to Vianna, since being accepted by catty secret societies founded in murder wasn't something to put on a resume.

The moonshine had created a flush of warmth in her chest, her muscles relaxing into a soft hum. The day was still early, early after-noon, and she needed a distraction from how tired she felt. She should go change her clothes and inspect the mark on her collar-bone that was a constant, low-throbbing pain. But she wasn't ready to see that. She rubbed the back of her neck and eyed the pantry. Cleaning seemed as good a distraction as any other. Looking down at her red beacon of a dress, she decided to leave it on. It'd been useless in making the desired statement, so its punishment was to suffer through the pantry with her.

An hour later, she'd emptied the shelves into sorted piles of "makes me gag," "what is it," and "hell no." None of it was edible or usable, so she scooped all the piles into the same trash bag, then wiped the grime from her hands onto the red dress. The only edible thing in the kitchen was the kerosene-flavored moonshine. She picked up the jar from the counter and took a swig to distract her rumbling stomach. Peeking around the kitchen archway, she eyed the door at the end of the narrow hallway. It was the only spot in the house that offered potentially worse horror than the pantry: the conjure room. Maybe it was best to get it over with.

Large golden peonies bloomed across the wallpaper of the hallway. The busy pattern made the space feel even smaller. It was an impressive feat to make such a gorgeous flower cringe-worthy. Vianna swirled the jar of moonshine and glared at the door to the conjure room, which was fitted with a porcelain doorknob stamped with a tree, just like the master bedroom. The tree-knob rooms were off-limits. The house would rumble, rattling her down to her bone marrow whenever she meandered in their direction. He was silent now, and the door, like everything else, looked smaller than in her memories.

She'd grown up with the whisperings from witch classmates about the relics and ingredients Roots witches hoarded within the sacred walls of their conjure room. Legacy witches attended an all-girls private school until high school, where they were then released into the general public. Teachers at the private grade schools taught that one family should never collect more than their coven; those teachers never made eye contact with Vianna. Some rules didn't apply to the older legacy lines.

The most ridiculous rumor was that her mother had wrestled a rhinoceros for its horn while in Africa. Children were exuberant, if nothing else, in the stories they told. Vianna felt confident her mother had never traveled across the ocean, since leaving Salem was some bizarre betrayal of the coven in her eyes. She did, however, actually have a rhino horn. How she got it was anyone's guess.

After a brisk march down the hall, Vianna pushed open the door, and a puff of old leather, dust, and bergamot exhaled into her face. She paused, eyes downcast at the deep scratch on the wooden floorboards that butted against the edge of her toes. She tilted her head, following the scratches that curved into a large summoning circle in the center of the room. There were no markings or remnants of ingredients, just a clean slate ready to be used. She stepped into the room that was the birthright she never wanted.

Rows of floor-to-ceiling shelves lined the wall to the right. Tall glass bottles filled with infused oils cluttered the middle shelf. Roots, leaves, and flower buds floated in yellow with labels reading: rhododendron, hemlock, tutu, and odollam. Animal skulls lined the top shelf, filling Vianna with memories of Mother wearing them as masks while she summoned demons or drank too much and danced beneath the moon. Vianna washed away the memories with another swig of moonshine.

Straight ahead was an apothecary hutch atop a wooden desk with deep drawers beneath.

With a sigh and warm liquid courage heating her limbs, she walked across the circle. Loose, scattered papers covered the desktop, and she thumbed through them: a grocery list with *garlic* written at the top in Mother's scribbles, an advertisement for an art exhibit at the old Essex Museum, and another list with names Vianna didn't recognize. Legacy witches wrote nothing of their traditions or practices, unless in grimoires, in order to keep knowledge from the wrong hands.

She had no idea what to do with the room or its contents, but throwing it all in the same trash bag as the pantry goop didn't feel right. Maybe if she knew exactly what it all was, she'd know what to do. She set down the moonshine and found a blank sheet of paper and pen to catalog the witchy ingredients as she pulled open tiny drawers of the apothecary cabinet. A ring with a red stone rattled when she pulled open a cubby, and when she opened a long compartment stuffed with locks of hair and handwritten labels of every major name in Salem, her face pinched. She looked closer to see clipped nails instead of hair caught in the honey blob on some of the tags. She didn't want to know how Mother got those. The smart move would be to light a match and run away with the moonshine, but instead, she rummaged through more drawers with abandon.

There was something alluring in exploring what had been off-limits as a child. The third wall was covered with cubbies painted in chipped black paint and adorned with wooden embellishments saved for royalty. She started in on them. Labeled jars crammed into tiny spaces: mouse dung, mummified animal remains, a bezoar stone from a cow, henbane, crushed coral and pearls, heart of a stag, ambergris, frog legs, and dried fish eggs. The number of drawers was endless, and each label more mind-boggling than the last. She turned her attention to the larger drawers, which were low to the ground, and pulled open the third one from the left. The rotting smell of mold punched her in the nose, and she covered her mouth, gagging at the sight of a severed hand coated in squirming maggots.

"Holy effing goddess!" She slammed the drawer closed, but it was too late. The smell permeated the room, or maybe just her nose. Either way, everything smelled of rotting flesh.

"Not a goddess. Just Nancy." Grandma stood at the doorway.

"Nancy?" Vianna repeated, the room suddenly spinning.

5

Ghost From The Past

Acid chunks crawled up Vianna's throat, but she swallowed them down. She swiftly walked from the conjure room to the bathroom. The cross handles of the faucet squeaked as she turned them, and the pipes within the walls groaned as cold water filled the black leaf-patterned sink. She rinsed out her mouth, then reached for the towel, but the rack was barren. She wiped water from her chin with her forearm.

Gripping the edges of the sink, she leaned into the mirror to examine herself. Her hair was limp, dark bags drooped beneath bloodshot eyes, and her skin was paler than usual. The last couple of days—getting the call about Mother, driving out, and the funeral—hadn't exactly been kind.

Vianna rubbed her face with both hands, desperately wanting Grandma to be wrong. Nancy wasn't dead, and her hand wasn't rotting away in the conjure room. No. Closing her eyes and shutting out the haggard version of herself in the mirror, Vianna instead saw Nancy as she remembered her from childhood. They'd shared countless late nights in the candle den, and one in particular stood out from the rest.

After hours of melting batches of wax in cauldrons, threading wicks through molds, and tying wick rods, Nancy had decided a little mischief was due. She pulled a small glass jar with a dropper from the side pocket of her backpack. An enormous grin spread across her face. Exotic, brightly colored plants were Nancy's speciality in the garden, and she'd finally gotten her skunk cabbage to bloom, then steeped it in oil. She dangled the small jar in the air.

That night, they'd added their extra secret ingredient into the candles for the upcoming Imbolc festival. For years after, no one spoke of that night without a scrunched nose, and little-Vianna always giggled inside of older-Vianna's head. She opened her eyes. A small grin tugged at the corner of her mouth, but the trip down memory lane had gone on long enough. She needed to get back to cleaning the conjure room.

The hand wasn't Nancy's, and Vianna needed to dispose of it. She could bury it. The appropriate and more normal response for dis-membered body parts would be sorrow or concern for the horrible crime, but she'd lost those instincts some time ago. This wasn't the first time she'd handled remains, human or animal, and compassion did nothing for what had already been done. The numbness that spread through her was a comfort. She gave a quick shake of her hands to dry them, then wiped the remaining water on her dress.

An icy breath blew against her ear, and goosebumps rippled down her arms. She stiffened every muscle in her body. Movement flashed in the mirror, and she focused downward, into the sink, counting to five and hoping that ignoring the truth would make it go away.

She could spend the rest of her life with her eyes on her feet, or even better, with her eyes closed. Rationale went out the door when she was tired. Dragging her focus up to the mirror, she saw her.

Nancy. Her friend wasn't a little girl anymore, but there was no denying her identity.

She stood behind Vianna, staring into the mirror with her soft blue-gray eyes, lowered pointed chin, and stringy blonde hair. She had the same strip of missing hair in the middle of her left eyebrow. Prepping for Samhain one year, a spark from the fire had jumped out at her, catching her brow and burning the hair. She'd just grinned, saying it made her look badass.

"Nancy." The name felt cold on Vianna's lips.

Her childhood partner in crime raised an arm, and where a hand ought to be, instead, was a bloody stub with mangled chunks of flesh. Vianna white-knuckled the sink, unmoving. Mom had killed Nancy. She hated Vianna that much? Was this the only way left to hurt her?

The bathroom door slammed shut, and Vianna's breath caught. Nancy's ghost flickered in and out like bad radio reception, with the vanity lights flickering on the same wavelength. She had a good lick of power for being such a fresh ghost. In a flash, she went from hovering behind Vianna to sitting on the toilet. Metal handcuffs clanked against the faucet handles as she tugged her wrists, her reattached hands flexing over the sink. This was her death loop. Vianna's chest tightened, and she stepped backward, bumping into the wall behind her.

Nancy stuttered out an almost whimper, more of a rough gurgle, the type that came from crying so hard that nothing but stuttering heaves remained. Tears slid down her puffy cheeks. Vianna bit down on the inside of her cheek to keep from crying. She couldn't stop what was about to happen, she couldn't undo what had already been done, but she couldn't unsee it either. Over and over.

Frost spread over the bottom of the mirror, and Nancy stiffened, her eyes tracking upward as someone approached.

Nancy's chin wobbled before she spoke. "I-I don't know! The cat isn't mine. It's hers."

Vianna wasn't sure what cat was whose, since she was only getting half of the conversation, but the Roots household had never included a feline. The skin on Nancy's wrists bubbled with fresh drops of moisture, and she tried to yank her hands toward her chest, but the cuffs stopped her. Vianna's stomach dropped through the floor. She didn't need to see the red pincushion filled with needles or the tall glass bottle with one of Mother's concoctions to know what came next. Mother loved her needles, and her true talent didn't lie within embroidery. A sweet clove scent clogged the room, and the clanking from the handcuffs went into a frenzy.

"No. I'm sorry, Angeline. No, no." The heel of Nancy's boots scraped against the tiles, over and over as she tried to find traction to push away.

Three soft taps came in unison, and Vianna sucked in a breath. Mother's dermal hammer. A single long needle stuck out from the top of Nancy's wrist. She honked a wail of despair as more of the *tap-tap-tap* repeated. One after another, needles appeared, piercing into the flesh of her wrist. She begged for Mother to stop, but the only answer came in a repeated *thud-thud-thud* from the plastic hammer. An ash-gray color spread between the puncture wounds like a speckled rash. Her shoulders trembled, then shook in full spasms. Vianna sucked in a breath and looked to the doorway for escape.

"No more," Nancy mumbled between sobs. "I'll tell you whatever you want. I know where Vianna is."

Vianna whipped her focus back to Nancy, eyes wide and lips parted in shock. Nancy had been the only person Vianna kept in contact with from Salem, the only person who understood that running was her only option. Had Mother tortured her for that information? Vianna swallowed more acid.

The metal clanks from the cuffs had stopped, the scraping of boots against tile silenced, and only a soft whimpering remained. Nancy's arms had gone limp, her hands flopped over the edge of the sink. A gray rash spread between the protruding needles. Vianna's heart pounded, or maybe it was the hammer, but the pounding wouldn't stop, and her vision shook with each tap.

"Then what do you want?" cried Nancy. "I don't know anything else."

A deep rush of air filled Vianna's lungs, and her chest expanded. Mother hadn't killed Nancy because of Vianna. Had Mother known where Vianna was all along? Or had she not cared enough to know? Either answer hurt; not knowing the truth didn't make a difference. Vianna hadn't wanted Mother to know where she was, so the rest of it shouldn't matter. But her emotions weren't of the rational variety.

She shrank against the wall, inching toward the door, reaching for escape, but the doorknob refused to twist. The lightbulbs grew brighter, blinding even, as Nancy's moaning echoed between the walls. With an open hand, Vianna smacked her palm against the door, gritting her teeth against the sounds she knew would haunt her long after.

"Burns," Nancy mumbled. "Please. Stop."

The door wouldn't budge, but Vianna knew this game. In order to escape, she'd have to face what was behind her. She turned toward Nancy, her back scraping against the indents of the door as she pressed against it. The rash on Nancy's wrists had turned black. Her head hit against the wall with a repeated *thud*.

Metal clicked, and a cuff fell against the counter. Nancy sobbed, snot running from her nose as her arm fell limply into her lap. Her other arm still hung in confinement, but her gaze was fixated on the sink counter and her chest convulsed in delayed hiccups. She could see something Vianna couldn't.

"You can't leave," Nancy whispered, eyes still on the counter. "It's spreading."

The swollen rash was almost twice the size of a few moments ago. Nancy jerked with her still-cuffed arm, then whimpered. Mother had a multitude of tactics when it came to torture, and letting a poison slowly spread to break a person was common, but this didn't feel like that.

Vianna faced back toward the door, jiggling the handle and smacking her palm against the wood, but it made no difference. Nancy's defeated sobs changed to a growl, then to a shriek of rage that made Vianna clench her fists, but she didn't look back. Glass shattered against tiles, and Nancy's boot slammed into everything she could reach to kick.

"I curse the day the Roots witches were born," Nancy hissed.

Resting her forehead against the door, Vianna inhaled deep breaths despite the ache in her chest. She'd wished the same thing plenty of times. The words hurt, but she understood. Metal clanked, but not the same handcuff sound from earlier. Vianna looked over her shoulder. Nancy had picked up a handsaw, the mystery object she'd been fixated on. More acid chunks tried to push up from her gut, and Vianna swallowed them down.

"H-hurts," Nancy stuttered. Her eyes flicked to the door, then to her wrist hanging in the sink, before she squeezed her lids shut. Her shoulders raised and nostrils flared before she set the metal teeth of the saw against her own arm.

The scene faded, and the door creaked open. Vianna stumbled into the hallway and looked back with ragged breaths. Nothing of the nightmare remained, only a clean washroom and the lingering sweet clove scent. Her hands trembled as she reached for the wall to steady herself. Ghosts of witches had more power; the living could get stuck in their death loops, and their deaths were often the most gruesome.

"Inform Nancy to stop clogging the lavatory sink. The house throws a hissy fit like a toddler every time she does." Grandma stood with her fists on her hips in the hallway.

"She was forced to saw off her own hand. I'd do more than clog a damned sink." Vianna headed for the stairs. She'd had enough; it was time to change.

6

Launch Mode

Now that the funeral was over, the red dress felt like a connection to Mother, and that was the last thing Vianna wanted after being forced to experience Nancy's death loop. There was no surprise in Mother's murderous extracurricular activities, but it was the *who* of the equation that had Vianna reeling. Witches, especially those who were coven-bound, were not open game. Mother had lost her freaking marbles. And why did it have to be Nancy?

Vianna let out a growl of sad frustration as she stormed down the upstairs hallway to the main bedroom, flinging the door open and slamming it against the wall. The house gave a hiccup of a growl, and she flinched. Letting her anger get the best of her was easier than drowning in sadness or guilt.

"Sorry," she mumbled. "I didn't mean to."

Fluffs of insulation flew through the ceiling vent and into her face. She swatted at them, unsure of what they meant, then crossed the room to the dresser.

When Vianna had run away, the only person she felt guilt over leaving behind was Nancy. And now her only friend was dead. If Vianna had stayed, she liked to think that Mother wouldn't have dove off the deep end. Or in her case, the deep-er end.

She picked through wrinkled balls of clothes in the drawer until she found a T-shirt and shorts. After slipping out of the dress, she stopped in front of the mirror, pausing to look at the mark on her collarbone left by her ancestors. It was swollen and red, exactly like a burn, but in a definite shape. A jagged line reached across her skin, with six small lines sprouting on each side of the main vein. It resembled a lightning bolt. She touched around the edges, getting a feel for the size. No, not a lightning bolt, it was a tree branch. There were twelve sprouts and eleven generations between Vianna and Grandma Susannah. Vianna made twelve.

The mark had to represent the Roots mantle. Her gut clenched, and a sheen of sweat broke out across her forehead. She couldn't think about what that meant. It was all too much. She turned away from the mirror and tugged the T-shirt over her head. Pulling out her laptop—that was almost as old as she was—she clicked it on and pinched the pressure point between her thumb and pointer finger to fight off the incoming headache as she waited for it to boot up. Her neighbor had the same Wi-Fi password as always, and she hopped onto the network. One day she would upgrade her prepaid flip phone.

There was no funeral announcement or obituary for Nancy Williams, which wasn't too surprising since the covens didn't advertise their business. Nancy's mother had died in a car crash when she was three, and the family line hadn't been legacy or demon-bound, but they'd been around for a few generations. Some of the older witches had taken pity on Nancy and allowed her to bounce from household to household. It was a fostering system, of sorts, that left Nancy constantly shuffled and with no real family.

Not sure what she expected to find, Vianna shut the laptop with a huff. There was a dismembered hand to dispose of and a house to clean. Those were the things she could do something about. She didn't know what happened when a mantle passed, and she couldn't help Nancy, not anymore. But it bothered Vianna that no one would be worrying over Nancy. She'd be forgotten in the realm of witches.

Downstairs, she looked under the sink and in two cupboards before finding a pair of black cleaning gloves. Armed with another swig of moonshine and a bucket from the pantry, she stormed into the conjure room. The large drawer sagged open, waiting, and she held her breath as she inched forward. The floorboards creaked with each step, and she scrunched her nose in anticipation. With a deep exhale and one squinty eye, she leaned over and peeked at . . . an empty drawer.

It was the same drawer; she was sure of it. She checked the neighboring drawers but only found a mummified squirrel, a deer's leg, and jars of a jelly substance in shades of green and brown. There was only so much nasty she could handle at once, so she closed the drawers.

She rotated in a circle, scanning the floor. The hand hadn't crawled off on its own. It couldn't have. But it was gone. Walking softly down the hall, she stopped before the hallway opened to the sitting room and tilted her ear to listen for noises.

A repeated shuffle-thud came from the upstairs bathroom, but she knew that was Earl. A scraping noise against the floor came from her childhood room, but she knew all too well about the death cycle in that room and shoved that thought aside.

"Were you struck dumb as a wooden spoon?" Grandma's voice made Vianna jump.

"Fuck the goddess, Grandma!"

"I will not. Ladies do not use such language or speak of such things. Nor do they perform such activities with other ladies."

Grandma looked around the corner. "Are you having an episode of some variety?"

"Shh," Vianna hissed. "I'm listening for the missing hand."

Grandma waved an arm, and the rope around her neck swung with it. "Missing? You must be drunk."

"Then who took the hand?" She jabbed a thumb toward the conjure room.

"Why the house, of course. That daddle was his." Grandma's tone made it clear how daft she felt the question was. "Your mother gave it to him."

Vianna frowned. The house taking things wasn't unheard of. As a child, it was the things Mother didn't approve of that went missing: T-shirts of Vianna's favorite bands, music devices, make-up, or anything that distracted from the craft. Even her science textbook had gone missing after she'd shunned winter solstice prep to study for a test on chromosomes and enzymes the following day, which she'd ended up failing. She rubbed her temples, debating getting shitass drunk on moonshine instead of dealing with the house of horrors.

"If you don't get rid of that festering hand," she said to the house. "I will tear this place up, board by board. You know I will."

Silence answered her half-empty threat. Even the ghosts upstairs stopped moving, but no hand appeared. Familiars weren't obligated to obey. They shared their magic with a witch by choice, not servitude. She pictured a hand chasing prospective buyers out the door, leaving a trail of maggots as Nancy screamed from the bathroom. *Lovely.* She knew she would have to sell to a witch considering the neighborhood, but it was a limited circle of founding coven witches who wouldn't blink at random body parts.

There wasn't a lot she could do beyond play hide-and-seek with a demon, and there wasn't any scenario where that turned out in her favor. The hand would show up when the house wanted it to, but it wouldn't explain why Angeline had done it. Her mother couldn't have hated Vianna that much, to kill her grade-school friend just for who she was. Nancy had spent every day after fifth grade making candles and binding dried herb bundles with Vianna. They weren't strangers. Nancy's death—the where and the how—made little sense.

When nothing made sense, brainless activities helped. Three stuffed plastic bags from her pantry loot and a set of burned-out nostrils from sniffing bleach later, moonshine sounded like the perfect reward. She threw a bag over her shoulder and went out the front door to the garbage bins tucked into the side of the house. When she used her hip to bounce it over the ledge, the bag tore and spilled moldy slime down her bare leg. She tipped her chin toward the sky and groaned.

"Vianna?" Charlie Barton strolled out from behind Vianna's Ford wearing pressed khakis and a powder-blue polo shirt. His cologne smelled like a pinecone disinfectant and overrode the blooming wisteria.

"What are you doing here?" She bent and picked up trash scraps, tossing them into the trash bin.

He raised a brow at her. "Nice to see you, too. Funeral days are rough, this one especially, it seems. Are you handling the trash?"

"Yeah, I know." She sighed. "Loose trash in the bin or whatever, but the bag broke." She flung the crusted milk carton in.

"How 'bout you take a break, and I take you out to dinner?"

A slight breeze sent goosebumps up her exposed legs, drying the rest of the slime from the trash to her skin. She shut the lid to the trash can. "I don't understand. Did the coven send you, Charlie?"

"Charles," he corrected.

Vianna raised her hands in surrender, and he chuckled.

"I may not have run away, but I wanted to set myself apart from who I was. I like to think I've changed. It's Charles now."

That was an unexpected reply, and something she understood. "Fair enough, Charles."

"No, the coven didn't send me." He frowned. "I'm here because I want to be. I'd like to catch up. And I've gotta hear the story of the infamous legacy who vanished in the middle of the night." Charlie flashed his million-dollar dimples.

"Umm . . ." There were so many reasons to pass. Her not staying in Salem, and his ties to the coven she'd done everything to escape, were at the top of the list. "I don't think Tiphonie would appreciate you being here." Vianna wasn't interested in games or drama.

He shook his head. "I went on *one* date with her. I'm not interested in another. I *am* interested in taking you to dinner."

Vianna's stomach growled. A real meal, one served hot and not wrapped in plastic, sounded better than clearance crap from the convenience store down the street. Or maybe that was just her inner younger-Vianna blushing at the attention of the Prom king. But, there was the potential he'd know something about Nancy.

She chewed on her lip. "I'm not dressed for anything nice."

"Would you like to change?" he asked.

She chuckled and shook her head. "Nah. I'll make you slum it."

"Being with you is not slumming it, Vianna *Roots*." Last names were as valuable as currency in Salem. "Come on, I have a place in mind."

"Let me grab my purse, real quick."

Inside the house, she used a wet washcloth to do a quick wipe down from trash slime before heading back out. Charles stood waiting, holding the door open to a candy-red convertible. The sleek car made her rusted Ford look like a monster truck.

"Like it?" He nodded to the car and gave her a dazzling, dimpled smile as she got in. He jogged around the front of the car and slid into the driver's side, not missing a beat in his conversation. "She's a beauty. A Taycan Turbo." When she didn't reply, he clarified further. "An electric-powered Porsche. Just got her last month."

Charlie and Vianna had always come from very different worlds.

Last month, the steering wheel of her Ford fell into her lap when she tried to start it up, forcing her to play the damsel in distress card with the mechanic across the street from her apartment complex. He agreed to help after minimal tears and claiming what little cash she had. That expenditure had put her three months behind in rent, and the landlord wasn't buying the damsel trick anymore.

They drove with the convertible top down, making conversation impossible with the wind until he abruptly stopped in the middle of the road. She gripped the door handle and looked around, confused because there was no stop sign or street light.

"Wanna see something cool? It's called launch control." He waggled his eyebrows at her.

That was all the warning she got before the car jumped to warp speed in all of two seconds. Her cheeks rippled back in waves, and her eyes watered. Her mouth flew open in surprise, and a fly sucked down her throat. She coughed to dislodge it, but it was too late. She'd eaten it.

"You all right over there?" He slowed down as they turned onto a different street. "Awesome, right?" he hollered over the wind.

"Awesome" wasn't exactly the word on her mind. They zipped along back roads, and the full summer trees of Salem created a canopy of green leaves over the road. Old Victorian homes converted into businesses lined the street before he pulled into a cluster of vacant brick factory buildings. The air smelled of blooming flowers from the apple trees. He parked in front of a two-story with trimmed bushes and a shiny metal door that stood out against the brick. There were no signs for pizza or smells of sizzling fries.

She turned to him with a raised brow. "What's this?"

He beamed like a kid. "Trust me?"

Vianna wasn't big on trusting anyone, even Charlie Barton. "We'll see."

He got out of the car, and when she didn't wait for him to open her door, he scowled. "Too proud to let me open a door for you?" He gave a strained smile.

She paused, caught off guard. "Oh. Maybe you can catch me if I fall later or something?" Seemed like something chivalrous and all that.

He slipped his hand around her waist, and she let him propel her forward. The possibility that he was a serial killer leading her into his abandoned dungeon of torture crossed her mind, but then she remembered that was the TV show from last week, before the Wi-Fi was disconnected. Maybe that was for the best. It might have been making her paranoid.

Inside the building was an ornate, round cherry wood table in the center of an entry hall. A black-and-gold brushed vase filled with blooming pink roses sat in the middle of the table. The polished wooden floors contrasted with the red brick walls in a charming way. There were two doors and a set of stairs that butted against the far wall. The lingering scent of burned sage mixed with lemon. Had it just been the lemon, she'd have figured it was from hired cleaning, but the sage whispered of a recent smudging. Since men didn't practice the craft, that meant another witch had been there recently. Charlie headed up the stairs, and she followed, her fingers gliding across the polished railing.

"My imagination is getting the best of me, Charlie—ss. Charles," she corrected herself. "Are you going to sacrifice me to some demon?"

"That's only on Thursdays." He opened the door at the top of the stairs, and with a sweeping gesture, motioned her inside. "Welcome to my home. I'm a horrible cook, and my mother didn't want me to starve, so she hired a personal chef." Without taking a breath, he added, "Plus, it's the summer film festival, so the restaurants are overrun with tourists."

Tingles bounced in her stomach at his closeness, and suddenly

Vianna felt like she was sixteen and in high school, turning beet red at even a glance in her direction from Charlie. He'd been class president and was always surrounded by the popular kids, making even a stolen glance or smile feel special. And here she was, being wined-and-dined in his home, just the two of them. Maybe things had changed a lot more than Vianna realized.

Nancy would get a kick out of it all, but she was gone. That reality was a slap to the face, draining any playfulness from the moment. Vianna was here to get answers.

<h1 style="text-align:center">7</h1>

Million Dollar Cheeseburger

Charles's loft was straight out of an interior decorating magazine, one with captions like *Industrial Chic for Bachelors with Money.* There wasn't a single pile of clutter; instead, the shelves had those unusable twisty glass vases, small potted succulents, and a few metal picture frames that were mostly of him or his mother. Tin tiles lined the ceiling, and a sloppy white paint job, probably called "vintage," covered the brick walls.

He pressed the button on an intercom system. "Austen, two for dinner and a bottle of red, if you could."

A male voice answered, "Yes, Mr. Barton. My pleasure. I'll send Alice with the wine right away."

Charles took off his jacket and hung it on a tiered hook system on the other side of the door, then turned back to her. With another grand, sweeping gesture, he asked, "What do you think?"

She gave an affirming nod that seemed appropriate. "It's nice. Industrial chic." And lacking warmth.

"Thank you." His eyes filled with pride, and she felt squeamish that her opinion seemed to matter. It shouldn't.

Footsteps drew their attention from across the room, and a server in black pants and a button-up shirt with a black apron stood at the top of the winding staircase in the far corner. She was a petite blonde with flaming red cheeks, but she wasn't what captured Vianna's attention.

A small half-wall had hidden an alcove when she first entered. In the center was a winding staircase that stretched both up and down. Art hung on the walls with lights like a professional exhibit, and a large abstract painting in deep reds and oranges drew her attention. She crossed the room to get a better look. The paint was thick, highlighting the texture of each brush stroke. And despite not being into art, she couldn't look away. Moving around the server, Vianna stepped closer and noticed accents of purple swirled into the corners of the canvas.

"I'll take that." Charles's voice brought her back to reality. He held two wine glasses and nodded in dismissal at Alice.

Had the server offered it to her? Time felt fuzzy. Food would be good. Her brain was probably frizzing out with all the bleach she'd used in the pantry. He held out a glass, and their fingertips brushed as she took the wine. He stepped closer, invading her personal space. Her heart fluttered, and she took a step back as she sipped her wine.

"My mother painted it." He nodded at the painting.

"A coven witch who paints?"

Painting wasn't a proper hobby for a legacy witch; it was too messy and—she didn't know—good? Creative? A proper coven witch had no time for hobbies that didn't benefit the coven. Unless you were Rose Barton, apparently.

Memories floated across her mind, uninvited. The toe of Mother's boot tapping as she peered down at Vianna. *I don't have time for your nonsense, Vianna. Behave. You are a future coven witch, not a child. Just like I am a witch, not a mother.* She'd always snarled the word *mother*.

Charles slid beside her as they studied the painting. "She recently got back into it. She was a painter before she joined the coven—family trade from her father."

"Before?" That implied his mother had a life before she was a witch. That would mean she wasn't a legacy witch, was possibly even a first generation. But the Barton's was a legacy line.

Charles nodded. "My aunt died very young, and my mother was her best friend. She continued the Barton legacy when she married my father."

"I've never heard of a mantle passing like that." Legacy witches passed their surname and mantle through the maternal side. Marrying to gain a legacy name shouldn't have granted Rose the same privileges. How had there never been gossip about this when they were younger?

He shrugged. "The Barton line would've died off if she hadn't."

The line would die regardless, since Charles didn't have a sister, which was also odd. Rose Barton had stumbled into a loophole that made her a legacy witch. Maybe they hoped Charles would marry a witch who'd take the Barton name as his mother had.

She gave a sideways glance to Charles as a feeling of concern swirled in her gut. Having your aunt die could be rough. She lifted a hand to squeeze his forearm in comfort before thinking better of it. The corner of his mouth twitched as he turned toward her. His fingertips brushed a lock of her hair, then trailed her jawline. The urge to lean into his touch felt like a pulse inside of her. He wanted her too; that much was obvious. Was it so bad to comfort him?

She took a step back and exhaled a long breath, steadying her heartbeat. The air felt heavier than a moment ago. Maybe the issue was that it'd been too long since an attractive man flirted with her, and she didn't count her landlord's greasy son, James, who showed up at all hours offering to fix things that weren't broken. There was too much going on. Her head was a mess. She needed to be clear.

"I'm only in Salem until I can sell the house. I'm not sticking around." Just because she wanted free food didn't mean she'd lead him on when she had no intention of following through.

His forehead wrinkled. "You're selling the Roots family home? An original house hasn't gone on the market since . . ." His voice turned to a whisper. "I don't even know when."

An original house referred to those passed through generations that traced back to the founding fathers of Salem. More specifically, the pure bloodlines filled with witches and politicians. The two groups were often linked.

"I don't belong here. Never did." She took another sip of her wine.

Charles motioned the way they'd come and led them to a sliding door on the other side of the loft. "Let's eat out on the deck. I'll light the fire-pit."

His hand slid to the dip in her lower back as he guided her. That's when Vianna saw the ghost sprawled over a white patio couch, a spandex dress hiked around her hips, displaying her lack of panties. Vianna stumbled over the ledge of the sliding door. A needle flopped from the ghost's scabbed arm, giving a no-brainer explanation of how she died. The woman could be a former tenant, a guest of a former tenant, or a whole host of other things. It didn't mean Charles knew her.

The large couch and a rectangle stone table dominated the patio that was the length of half of the building. Fancy pillar lamps with gaslit flames lined the railing behind the couch. Vianna sat with her back to the ghost, stiff cushions scratching against the back of her legs. Charles sat beside her, flicking a switch hidden in a strip of shimmering granite stones in the center of the table, and a blue flame rippled from beneath the rocks.

He leaned into the corner of the couch as he drank from his wine glass. She took a sip of her own; it was a hell of a lot smoother than Mother's moonshine. The glow of lights from downtown highlighted the treetops, and distant music from a band with horns—one very off key—created a festive ambiance.

"So, what have I missed in the last ten years? Anything interesting?" *Maybe something about Nancy?*

"Let's see." He draped an arm over the back of the couch. "You've missed thousands of tourists looking for witches, covens fighting over initiates and territory—and I opened an art gallery."

"An art gallery? With your mother, I assume?"

The ghost of the woman in a purple spandex dress had stood and now twirled around on the patio with her arms out, giggling as she stumbled in her strappy heels.

"The gallery is mine, but yes, her art is on display, along with other artists. My mother travels a lot, and I got in the habit of accompanying her. Discovered I have an eye for what sells."

Alice reappeared with a tray, walking through the dancing ghost who took a face-first dive through the table. Vianna focused on Alice and the lowered tray she offered, hoping her face hadn't cringed too dramatically at the ghost's performance. Vianna peered at the tray and into tiny cups of . . . fish eggs? She was hungry, but that wasn't food by her standards. Memories of the squirming maggots on Nancy's hand made her stomach flip. What was wrong with a good old-fashioned pizza or grilled cheese? Her mouth watered at the mere thought.

Charles laughed. "You'd be horrible at poker." He turned to Alice. "Have Austen make something more *casual*."

Alice batted her lashes excessively. "Of course, Mr. Barton."

Her attention seemed like it was aimed at flirting with Charles, not poking fun at Vianna. Although, it could be both. Alice left with her slimy fish balls, and Vianna turned to look at Charles. It was clear he had his pick of women, just like in high school. He was good-looking, successful, and kinda nice, but something was missing. She wanted to rustle his hair and leave piles of clutter in his house to disrupt the pristine order of everything, but she didn't imagine that would go over well.

"You mentioned witch coven drama? Sounds like the same old, same old." She refocused the conversation back to getting information about Nancy.

"Just the usual. You know all about that," Charles said. "Which family names have what right to what area for business."

Getting the right information was going to require a more direct approach. "Do you remember Nancy? She was in our grade."

That might have been a little too direct. Her focus was shot, and her insides felt like a disturbed ant pile. Somehow during the interaction, Charles had migrated closer to her on the couch—his knee pressed against hers. She took another drink of wine.

His brow furrowed. "Nancy? You mean the witch from the Mabon Coven who went missing?"

Vianna tilted her head in question. "She's missing? I didn't know that. I couldn't get a hold of her since I got back, and we were friends back in the day."

He placed a hand on her leg. "I'm sorry. I didn't know you were that close. It was about a month ago that I heard whisperings. You'd have to check in with the covens for details."

Vianna nodded her head as if that were a possibility. She didn't need leads on how to find her; she knew exactly what happened to Nancy. Vianna wanted to know why. Charles changed the subject to stories of travel and unique artists within his gallery, but Vianna's attention wouldn't leave Nancy. Killing a witch brought larger repercussions than your typical murder. And why the hands?

Charles moved on to former classmates and where they were now. She nodded along. Was it possible the coven planned the kill, or was her mother working rogue?

Alice came back. "Would you like dinner served here?"

"Yes, Alice. That would be excellent."

The smell of fried food made Vianna's stomach rumble, and trays of cheeseburgers and fries appeared. She rubbed her hands together and focused on the glory before her. The burger filled both hands, and she took a large bite. The lettuce even had a crisp snap, and a pickle spear peeked out from the fries. This date was climbing the ranks.

"So, where did you disappear to in the past ten years? Travel anywhere exciting?" Charles asked before taking a bite of his own burger.

She swallowed the bite in her mouth. "Oh, yeah, Boston is super exotic."

His brow raised. "You were that close? I'm surprised your mom didn't haul you back."

"There's a saying about that, I think. Hiding in plain sight?" She ate a fry. Only she hadn't been hiding as well as she'd thought. Mother knew where she was all along.

"What were you doing in Boston? I hope not falling in love with some handsome, rich guy who has already swept you off your feet." He grinned.

"News travels fast." She took another bite.

His expression dropped. "You're with someone?"

She debated lying, but shook her head. "I'm teasing. I'm too busy for relationships." Most of her nights were spent finding new candle designs with dried flowers, but he didn't need to know that. She wiped her mouth with the cloth napkin and slumped back into the couch. The ghost had reappeared, tying up her arm—a needle close by—bopping her head to the beat of music only she could hear. Definitely an overdose.

Charles chuckled. "You look like a satisfied woman."

"I am." She smiled. Music from the festival picked up in tempo as a trumpet finished a long solo. "The band isn't too bad."

"We can walk down to the festival, if you like."

She shook her head. "I'm too full to move. Plus . . ." She grimaced. "Tourists. Yuck."

"Agreed." He picked up his wine and leaned back, draping an arm across the back of the couch, this time behind her.

Her hair tickled her neck, and she guessed his fingers were playing in it. She swallowed and sat up to reach for her own glass. Teenage-Vianna would have melted into a puddle of lust, but something felt off.

"You were always pretty, but you've grown into stunning, Vianna."

She gave a nervous chuckle. "Pretty sure you barely knew I existed when we were kids."

He leaned forward, fingertips tracing her thigh. "I was a dumb kid."

She gave a gentle squeeze to his fingers and stood. "The food was good. Thank you. I better get going, though. I'm sorry, I've got a lot to get done at the house."

It was clear that teenage-Vianna and adult-Vianna weren't one and the same. She was still attracted to Charles, obviously, but her focus was on the house and Nancy, not strolling down memory lane. The growing urge to give him what he wanted, to sit back down and see where things went, felt like a prickle beneath her skin, and she second-guessed her resistance.

"I'm glad you came over. I've *really* enjoyed your company. Maybe we could meet up tomorrow?" He set his glass on the stone table and stood.

Following him inside, she grabbed her purse. "I'm not staying in town very long."

"Yes, you've mentioned that." He grabbed keys and looked back with a smirk. "You're preparing a house that's been in your family for twelve generations for the market. Sounds like an extensive project that might keep you here for a little while. Plus, you clearly need food with how you devoured that burger. Hopefully, my company isn't *that* bad."

She smirked. "No, not that bad."

"Wow, such glowing words. Careful, you might inflate my ego too much."

"Ha. You've got plenty of people around for that."

As they left, he locked both doors, upstairs and down. This time, she let him open the car door. The drive back felt faster than the drive there, despite not using his special launch feature. He pulled into her driveway and turned toward her with a dimpled smile.

"See you tomorrow?"

Fresh air cleared her mind, and the feeling of festering ants had gone away. She stepped out of the car and shut the door before looking back. He truly was striking, confident, and once upon a time she'd have fallen over backward for this exact evening. But now, he felt . . . she didn't know the word. She just didn't feel comfortable with Prince Charming. "I've got a lot to get done, and I don't think it's the best idea, but thank you again for dinner."

His smile only widened. "I'll call you tomorrow. Maybe you'll have some free time."

He sped off before she could reply, and she shook her head. Never in a million years would she have planned on spending time with Charles Barton. She walked up the steps, and surprisingly, the front door slid open in welcome.

8

A Secret Odyssey

Despite having the world's longest to-do list, Vianna decided sleep came first. Tomorrow she'd handle sorting through closets and hunting down the missing hand. She spread the tattered gray comforter from the hall closet over the bed. The garlic scent had dissipated until she flopped onto the mattress and a puff engulfed her. Even the pillow she'd brought from Boston with drops of lavender oil couldn't compete with the fumes.

Crickets chirped from the open window, and a faint breeze offered relief from the summer heat. She sprawled on top of the comforter, and instead of passing out from exhaustion, her mind buzzed, replaying the day. Sleep had eluded her for as far back as she could remember. As a child, the fear of monsters kept her eyelids peeled open. As an adult, she realized there was relief in closing her eyes against the terrors because they couldn't touch her, but logic didn't change the hard-wiring in her brain.

With a huff of defeat, she rolled onto her back and stared at the crack and weird blobby stain on the ceiling. No matter how hard she tried, she couldn't shake the questions about Nancy's death that seemed to multiply by the hour. The memory of her pleading haunted Vianna. Killing a witch was punishable by death and would bring dishonor to an entire line. Nothing mattered more to Angeline Roots than the honor of her legacy name. The pieces didn't add up.

Ten years of silence had left Vianna on the outside, but now she needed back in for a hot minute. She had to know why Mother killed Nancy, had to know if it was her fault. There was a cheat to get her up to speed, a place where things were documented and coven activity held accountable. She needed to visit the coven caves. After sleep, though.

She yanked the pillow over her head and squeezed her eyes shut. After a few minutes turned into a few hours of tossing and turning, morning spilled through her window in cotton-candy-pink bursts. With a groan of acceptance, she pulled herself upright, fantasizing about coffee.

A list of things to clean out in the old house rattled through her head as she pulled on shorts. The closets were likely to be a nightmare, but her mind wandered to the log books listing coven assignments that were tucked away in the coven caves. Information would give her some idea of what Mother had been up to, besides killing other witches.

Vianna slipped on shoes and reached for her truck keys from the top of the dresser, then stopped. No. She was staying here and cleaning, not getting distracted in whatever mess her mother had caused. Practicality was the obvious choice: clean the house, sell it, and keep her nose out of the rest. Still, there were a lot of unanswered questions, and ignorance was never bliss.

She'd work slower if distracted, and a quick field trip might help her focus. If Vianna wanted to find Nancy's hand and release her ghost from being tortured in the bathroom, understanding why she'd been in the house could help. Any clue would help. It wouldn't take long to poke around the logbooks. Plus, she could swing by the market afterward for food. With her decision made, she grabbed the keys, hopped out the front door, and slid into her beat-up Ford to drive across town.

Two blocks down, the stoplight at the intersection was still the longest in the world. Rolled-down windows didn't help with the lack of air movement. Morning sun burned on her forearm, and she pulled down the visor even though it shaded the dashboard instead of her arm.

She pulled into the small parking lot in front of a three-story brick building with a hanging metal sign that read Salem Library. The dirt parking lot was half-full, and all the vehicles had local license plates. Gravel crunched beneath her soles as she closed the truck door with her hip. The cobblestone walkway was only a few feet, with well-trimmed hedges lining both sides. When she opened the door, a wave of cold air-conditioned air washed over her with a welcome chill. A small boy in overalls played with a wooden push train on the floor by the front desk. His freckled nose scrunched at her entrance, and he sent the toy careening in her direction, but it faded to a puff of air as it ran through her feet. The ghost child vanished with his toy.

There was no librarian at the front counter, but a few people lingered in the stacks closest to the front desk. An elderly white man in a brown sweater leaned on his cane as he hobbled down a row of books, angrily mumbling to himself in a language Vianna didn't recognize. She snaked through bookshelves and open study areas with tables toward the back corner of the building. The coven caves were one of the few places her mother allowed her to spend her spare time, and these walls had become her haven.

Mistress Layton sat on a chair in the corner, crocheting the same brown mess of yarn as always. The years of age hung from her cheeks and arms since the last time Vianna had seen her. Yarn bulged from a bag bedazzled with gold stars that sat at her feet. Vianna shook her head and smiled. She didn't remember the old coven librarian as much of a bedazzler.

"Blessed moon, Mistress Layton." Vianna beamed.

"Little Vianna Roots!" The old witch stood and hobbled toward her, and Vianna met her halfway before being embraced in a hug that smelled of sunflowers and sugar. She held Vianna back with both hands and appraised her.

"I saw you at your mother's burial. Spicy as ever." The old witch winked. "I didn't want to bother you during such a sacred time, but I'm happy to see you're back. The coven could use some fresh Roots blood."

A frown tightened Vianna's lips. "I'm not back, not like that. Just handling family affairs and then I'm leaving."

Mistress Layton gave one of those smirks that seemed like she knew something others didn't. She probably did.

"I was hoping to poke around in the caves a bit." Vianna gave a smile she hoped was as endearing as it was ten years ago.

Technically, as a solitary witch, she couldn't enter the coven caves. Only coven-bound witches had such rights. However, children of legacy witches were allowed. Vianna was still the child of a legacy, but she was solitary, making her both allowed and forbidden.

"Have at it, darling. A few others are mingling, but not much of a crowd." The old wooden chair groaned as Mistress Layton settled back down.

With four major covens and a constant rotation of lesser established covens, there was always someone in the caves. She pulled the spine of Homer's *Odyssey* at the end of the shelf, and the bookshelf beside Mistress Layton clicked open a crack. Using her toe to nudge the secret door open wider, Vianna slipped through. On the second step down, the wall closed behind her with a soft click.

She trailed her fingertips along the polished marble of the banister, and her eyes adjusted to the dim light after a few more stairs. Although the caves were underground, they were lavish and well-tended. Connections with the deepest pockets in Salem meant witches weren't just dancing around bonfires; they roosted in the most extravagant homes and swayed every local election. Coven witches were hired enforcers who whispered death in the middle of the night to those who dared run against their candidate. In return, politicians gifted generous donations, and the coven caves were a testament to just how generous.

Ornate black chandeliers hung from the ceilings of patterned stonework. At the bottom of the stairs, a common area sprawled with lush sofas, chairs, and piles of pillows. A fire crackled in the carved mantel that stood taller than Vianna. Archways led in all different directions to long tunnels. Each coven had its own cavern that varied in depth and size.

Vianna kept her focus locked straight ahead to draw as little attention as possible. Who sat with whom and the political hierarchy was a high-stakes game. Added to that was the high volume of ghosts who paced among the living in their period clothing: flapper dresses, cover it all puritan smocks, and large Southern Belle hemlines. The familiar copper tang wafted from the entrance to the cutting room on the other side of the fireplace. Cutting was basic knowledge for witches, since most spells required sacrifice. Competitions of cleanest cuts, most blood spilled, and artistic scars were a common pastime. As a legacy, Vianna was more than proficient in understanding how to cut and even how to stitch herself, but she'd never felt the need to get into competition over it.

An archway set in darker stone marked the Original Blood entrance. She stepped over the symbol of a deformed star engraved on a footstone, making the new marking on her collarbone flare with heat. Each coven used hexes of protection at their cave entrance, and the star symbol caused five points of pain for five days straight, supposedly. She'd never seen the curse in action, but witches weren't known for bluffing.

The entry room held records of births, marriages, convictions, and deaths in leather-bound books lining shelves that stretched from floor to ceiling. While the room was empty of the living, a familiar ghost paced the shelves, running her fingers across the spines. Her peasant dress was identical to Grandma's, only a deep blue and torn at the collar and sleeve. For the blink of an eye, smudged footprints on the polished stone trailed behind her before lifting away like fog on a bathroom mirror.

The next cavern further in were the research stacks: books on herbs, foliage, animals, bugs, fungus—basically any ingredient needed for magic, but no actual spells. Being taught a spell or hex was an honor. Writing spells meant anyone could learn generations of secrets instead of earning the right—which was why families reserved writing down spells for their grimoires.

Cleansing sage burned from pillars in the corners by the stacks, and several witches were curled into overstuffed chairs and couches with books on their laps. The stacks were three times the size of the family records room, and a smaller version of the fire mantel from the common area was nestled into the back wall.

The assignment logs were in a deeper cave, so with her head held high, she walked past several of the scowls she'd attracted, through a tunnel with narrow strips of wood between tiled stone. The logs contained every assignment, along with the payment and split of dues to the coven. Witches were for hire: the common hex, love potion, bout of bad luck, fruitful harvest, nasty infection, or even a simple tea to soothe a common cold. Assignments for the Original Blood Coven were more costly—and more deadly. Vianna didn't expect tea prep to appear in the logbooks with Mother's name.

Since the Original Blood Coven was the most sought after on

the East Coast, their books were extensive. An hour or two might've been an underestimation, but she was here. *A job halfway done isn't worth doing.* Mother's words echoed in her head, and as much as she hated them, she lived by them.

She moved through two more archways then stopped short. There was another witch in the cavern with a book propped on long almond-colored legs stretched over the thick wooden table. Crossed ankles showed off purple heels, and she wore a black skirt with graffiti patterns in bright colors. Lollipop and candy wrappers littered the table, and Vianna recognized them.

"You," she blurted.

The woman closed the book and raised her eyes to Vianna but didn't change her position.

"You were the groundskeeper with the candy yesterday." Vianna tilted her head as she tried to piece together who she was. She had dark brows that matched her curly hair and didn't seem familiar in any of the older witches she knew. "Coven witches don't work at the cemetery."

Such a position was beneath a bound witch. They only worked for their coven.

"I finally get to meet Vianna Roots, the infamous runaway legacy." The woman tucked a silky curl behind her ear. "I'm Sandeen Layton." She stood and slid her book onto a shelf behind her.

"Layton?" Vianna echoed the last name as she processed.

Mistress Layton was a member of the Original Blood Coven—which explained why Sandeen had access to the caves, but not why she worked at the cemetery. The librarian had one child, a young boy. Realization dawned.

"You're Mistress Layton's son—kid." She wanted to kick herself for blurting before thinking.

"Daughter," Sandeen corrected. Vianna didn't miss the tightening in the woman's jaw. Men were forbidden to learn the craft, and

Vianna didn't imagine a transgender witch was met with kindness or acceptance.

"Are you a witch?" Vianna asked.

Of course she was; she was in the coven caves studying. Her ability to think before she spoke needed more than a little work.

Sandeen leaned against the shelf with her shoulder. "A solitary witch. Just like you, kinda."

They were both tolerated and scorned by the society they were born into. They had a bit in common. Vianna eyed the row of books behind Sandeen.

"Didn't look like you were on good terms with your mother at the cemetery," Sandeen said.

"Wow. Just gettin' right to it?" Vianna was used to veiled words filled with layers of meanings and assumptions from other witches. Directness was refreshing. "I despised my mother."

"She was one hell of a witch." Sandeen whistled.

Vianna shrugged. Assessments depended on the variables judged. "Well, it was nice to meet you. I'll let you get back to it." She nodded a polite goodbye as she went to the shelves with the most recent assignment logs.

Sandeen followed. "What are you looking for? I can help."

"I spent my childhood in these stacks. I'm good." She reached for the logbook from last month. Her mother died almost two weeks ago, making this month's logbook useless.

"Angeline hadn't been assigned jobs for almost six months." Sandeen pulled a book with older dates scrawled on the spine and plopped it on the table. "I spent the last eight years in these caves while you were . . . whatever you were doing. So I can help."

Six months since an assignment? That wasn't normal. Vianna sat in a chair carved from a tree stump. "I was avoiding this town. That's what I was doing. And I was gone for ten years, not eight."

"Ah, well, eight years ago was when I told my mother I was a witch. So the caves had two years without either of us."

"Oh." Vianna nodded. She knew all about hiding in the nooks and crannies of the library, burying herself in books. It was a good place for those who belonged but didn't fit.

"So you're a solitary witch who sneaks around the coven caves by day and a groundskeeper by night?"

"You can call me Dee for short." Sandeen gave a smirk.

Vianna thumbed the edge of the book she'd pulled down. "Was my mother the only witch not getting jobs?"

Dee's forehead crinkled as she considered. "Rose Barton's been assigned more than others, and every witch had fewer jobs because of it, but your mom seemed to stop getting coven assignments altogether."

Rose was Charles's mother. The Barton name was coming up a lot.

"There are rumors of the coven mother pushing for a union with Charles and Tiphonie." Dee shrugged. "I assumed that's why Rose was being buttered up by Josephine. Not too many eligible bachelors floating around Salem. And the precious coven-mother-in-training has to have a proper match."

Tiphonie's interest in Charles added to a long list of reasons to stay away from him. Regardless of what he said, there must've been more than just one date between the two.

"Salem hasn't changed a bit." Not that she'd expected it to. "Hey, do you know the story of why the coven allowed Rose to take on a legacy mantle, despite being a first-generation witch?"

Dee raised a brow. "I didn't know she was only a first generation, but it's common knowledge that she saved the great Barton line after the accident with the young Barton witch."

"What happened to her?"

"She drowned a year after her mother died of an allergic reaction.

It wasn't until a few years later that Rose hooked up with Charles Senior, but somehow it all worked out."

That painted a clearer picture of Rose, but what did it have to do with Mother or Nancy? Mother not getting jobs from the coven explained the lack of supplies beyond home-made moonshine in the house. She flipped open the logbook.

Dee stood, and Vianna expected her to leave. Instead, she pulled two more books from the shelves and plopped down on the other side of the table with a smile. "I'll see if anything looks odd in the six months prior to the logs you have."

Dee flicked over a mini-bag of Sour Patch Kids, and Vianna grinned as she took it.

9

Baby Witch

A few hours later, Vianna gave her goodbyes to Mistress Layton and Dee and drove to the market, where she scored off-brand coffee and melted chocolate from the clearance section. Then she stopped by the shipping dock in the back and snuck off with a couple of sturdy boxes to use for packing. She twirled her silver infinity-loop ring on her middle finger as she kicked into autopilot and drove down a back road to the house.

The coven caves had dug up as many emotions as her old home. Emotions she'd long since shoved deep within, where they belonged, but they'd resurfaced with the ease of spring blossoms. Something shifted in her back pocket, and she pulled out a mini pack of jelly-beans, then chuckled. Mistress Layton had always slipped candy in her pockets as a kid. Like mother, like daughter. She supposed there were good memories of Salem if she thought about it, but the bad ones had a habit of taking up more space and time in her head. She ripped the bag open and picked out a green jellybean.

Dee had been a pleasant surprise. They'd scoured her mother's assignments over the past two years, but there was nothing in the logs about Nancy. What few assignments that were in the logbook for Mother were spells that younger, inexperienced witches could've handled. Losing favor with the coven mother might put you on a list of crap assignments, but not when you were Angeline Roots. Mother always landed big cases that brought in a lot of money; for the coven to turn their nose at that was unheard of.

Something nagged at Vianna about Tiphonie and Charles. The Parker line was stronger, more established, than the Bartons. The pairing was more beneficial to Charles than Tiph. So why was Josephine schmoozing Rose when it should be the other way around? Maybe none of it mattered, and Vianna was letting nonsense cloud her thoughts after spending time with Charles, but she didn't think so.

She parked the truck in front of the house and let her head rest on the steering wheel. The thump in her chest beat faster, but there was no reason for it. There was no Mother with a whipping stick, and she'd never again sleep in her childhood bed.

Grabbing the brown bag of groceries, she slid down from her truck and noticed a cloth sack on the porch with a single red rose. She hitched the groceries onto her hip and paced the area for markings or smudges to signify a trap, but found none, so she peeked into the bag. The smell of melted cheese and sausage wafted upward, making her stomach rumble. Unfolding the note that sat on top of the takeout boxes, she frowned.

Vianna,

I enjoyed your company last night and look forward to seeing you again. Something came up tonight, but I'm all yours tomorrow. Lunch is on me.

Yours truly, Charles

The irony wasn't lost on her. She'd have done anything for Charlie's attention ten years ago, and now that she had it, she wasn't sure she wanted it. She rubbed at her collarbone, then flinched because the mark was still tender. Whatever was going on with him or her feelings toward him, the food smelled orgasmic.

She juggled both bags, and the door swung open to Grandma Susannah. Vianna walked through her and toward the kitchen, shaking off the chill down her back.

"A trap was left on the porch." Grandma's beady eyes narrowed. "Have you fortified the perimeters?"

She set the bags on the kitchen counter. "Maybe missionaries left a Bible to save your soul." They were a little late. There'd been nothing salvageable under this roof for centuries.

"Do not get smart with me, you lackluster nitwit." Grandma hovered over Vianna's shoulder. "You are in over your head."

Vianna gave a slow, tired shake of her head. "It was just food, Grandmother. Charles Barton dropped it off. And maybe I wouldn't be so in over my head if you'd tell me why Mother killed Nancy."

"Nancy got what she deserved." Grandma's voice rose into a shrill. "You haven't answered my question. Did you fortify the perimeters?"

"I'll add it to the list." The very bottom of the list. Grandma was paranoid, and Vianna had no idea what she was supposed to fortify against.

Vianna turned her attention to the decadent smells permeating from the paper bag. She picked up the plastic fork on top of the container and pulled the boxes out, then slumped into the wooden dining chair. Opening the flaps revealed a circle of sliced sausages spread over a heaping portion of the good mac 'n' cheese—the creamy yellow kind instead of the bright orange stuff. She stabbed a sausage with the fork and scooped up pasta shells along with it, then took a bite.

Still warm, creamy cheese made every taste bud jump for joy. A deep groan of appreciation rumbled up her throat. It really was the good kind.

She opened her eyes just as Grandma vomited green chunks coated in white acid pus over the table, splattering Vianna's face and chest. It didn't matter that she couldn't feel the chunks, she could see them, and the smell alone challenged her perception of what was real and what wasn't. Her stomach convulsed, and she covered her mouth.

Vomit was a regular tactic when Grandma didn't get her way. Vianna wasn't giving into the theatrics by giving her the reaction she deserved. With effort, she swallowed her bite, boxed up the leftovers, and shoved them into the fridge. There was nothing to say. Ghosts weren't rational, much less grandmothers.

She pulled out the cleaning gloves and a rag from beneath the sink. Lemon disinfectant soothed her as she scrubbed the already-clean table. Sometimes the motion of cleaning distracted her brain from the vomit and severed hands that were a normal day in the Roots house. After the table, she moved to the baseboards. Maybe if she went through every closet and cupboard, she'd find some clue as to why Mother had started behaving like a solitary witch. The coven logs had shown inactivity for close to a year. Maybe Vianna would even find Nancy's hand in some forgotten cupboard so she could put her friend to rest—or, knowing her luck, she'd find more hands. Maybe she could form an entire collection.

After the kitchen baseboards were spotless, she moved into the living room. Dust coated every surface, but time sped up as she went to work, and the room was dust-free before she realized. She grabbed the cardboard boxes from the back of her truck. There was enough crap in the house to fill three times as many boxes, but she'd load dishes and knick-knacks for starters.

A box sat on her hip as she looked at the rows of picture frames on the mantel. Each set of cold eyes was a distorted version of herself. Some had the same long dark hair, some the mole on their chin, some the full lips, even if always set in a frown, but all of them had the same perfect posture. They were proper witches, each and every one.

Her eyes flicked to the wingback chairs by the bay windows as memories flooded in of holding that "proper posture" while balancing books on her head for hours. A Roots witch was always in control, and that included posture. Vianna slumped her shoulders and moved to the built-in shelves that lined the fireplace. She'd box up the picture frames later.

Antique sewing boxes and vintage embroidery tools filled the shelves. She might get a little cash for the stuff at a pawnshop. A low rumble came from within her chest instead of the house, and she paused, her hand on a vintage thread-spool display. Someone knocked on the front door, and Vianna jumped in surprise, knock-ing over spools of blue threads. She glared at whoever was waiting on the porch. There wasn't a single person she could think of who should be knocking on that door right now.

She set the box she'd been filling on the merlot-striped fainting couch, then moved to the door. Opening it by only a small crack, she peeked at the man standing on her porch. He wore an open plum cardigan with the sleeves pushed back, revealing raised scars criss-crossed on his black skin. The cartilage between his nostrils was pierced, and he sported a mo-hawk of locs.

"You are Vianna, yes?" He raised a brow at her, and she opened the door a fraction further. "Ye wear the same scowl as your ma."

She flinched at the comparison. "Can I help you?"

He leaned closer, pushing the door further open and invading her personal space as he inhaled. The scent of burned wood rushed over her, and she nudged him back with a hand to the chest. "My mother's dead, and I can't help you. Find someone else." *Holy goddess. Anyone else.*

"Unacceptable." He shook his head, then barged into the house.

Vianna stumbled backward, and the house grumbled inside of her chest. "Excuse you. You're not invited."

Making himself at home, he settled into the red cushions of Mother's embroidery chair and smiled. Vianna left the door open, since he'd be leaving any second, and stepped into the sitting room.

"His kind is not welcome here," Grandma hissed as she crossed the room toward him.

Vianna wasn't sure which "kind" she was referring to, but anyone barging in wasn't welcome.

"He reeks of hoodoo," Grandma growled as she circled the chair he sat in.

That clarified Grandma's reaction. Hoodoo practitioners had a habit of undoing the harm witches spread. If not for hoodoo, witches would rule unchecked in the terror they inflicted. Witches hexed. Hoodoo healed. The real curiosity was why a practitioner would show up on a legacy witch's door, especially Mother's.

Vianna folded her arms over her chest. "This is the part where you tell me who you are." Or the part where he left, but he clearly had something to say, and unfortunately, she couldn't ignore the living like she did the dead.

His casual posture stiffened the slightest fraction. He expected her to know who he was. "Csada Laguerre. I've come to make an offer on the house." He crossed an ankle over his knee and stretched out in the chair. His cargo pants were rolled up, showing off hemp sandals.

Vianna's brow shot up. "You?"

"Yes." He nodded, unaffected by her shock.

She desperately wanted to stick to her own path of shelf stocking and plotting a maybe-one-day boutique. This could solve everything. The normal rumble of the house was the faintest whisper of a whine, easily confused with creaking wood joints. An unexpected slice of guilt slithered through her.

"Name your price." Csada's smile wasn't the warm, welcoming kind, but the confident grin that came right before a fatal blow.

Grandma stopped pacing and spat at his feet. The offer was too perfect in its timing, too perfect of a solution. Vianna narrowed her eyes and resisted stepping further away like she wanted. "This is coven territory. You couldn't possibly want this house."

He gave a casual wave of his hand in the air. "Times have changed. Your neighbor, three doors down, is an ordinary citizen. No legacy. No craft. Maybe it's time to mix things up."

Vianna hadn't planned on selling to an ordinary citizen. There were plenty of witches, of all flavors, coven-bound or not, to make a market for the house to sell. Grandma flashed in front of Vianna, nose to nose, making her startle. She hoped Csada didn't notice. "That dandy prat is nothing more than a heathen philosopher," Grandma growled. "You are not selling."

"How did you know I would be here?" Vianna asked. She didn't trust anything about him or the offer.

"Yesterday was your mother's funeral. Was it not obvious you would resurface?" He leaned his elbow on the ornate wooden armrest of the chair, resting his chin in the crook of his thumb.

Sure, it would have been obvious to a coven-bound witch, but legacy funerals weren't advertised to the public.

"How did you know the funeral was today?"

He broke into a broad smile. "Witches love their pillow talk."

Vianna wrinkled her nose. That was more information than she wanted.

"Throw him out. Right this instant." Grandma jabbed her finger at Vianna's chest.

"Enough. I'm bored with this chitter chatter." Csada stood and his upper lip twitched. "Do not play coy. You are the witch who ran away, are you not? Your mother is dead and you don't want to be in Salem. Sell me the house. Name your price." He pulled a pocket-knife from his pants pocket. "We will make a blood pact. Then you can trust me."

Nope. All the nope. "A legal document will do just fine."

The corners of his mouth tightened. "We can handle this now. No need to complicate matters. You want to leave. I want to stay. What is your price?"

A creepy-crawly feeling clung to her skin. Yes, she wanted to leave Salem, but . . . something wasn't right. She couldn't leave the family demon to just anyone, and she needed to know what had happened to Nancy. Not just what happened, she realized. She wanted to put her friend to rest instead of leaving her to haunt the bathroom. Nancy deserved more.

"No." She didn't offer an explanation. Her gut clenched at losing the opportunity that had been so close.

"Your manners are lacking, *baby* witch." There was no playfulness in his tone.

"Get him out!" Grandma screeched as she flashed in and out of existence around the room at disorienting speeds, making Vianna dizzy as she tried to track her.

The house rumbled within her chest, stronger and surer than before, and she scanned the room for every potential weapon. The drawer in the console table beneath the stairs held a blade to open envelopes. On the other side of the room, a fire poker dangled from the hook on the hearth, but several pieces of furniture stood in her path.

Csada flipped open the pocketknife and slid the blade across his palm. "This is the last time I will offer such generosity. Sell me the house."

A cold frost webbed over her insides, and she shook her head. "I said no." Whatever he offered, it was wrong. She wasn't interested.

His chin lowered, his eyes narrowed, and he began to mumble words under his breath that she couldn't make out. She leaned in to hear him, then pulled back at Grandma's flickering ghost.

"Out, out, out!" Grandma screeched.

The floorboards of the house shook and both Vianna and Csada stumbled, his lips still whispering. Drawers opened and slammed shut. Vianna covered her ears and hunched her shoulders.

"You're under attack!" Grandma growled, each word spoken from a different corner of the room and sounding as though she were underwater.

Vianna gasped in a breath, stabilizing herself and focusing on the threat. "Get out." She crossed the room and shoved Csada with a hand. "Out!"

He flicked her hand away, then jabbed his palm into her sternum, and she flew back, stumbling against the console table pressed against the wall. Grandma yelled, the house rumbled, and Vianna wanted to hide in the closet. But she wasn't a little girl anymore, and there was nowhere left to hide.

10

Demon-Bound

The console table jammed into Vianna's back as she tried to create more distance from Csada. He kicked a side table out of his way, then stalked toward her.

"You don't deserve this house. You're too weak."

His hand struck out like a snake's head, latching onto her neck. Candles crashed to the ground as her hands flung out over the table-top. The house rumbled as an earthquake shook the ground, and he tilted his head to the side.

"You've already bonded with the house, I see. No matter. He will come to respect me."

Respect him? He didn't want the house; he wanted the Roots family familiar. Csada squeezed harder on her neck, and stars danced in her vision as she gasped for air. The small drawer of the table flung open, whacking her in the leg, and Vianna reached a hand down, stumbling for a weapon. Her fingers wrapped around a blade, and it sliced the side of her palm. Wetness slicked across her hand. She was bleeding. Legacy blood. She fisted her hand and squeezed against the sting.

She pulled her knee up hard, straight into Csada's crotch, and his grip dropped as he staggered backward. Memories shook loose, and Mother's voice whispered in her ear. Without thinking it through, Vianna repeated the words echoing in her head. "By the blood that came before me, the life that feeds the land beneath me, and the birthright bonded to strengthen me, you are banished from this house."

The floorboards groaned, the windows flung open, and a heavy wind tore through the house with a moaning howl. Ghostly-pale hands reached toward Csada from all sides. The faces from the mantel came into focus. They weren't like the living, but an army of flittering spirits that weren't formed enough to be corporeal. Their shrieks rippled through the house as they pulled at Csada's shoulders and arms.

He swung out, finding only air for his fists to swipe through. Roots witches of the past dragged him across the faded rug of the entryway. The whites of his eyes bulged and his arms outstretched as the ghosts swept him out and onto the porch. The front door slammed shut. A repeated *thud-thud-thud* came from the other side of the door, and Vianna knew Csada was falling down the porch steps.

The house was quiet but for Vianna's heavy breaths. In and out. Her heart hammered. The wind was gone, and the shrieking stopped. The new mark on her collarbone burned, and she rubbed at it, accidentally smearing blood across her skin. She pulled her palm back to look at the cut. It wasn't deep enough to need stitches. Outside, a motorcycle roared to life, then the single headlight flashed across the window before it zipped down the road.

"You've started something you can't finish." Grandma's nose poked between the curtains as she glared out the window.

"I'm not the one who started anything," Vianna said. She walked to a linen closet next to the laundry room and pulled out a first aid kit. "What just happened? How were all the ghosts able to do that?"

"You called for help. We answered." Grandma huffed from the other room. "You're confused by the simplest of things."

"I can call on witches past, anytime I want?" Vianna never imagined she'd need to call on a gang of murdering witches at the snap of her fingers, but it'd come in handy. She swiped a disinfectant wipe over the cut before slapping a Band-Aid on it.

Grandma appeared at Vianna's side. "Only when in the house. And only those of your blood."

And they could physically touch when called on—that would undoubtedly haunt her nightmares. Vianna put the first aid kit back, then turned and went into the kitchen. She unscrewed the jar of moonshine on the counter and took a drink.

Grandma followed and hovered at her side. "The mantle has not fully passed. The connection with you feels off. Distant. What did you do?"

"I don't remember asking for some special connection," Vianna said.

"Your mother," Grandma said. "Where was her ghost?"

Vianna drummed the countertop with her fingers.

"Vianna Roots, answer your grandmother!"

She turned and faced her. "I didn't want any of this."

Grandma stepped closer to her. "What did you do?" she snarled through yellowed teeth.

"It's my life, and she is no longer a part of it. I made sure of it. She's bound to her grave."

With a blur of white, Grandma smacked Vianna across the face. Her wrinkled hand was only a gust of wind that moved Vianna's hair, but one day, Grandma would be strong enough to become a poltergeist.

"You're a lubberwort-barnacle upon our family. You are weak until she passes the mantle, and you've prevented her from doing that! You won't be able to protect what is ours," Grandma snarled.

Vianna nodded. "Maybe."

She'd lucked out remembering the chant she'd heard from Mother when she was little. Grandma was right in one thing: Vianna was vulnerable to attack. But she didn't have to be. There was an arsenal of weapons within these walls, and a manual to help her use them.

Vianna walked through Grandma, out of the kitchen, and down the peony hallway to the conjure room. She stopped at the edge of the engraved summoning circle on the floor, scanning the rows of drawers. A grimoire had to be larger than the average book. She frowned at the larger compartments by the floor where Nancy's hand had been. Reliving that experience was at the bottom of a long list of no-thank-you. With a deep breath, she faked being strong and started pulling open drawers.

"What are you still doing here? Go dig up your mother. Undo the wrong that you caused." Grandma appeared in the corner by a tower shelf system filled with push-pin cushions.

Digging up a body in the cemetery was not happening. "Where's the grimoire?"

Silence answered her. She pulled open a drawer filled with animal horns, one of which looked like the infamous rhino horn. The next drawer was a folded goat hide.

Grandma finally spoke. "You cannot find what is meant to be offered."

"Offered?" Vianna repeated. "By whom?"

"By Shuck, of course."

Vianna hadn't heard that name for a long time, and only in whispers through closed doors. Shuck. He was the family demon who possessed the house.

The desk against the wall shuddered, and a secret compartment popped open from beneath. "Oh," she breathed out. There was no game of keep-away or hide-and-seek, and Vianna raised a brow in surprise.

She pulled back the mahogany leather chair and lowered into it as she gave a closer look at the desk. The secret cubby hung from the bottom of the single drawer beneath the writing surface. Using both hands, she reached in and pulled out a large, heavy book with leather binding.

The cover of the book was soft as velvet as her fingertips traced the embossed family tree in the center with roots that stretched downward. There were answers and protection within the pages before her. But could she dabble in the same magic, with the same demon, and not become like all of those before her? She wasn't sure, but she couldn't leave Nancy to live for eternity in the bathroom. And what would happen if whoever bought the house didn't get along with Shuck? She hadn't considered him as a him until his rumbles started rumbling her bones. It would take more than light cleaning and minor repairs before the house would be sellable.

She chewed on the inside of her cheek and fidgeted with the edge of the book. There was no one left to handle this paper vault of secrets, this house and everything in it—no one but her. She cracked open the grimoire.

The first page was a list of names, some that she knew from the photos on the fireplace mantel in the living room, the first being Susannah Roots. The name below that was scratched out, Bethiah Roots. Halfway down the list, another scratched-out name, Lily Roots. The final name was Vianna's, in an elegant cursive flare that wasn't Mother's.

The next page was an agreement. She read the words three times to make sure she had them right. Bound in eternal servitude to one another, the Black Shuck would walk alongside the Roots clan. *The Black Shuck?* She hadn't thought to link the name with the myth.

Demonology was standard study for witches, and the lore on the Black Shuck claimed the demon was a large black dog, not a house. That almost explained the deep growls he liked for communicating. She kept reading.

Each Roots witch became the new ward, bound to Shuck, after the mantle passed. At the bottom of the page was a hand-drawn sketch that looked like the burn on her collarbone, and she reached for her own marking. When her ancestors had come to her at the grave, they'd branded her as their own, passing the mantle. She was next in line, regardless of what she wanted. The blood bonds she was born into were impossible to escape. Running away had changed nothing. The results were the same. Vianna was demon-bound. She twirled the infinity ring on her finger.

Witches who weren't demon-bound were mostly wishful herbalists, and Vianna liked that role. Understanding the benefits of the garden, of the world around her, gave her a sense of hope that not all magic was hurtful. Demon-bound witches were another beast entirely. Their ability reached far beyond understanding the elements of the earth and how to use them. Bonding with a demon gave a witch unearthly powers, and not the kind that made the world a better place. What kind of power, and to what degree, depended on the demon.

A tingly numbness spread through her limbs as her new reality seeped into her mind. Flipping through the pages only worsened the growing dread. The spells were a collection of ways to inflict harm. One after another, more variants of horrible actions: hallucinations, summoning fear, hexes, bad luck, insect plagues, and even one about raising the dead. All of it was too much for one person to know, too much potential to inflict pain.

She paused at something hopeful. An ancestral talisman for protection could help, until she read the ingredients. She was pretty sure she didn't have any ancestral bones lying around. Flipping more pages, she found an echo call to locate something lost. That was an interesting option for Nancy's hand. But Vianna needed something connected to what was lost, and she doubted that childhood memories counted. Numerous afternoons in the garden collecting herbs or candle room shenanigans together as little girls left Vianna with nothing more than a weighted feeling of guilt, because none of it mattered now. Vianna was useless in helping her friend.

She turned through more pages. Each spell had basic craft similarities: a different oil or herb-infused candle, an incense with various bird feathers to spread the smoke, ingredients to be mixed with a mortar and pestle, and a chant. The most important part of each spell came at the end, where she called on the bond with Shuck.

Vianna looked up from the grimoire, settling her attention on the squat black candle on the desk. She had countless recollections of Mother lighting candles or even the living room fireplace with a snap of her fingers.

Letting out a deep breath to release the bouncing jitters, she rubbed her hands together. There was no rumble within her bones from Shuck, so she closed her eyes to focus. Nothing happened. She opened her eyes with a frown. There was nothing in the grimoire about how to connect with a demon. They were bound. That was the end of the explanation.

"Well, I'm here. I'm trying. Now what?" Vianna spoke to the empty room.

The silence stretched on. "Helpful," she grumbled.

She'd had the mantle for all of two days and was already failing at being demon-bound. Maybe she didn't have what it took to be good at any of this, but that didn't settle right either. Vianna had always been more than just proficient at learning the craft. The rituals, the gardening, the planetary cycles, the symbols—all of it just made sense to her, and she'd been at the top of her class as a young witch. She had the knowledge, the last name. She should have fit, but she didn't. Seeing ghosts made her twitchy and different. That, coupled with her discomfort in causing harm, had made her an outcast.

Cupping her hand around the candle, she pulled it closer. Maybe she was trying too hard. Next time the demon got all grumbly on her, she'd try then. Releasing the candle, she pushed the chair back and stood—then paused. A taut cord of tension pulled through her core. She tilted her head at the candle.

"There you are," she whispered as she extended a hand toward the candle.

The familiar grumble came in a soft wave. Vianna swiped her palm above the wick, and a flame jumped to life. She sucked in her breath, then grinned. *Magic.*

11

Weeds

Vianna stared at the dust particles that floated in the gold-tinted rays shining through the crack in the thick curtains. She'd been staring at the same nothing for the past hour. A solid four hours of sleep was what she logged for the night, which, to be honest, was about average for her. Waiting for things to go bump in the night had over-ridden slumber for as long as she could remember.

The smell of garlic lingered, and with it, the feeling that the room wasn't hers. Mother's belongings bulged from the piles of garbage bags stacked in the corner. One moment the room was her mother's, and the next, it was hers. Change was like that.

It wasn't just the master suite but the entire house, layered in memories and ghosts, that now belonged to her. Horror and pain was the Roots legacy. Vianna huffed and focused back on the dust particles caught in sunrays. They were just like her. Trapped.

Birds chirped outside her window, dispersing what lingering hope she had of extra sleep. She jerked the quilt down and swung her feet over the edge of the mattress. The garden had beckoned for days. She rubbed her hands over her face, then checked that the Band-Aid on the side of her palm was solid. The better shape the house was in, the higher its value. Even though cleaning the inside should be her priority—along with finding Nancy's hand and possibly learning about whoever Csada was—her fingers itched for the soil. Besides, her head needed space from the intensity of being inside the house. She slid into a pair of shorts and found her battered tennis shoes.

Once downstairs, she zapped a cup of clearance instant coffee, and then, with a porcelain mug cradled in both hands, she walked the perimeter of the backyard and made a game plan. Seasons had come and gone without the muck being properly turned into mulch. Instead, the bottom layers had turned to slime, then dried into patties of useless waste stuffed in every corner.

A breeze rustled her loose hair, and she closed her eyes, raising her chin to the sky so the warmth from the sun could soak into her face. For a moment, things felt peaceful and the glimmer of hope that everything would be okay threatened to bloom. Instead, she opened her eyes and drank shitty coffee. A long day of work was ahead of her.

The first step was to rake and bag the piles. After choking down half a cup of her coffee, she set it on the porch and got to work. With each bag filled, her muscles loosened into the heat of exertion, and with it, her mind too. She thought about Csada and his desperation over claiming the house. His words rattled her head. *Too weak for the house.* Had he approached Mother? She guessed not since he was still alive.

Maybe Csada was right, and she was too weak. Would the banishment hold? Grandma had said something was off with the mantle. Would calling on Mother make Vianna stronger? She wasn't sure she wanted to be stronger, not at that price. Vianna raked with more force.

The sun inched upward and away from the horizon as hours ticked by. Sweat dripped down her back and neck. She knelt on a towel and worked through the weeds that'd taken over the flower beds. The roots were hard to get out without snapping the tips. Just like an infection, you had to get it all, or they came back.

She needed to refocus on her priorities. Sell the house and use the money to open an herb shop back in Boston. Maybe even move out of the roach apartment owned by the creepy landlord and his greasy son. That was her plan. She didn't know how to fix her problems, much less Nancy's. Run and don't look back. The top soil was baked into a solid mud cake, and instead of kneading it, she punched at it. Run away and avoid, the classic Vianna move. She hit the soil harder.

The tips of Grandma's scuffed boots appeared on the soil in front of her. "The coven is here. You smell of a remedy critch, and your hair has evolved into a rat's nest. Fix it." There was a growl with the last two words.

Vianna gripped the base of a thick weed and wiggled to loosen the surrounding soil instead of pulling.

"Why aren't you moving? They are at the door. The coven mother is with them!"

Twirling the stem in a circular motion sometimes shook the root's grip. Whatever the coven was selling, Vianna wasn't interested. A squeak from the side gate announced the visitors. She yanked hard on the stubborn weed, abandoning the patient nettling. The stem broke with a snap, and the momentum sent her onto her ass, a broken white root dangling from her hand and draping over her knee. She tossed the fragment over her shoulder, and an impatient huff came from behind, but she didn't turn around. Instead, she focused on the next weed.

"I assume you didn't hear our knock," Josephine barked.

Vianna grunted as she shifted her weight against her new victim.

Maybe if she pretended her unwanted company wasn't there, they'd leave.

Tiphonie's squeaky voice came next. "That is not how you greet a coven mother."

It couldn't be just Josephine stampeding through her yard. No, of course not. That wasn't annoying enough. Her mini-me daughter had to be involved. Vianna gritted her teeth as she pulled on the stubborn stem. Josephine was not her coven mother.

Another root snapped. "Freya's cock!" Vianna growled.

Tiphonie gasped. "How dare you imply such a thing about the goddess! And in front of your coven mother! You'll be smitten."

Vianna couldn't help but laugh. A variant of smite was probably what Tiph was going for, but smitten was more entertaining. Vianna leaned on her knee and turned to look at the witches. They were dressed in matching pastel summer dresses. Josephine's red hair was back in a tight bun, but Tiphonie's was down and loose.

"I heard you visited the coven records." Josephine looked down her large, hooked nose.

Josephine's comment was technically a statement, not a question. There was no reason to answer. Vianna had spent her childhood in those caves. To take issue over it now was petty, even for the coven. What were they afraid of her finding?

"Only coven-bound witches have access to such places," Josephine continued.

Vianna wasn't in the mood for a game of state-the-obvious; the last two days had drained her of all proper protocol. "Children of legacy witches have privileges. I hadn't realized my birth status changed."

"At the time, you had a coven-bound mother." Josephine's face soured. It was unattractive, made worse by her white eyeliner.

"Did I miss the part where Angeline Roots stopped being my mother?" Vianna wiped sweat from her brow with her forearm.

"Death changes things, child. Don't play coy."

Something was wrong here. Something was off. Why did Josephine care whether she was in the caves?

"What do you want?" Vianna asked.

"Are you filling your mother's seat in the coven?" Tiphonie's nose crinkled as if a thought could smell.

The idea *was* rotten. "I am not," Vianna said. "I'm fixing up the house to sell it. I should be out of Salem by the end of the month."

"You'd never cut it as a coven witch," Tiphonie sneered.

Vianna couldn't help but agree with her. She turned back to the garden and gripped another weed.

Grandma still hovered in the flower bed. "Everything your family has done before you was for naught if you walk away from the coven, you skittish weevil."

"The coven will buy the house." Josephine straightened, tall and formal, but the tone of her voice betrayed her eagerness. "As is."

Rocking back on her heels, Vianna shielded her eyes as she looked up at the woman. There was no smile, no twinkle in her eye, nothing but stern business. She was serious. "How much?"

"We'll set up adequate payments that factor in your mother's debt." Josephine shrugged. "Your mother was behind in her dues."

There was no world in which Angeline Roots would disrespect the coven by being behind in dues. That was a crock of shit. But if they worked out a decent deal, this whole mess would go away. Then they could deal with Nancy's body parts and with the demonic possession. This could be the first break she'd caught since being back in town.

"How dare you consider selling our home to this treacherous witch!" Grandma lunged, but Vianna didn't flinch, and Grandma passed through her body, leaving only a breeze of freshly cut apples.

"Send over the offer, and I'll take a look." She turned back to the soil and pulled the stem she had her fist wrapped around. The root pulled out to the tip, looking like a tentacle from an alien.

"You will do no such thing." Grandma clicked her tongue as she paced around them.

"I'll be in touch." Josephine spoke at the same time as Grandmother.

Vianna hated when the living and the dead rambled at the same time. It turned her head into a jumbled mess. She didn't bother responding to either. Instead, she focused on the blissfully silent garden. They could see themselves out.

Grandma disappeared with the other unwanted company. Vianna was grateful for the peace. She cleared an entire bed and upturned the soil before planting moonflower seeds. With a deep breath, she looked at her work. It was a good-sized box, and she could tuck in a back row of lavender. Back in Boston, products such as candles, teas, and soaps sold faster when they had lavender buds. It wouldn't be that different in Salem. Only, she wasn't staying.

She didn't belong in Salem, but what about Shuck? If she left and turned the house over to the coven, would that break their bond? It wasn't her problem. She hadn't asked for any of this. An assortment of emotions surged through her, and she focused instead on tasks that made sense. Sorting through the pots in the greenhouse and counting bulbs eased her mind. A slick sweat slid between her breasts and across her brow as she hauled the larger pots to and from the greenhouse. She dumped the soil from the pots and merged it with other parts of the lawn for nourishment.

"You stink like a slave." Grandma stood at the back door to the kitchen.

Vianna grunted as she rolled one of the clay pots that was too heavy to lift. The metal clank of the latch on the side gate made her look up. Sun rays spilled over Charles in pressed khakis and with every hair in place. She frowned, then remembered the mac 'n' cheese still sitting in her fridge and his comment to meet up before he sped off.

"Crap!" she blurted out. "I forgot to call you." She'd meant to call and tell him she didn't have time for dates—especially dates with someone tied up in coven courtships.

He chuckled. "I'm unreasonably early. I couldn't wait to see you."

She pursed her lips. "We agreed on a time? Felt like you drove off without me agreeing to anything."

He nodded. "You're right. I was afraid you'd say no, though, and I desperately wanted a second date." He gave a hopeful grin, the same grin that had made young Vianna swoon. She'd grown up, she'd changed, but that grin still made her stomach do somersaults.

She was starved, and if the coven was going to buy the house, she had spare time on her hands. A few meals together wouldn't mess with whatever wedding plans the Bartons and Parkers were making. Plus, it wouldn't hurt to get away from Grandma for a few hours.

"I still need to shower." She plopped her gardening gloves into the flowerpot.

His eyes roamed her body. "I suppose I'll wait?"

"Price to pay for being early. There's"—what was there to drink?—"water from the tap." She motioned to the kitchen. "I'll hurry."

He put his hands in his pockets and grinned. "Sounds good."

The water from the shower rinsed away the dirt and barbs from the garden. She turned off the faucet and reached for the shower curtain, but hesitated, remembering the bathroom ghost with scissors in his eye. He was nowhere to be found, and she snagged a freshly washed towel. She'd done more laundry earlier and had never been so grateful not to smell garlic.

The wood floors were cool against her feet as she padded into her mother's bedroom, leaving wet footprints behind her. She frowned into the single drawer of clothes. Looking at the stacks of unglamorous T-shirts and cut-offs, she wondered if she owned anything that matched with khakis. Definitely not.

Her stomach growled. She hadn't eaten today. Time had flown in the garden. She got dressed—opting for a billowy tank-top thing instead of a T-shirt—shook out her hair, then jogged down the stairs. The living room was empty, so she poked her head out the back door, but the yard was also empty. She heard a low creak from the other side of the house, and walked across the sitting room, looking through the front windows. Charles lounged on the porch swing with one foot against a pillar, pushing himself into a gentle swing.

She opened the front door and approached. "Sorry to keep you waiting."

His gaze raked over her again, and this time it made her twitchy. He stood at her words and closed the distance between them. "I hope you're hungry because I had a special dish flown in." He stepped closer. "I wanted to make it up to you for canceling last night. And I know you're busy with flipping the house, so I'll even help around the house tomorrow to make up for lost time."

Vianna raised her brows. Maybe he was the Prince Charming that little-Vianna had swooned over. "You didn't have to do that. Let me get shoes."

She darted back into the house, then came back wearing flip-flops and her handbag clutched at her side. Charles was waiting at the car with the door open, a perfectly dimpled smile on his face.

12

Be Like That

The sun beat down in waves, and Vianna slid into the passenger seat, playing hot potato with the back of her legs on the leather. Charles was oblivious to anything besides the steering wheel as he zipped through side streets. Her dark tangles whipped in the wind, and she kept her mouth clamped shut in case of an errant bug. He pulled up to the tattered brick building where he lived.

Once up the stairs, he led her into the same flat with one large difference: flowers. Pink peonies, stargazer lilies, and red roses littered every flat surface and tabletop. The scent of wilted sugar washed over her, then settled as a weight of expectations on her shoulders.

"Wow." She stood in the doorframe. Her mind went blank.

Charles raised a brow. "They're for you. Like 'em?"

She rubbed at her neck and gave a thin-lipped smile. "There's . . . a lot of them."

He closed the distance between them, then wrapped an arm around her waist with the familiarity of someone who'd done it countless times. He kissed the top of her head, and the aroma of a dying garden thickened.

She sucked in her lower lip. Filling a room full of flowers was decidedly romantic, but a little intense. Her mouth felt dry. She shouldn't have come. What were his expectations?

This was a mistake. "Charles, I shoul—"

A generic ring went off, and he pulled his phone from his pocket. He looked up from the screen. "I'm sorry, Vie, but I have to take this. I'll make it quick. Alice will be up with wine."

He left the room. She set her handbag by the front door and wandered around to distract herself. Not a speck of dirt or even a fallen flower petal was amiss. Everything had a proper place. It made her skin itchy. She rubbed her arms. Movement chased the jitters away. Out on the patio, the prostitute was in the shooting-up-on-the-couch phase of her death cycle. Vianna moved away from the sliding door and wandered some more.

Like a magnet, she ended up in front of the wall-sized painting. The colors looked different. Maybe it was just in her head. She looked closer. The texture of a brush stroke on a new block of tangerine almost looked like a strand of hair was caught in the paint.

Alice appeared at the top of the stairs with a tray holding two glasses of red wine. She handed one to Vianna and set the other on a small table against the half-wall. Bite-sized, sugar-dipped pastries called to Vianna's stomach.

"Thank you." Vianna smiled and motioned to the painting. "It looks different from the last time I was here."

"Oh, yes. Mrs. Barton comes by often and adds to it. She was here just yesterday." Alice fidgeted with the display on the table, making sure the plates were in the center and the same distance from each other.

"He sure does like everything in its proper place, doesn't he?"

Perfectionism seemed to be a family trait if Rose dropped by to work on art hanging on her son's wall.

Scarlet coloring spread over Alice's neck and cheeks. She adjusted her apron so that it sat perfectly straight across her waist. "It makes him happy when things are orderly." A dreamy look crossed over her features. "I like it when he's happy."

That was more than a little creepy. Vianna's attention went back to the painting. Maybe making your boss happy wasn't that creepy; maybe Alice was just good at her job. Charles deserved to be happy. Proper order wasn't too much to ask. She straightened the hem of her shorts.

"Is there anything I can get you while you wait?" Alice asked.

The room felt hazy. For a moment, she felt like she might float. She shook her head. Some sleep and water would help. Her symptoms were obvious signs of exhaustion. A low rumble came from beneath the new mark on her collarbone, and the room felt more tangible again. She could hold on to her thoughts easier.

Since Alice was feeling chatty, maybe she could get information on the ghost on the patio.

"Alice . . ." There really wasn't a tactful way to broach this. "Did someone die here?" At least she hadn't used the word hooker. That counted as tactful.

Looking down at the tray still in her hands, Alice nodded. "Such a dreadful night. Poor Charles."

Poor Charles? Vianna kept her mouth shut.

"He brought the girl over for dinner on the patio and stepped out for a phone call. When I brought the food, she was on the floor." Alice's face crumpled like she might throw up. "Charles gave me the night off. Mrs. Barton showed up too. She even made me tea." Her expression of horror switched to a far-off look of contentment, as though the memory of tea brought her peace.

Vianna felt prickling inside and tried to shrug it off. Maybe the ghost hadn't been a hooker. Non-hookers wore spandex dresses. Or even if she was a hooker, that was Charles's business. Her attention wandered back to the swatches of color on the canvas.

Charles stepped up behind her, and she startled. He hadn't made a single noise before pressing up behind her. He was close enough that she could feel his breath against her ear, and her pulse quickened. A rush of excitement jolted through her at the idea of him wanting her. Why was she fighting this so hard? It was clear he wanted her. She was flattered.

"Looks like I interrupted an interesting conversation."

Aspen-scented aftershave cocooned her. Somehow, knowing he wanted her awoke every sensual nerve in her body. His fingers traced down the back of her arm. Her body betrayed her hesitancy with a quiver, and to her surprise, she leaned into him with a breathy sigh.

"Of course not, Mr. Barton." Alice picked up the glass on the table and handed it to him. "I was just answering Ms. Roots's questions."

"Maybe next time you can entertain our guests with more up-lifting stories. Why don't you check on the appetizers?" His lips brushed against Vianna's ear and sent a ripple of flesh bumps down her spine.

Alice nodded and scurried down the stairs. Everything felt hazy again.

"My apologies for stepping away, but it couldn't be avoided. I'd much rather be here with you." He nuzzled into her neck, and she let her head roll to the side, giving him full access.

She wanted to ask him about the ghost, but she also didn't want to upset him. His fingertips danced along her neck before he swept her hair to the side. It'd been too long since she'd been touched, and she groaned.

His arms slid around her waist, and he pressed against her. There was no doubt he wanted her. He palmed her hip and twirled her toward him. The movement made her stumble, and she almost took a nosedive to the floor, but he looped his arms beneath her legs and swept her into his arms. Her surroundings were muddled, and she rubbed at her temple. Had she eaten today? He sat on the couch with her in his lap.

"I think I need some water." She squirmed to get up, but his arm fastened around her.

"Hold up. You just about passed out. Let's give you a minute to catch your breath." He kissed her shoulder.

That made sense. Taking a minute was a good idea. His kisses trailed up her neck. Water also seemed like a good idea, but there wasn't any around, and Charles wanted her on the couch. She took a deep breath and settled into his arms. The same rumbling from before shook within the center of her collarbone. She brushed against the area with her fingertips, then dropped her hand, ignoring it.

"It's official. You're swooning for me." His fingers slid under her shirt and crawled up her spine.

In response, she arched her back, and he pulled her up against him. "Good girl."

She'd heard those words before, and the memory made her flinch. The closed door to her childhood bedroom flashed in her mind, then turned blurry. Her thoughts felt just out of reach, as though she were drowning in an ocean of blurred obedience.

He leaned in and brushed his lips against hers, then pulled back. "I want you to kiss me."

His stare was unblinking, and something about this moment felt like a challenge, but that didn't make any sense. A kiss was simple enough. She fisted the buttons of his polo shirt and pressed her mouth to his. His lips parted, and a tangy spice flooded her senses as he groaned. Her bra snapped, releasing her breasts. She jumped in surprise.

A small voice in the back of her mind was screaming, but his touch felt good, and she was making him happy. He was a good guy. This wasn't bad. A gnawing feeling in her gut grew as he unbuttoned her shorts.

"Appetizers are served." Alice reappeared with another silver tray and a beaming smile. "Just like you wanted."

Charles rumbled with a sigh. "We'd like some privacy."

Alice nodded with a dopey grin and set the tray down before disappearing.

Charles pulled her attention back by tracing his hand along her neck. "Where were we?"

The scent of his cologne was stifling as his hands roamed beneath her shirt, and with that, came another bout of dizziness. A few more deep breaths would steady her, but she didn't want to upset Charles. He wanted this. A bark, an actual dog bark, snapped in her head like a bucket of ice water to the face. Alice's flushed face and eagerness to please popped into Vianna's mind. She sat upright.

"What's wrong?" He gently squeezed her nipple, then tugged.

Instead of heated butterflies, she felt the prickling of dread. He nuzzled the tip of his nose into her neck, but this time she pulled away. With her hand on his chest, she pushed him back, then slid off his lap and onto the couch. The cushion was stiff, and the fabric scratched against her skin.

A deep frown settled on his face. He rolled out his neck and took a deep breath. "You sure make a guy work for it, don't you?"

Her eyes widened, and her jaw dropped. Work for it? She'd made it clear this wasn't going anywhere, couldn't. Well, she had until she'd gotten here. And then suddenly she was throwing out as many mixed signals as there were flowers in the room. She rubbed at her temples as she tried to sort the mess in her head. None of it added up. Fresh air and water. That was the new plan.

She stood and wrestled with her bra strap. A trickling discomfort at the thought of upsetting Charles nagged at her.

He patted the couch. "Come, sit down. Have some pâté."

Charles was as appealing as chopped liver, and still, even a negative thought toward him made her feel guilty. Something was very off.

She rubbed at her collarbone, then stormed toward her purse and the door. "I'm sorry, but I can't stay. I've just got too much going on."

"You can't be serious."

She'd made it down the stairs and out of the building before she heard his footsteps on the stairs.

"Vie! Where are you going? Hold up!" He scrambled through the door of the outer building.

A breeze of fresh air was a relief. The need to please Charles lessened, and in its place, the growl from within her roared. *Shuck.* She shook her head at her own stupidity for not listening to the warning. The scowl on her face was half at Charles and half at herself. Something was wrong with his place. He wouldn't have put something in her drink, would he? No. She was just out of sorts.

She wrapped her arms around herself. "I need to get home. I told you, I'm not staying in Salem, and I'm not looking for a relationship. Let's not drag out the goodbyes."

He reached out to her, but she shrugged her shoulder and stepped away.

"You're overreacting. You want me. I know it." His jaw clenched and his eyes narrowed. "Maybe you're just scared."

"I'll just walk home. Salem's not that big."

"Fine." He folded his arms over his chest. "Be like that."

A long walk was better than his company anyway. She didn't answer but turned away and headed home.

13

A Magic Broom

Vianna wanted to punch something, but instead stomped her feet as she walked down the sidewalk. She knew better than to mess with Charles Barton or anyone with a legacy last name, and even worse, she'd ignored her internal alarm and . . . Shuck. The situation could have been a lot worse without the family demon—that wasn't a thought she'd ever expected to have.

She slid on sunglasses and whipped her hair into a sloppy bun as she passed one of those tiny mailbox houses filled with books. The cracked sidewalk led her through an old neighborhood that sat between Charles's loft and the tourism mecca center of Salem. Her own home was beyond that. The sun baked her skin and her chapped lips, reminding her she still wanted water. She'd have to suck it up. Wasting what little money she had on a five-dollar tourist bottle of water wasn't happening. This day was bad enough without compounding more stupid decisions.

The large, two-story witch museum loomed just a block away. It sat right on the corner of Essex Street, and even in the off-season, the crowds were heavier through this part of town. Unfortunately, the number of ghosts was also higher since the buildings had been around for centuries. The older the property, the more likely a ghost lingered. These ghosts were older and often not caught in death loops, but in simple routines from a different time. They were far more tolerable than the others.

The crosswalk at the stoplight blinked a red hand, and she waited alongside a small group of tourists, who chatted with each other in West Coast accents. She looked down Essex at the row of painted signs that hung from the shops: The Green Witch, Quackery, Books and Nooks, and Sticks and Bones. Most of the little boutiques were nothing more than a ploy at making a buck, but there were a few with hidden knowledge and culture tucked into secret corners. Sticks and Bones was one of those.

Vianna hadn't thought of Tucker Etienne for a very long time—not since grade school. Vianna had gone to public school during the day and then craft classes in the evenings, until Mother discovered Tuck. He and Vianna were best friends for a full year. He was the first person besides Mother that she'd told about the ghosts, and Tuck hadn't freaked out. Instead, he'd thought it was the coolest thing ever.

When Mother discovered her legacy daughter was fraternizing with a hoodoo practitioner's son, she'd pulled Vianna from public school entirely. She'd seen him a few times after that, but only in passing and nothing more than a head nod of acknowledgment. His family owned the shop just a block down, a shop that specialized in hoodoo for locals and voodoo for tourists.

The red hand still flashed to go straight, but a stick figure flashed white toward the row of shops. In a perfect world, the banishment against Csada would be the end of him. And maybe it was. But in a perfect world, Csada never would have turned an offer on the house into an attack. She needed more information, and if anyone could shine a little light on Csada, it was Tuck. She turned right.

The same stacks of candles, T-shirts, and hanging crystals she remembered from ten years ago still filled the display windows. Even the thrift store had the same glass cabinet of antique dolls painted to look like zombies and monsters. She paused with a group of tourists caught in the same web of fascination. The artist had added two new ones: a Victorian doll with a thick tentacle and large suckers ravaging her face; and a black doll-turned-vampire, who'd just finished an overly messy meal of intestines. As creepy as they were, they were damn good art, better than Rose's splattered paint. She pushed the thought of Rose from her thoughts, not ready to sort through what had just happened with Charles. She shook out her shaking hands and moved on from the store window.

Two shops farther down, she could see the hanging wind chimes made of bones just past a floral nursery worthy of even the locals. The nursery owner wasn't a witch, but she knew her local gardening just as well, and the best collection of vines filled the shop's back patio. It took effort not to veer into the nursery but the hoodoo shop instead.

A metal bell announced her arrival, then was replaced with a steady drumbeat and chanting. Tall wooden shelves stuffed with voodoo dolls, hex candles, tarot cards, and animal bones wrapped in twine crowded the small space. It was all for the tourists. There was a backdoor to the shop where locals entered. Vianna didn't dare use that entrance in case she triggered some sort of curse that turned her fingernails into slugs or something.

Sage and a mystery herb with a tart bite hung in the air. Allspice maybe? The resulting aroma was more like dinner than a spell. A group of teenagers huddled around a Ouija board tucked beside a prayer altar to some goddess on a wooden desk. Scraps of paper were left out to send requests to whichever spirit the statue represented.

The register was somewhere on the other side of the room. Vianna wove her way around the large baskets filled with bound scarves and bundled herbs until she saw the woman behind the register. She had a painted skeleton face, top hat on her head, and a vest worn like a corset, advertising impressive cleavage. She didn't look up as Vianna approached, her attention on the phone in her hand.

Vianna chewed on her lower lip in hesitation. Tucker might not even be around, or he might not remember who she was. They didn't exactly come from the same side of the tracks, and it'd been fifteen years.

"Hey." That seemed as good a start as any. "Is Tuck around?"

Top-hat girl looked up with a pout, then looked over Vianna. After a pregnant pause, she nodded her chin at the archway behind the front desk. "He's in back, per usual." She rolled her eyes and went back to her phone.

Vianna took that as the go-ahead and headed behind the counter. She peeked into the first open door to discover a bathroom with no ghosts—must be nice. That left the closed door with chipped orange paint or the midnight-blue velvet curtain at the end of the hall. There was a muffled noise coming from behind the door. Leaning her ear closer, her hand hovered in a knocking position. The noises turned to gunfire on the other side.

She twisted the knob and shoved the door open. "Tuck?"

Unsure of what drama she'd landed herself in, she froze as she took in the scene. Giant television screens were on two different walls, with a corner desk littered with monitors. The gunfire came from the speakers mounted into the corners. There were no windows, and the walls were painted a deep midnight blue.

A thin black man with a high fade showing off tattoos of reaching hands at the base of his skull sat at the desk wearing headphones.

He didn't bother to turn around. "Ashley, I'm not calling on your ancestors to follow Ruby. She broke up with you. Stop being a stalker. Go do something productive. Count something or whatever it is you do."

"Uh, not Ashley."

He spun the cushioned chair, and the same blue eyes from childhood narrowed at her. "No. You're not." He pulled off his headphones. "But you look familiar."

She gave an awkward fist bump toward the ceiling. "Long live the Parrots?" All right, not the smoothest introduction, but he had to remember their school mascot.

"Vie?" He chuckled, pushed himself off the chair, and his long legs made it across the room in three strides. He wrapped her in a hug. "I'd know that awkward socializing anywhere. Last I heard your name, you'd done the impossible and escaped this hellhole." He pulled back and gestured toward a couch that looked like a giant gray pillow.

Relief came in a flood that made her smile. She flopped onto the couch, the cool leather soothing on her skin after it had roasted in the sun. She hadn't realized her feet were aching until she sat down. "I'm just here to handle the estate. I'll be out of here as soon as I can."

Tuck pulled a vape pen from a drawer in the desk and took a puff as he sat back in his chair. "Yeah, I heard about your ma. I'd say I'm sorry for your loss, but . . ." His shrug encompassed the whole of Vianna's miserable childhood. "What brought you to my door?"

"Just passing by and turned right. Ended up here. I was surprised Mama Miriam wasn't out front."

He frowned. "Ma died a few years back."

"Oh, I hadn't heard." Unlike her mother, Mama Miriam had been beloved by the community. She was the pillar of healing and generosity that the new Salem was built upon. "I'm sorry."

"Death comes for us all. It was her time."

They both settled back and relaxed in silence. Tuck blew a puff of smoke, and Vianna was content to sit and breathe.

"I was kinda hoping you could give me the lowdown on a local practitioner."

Tuck raised a pierced brow. "That's a curious request, coming from a witch."

"He stopped by my home. Offered to buy the place, and he was less than rational about it. Said his name is Csada."

"Csada Laguerre?" Tuck took another inhale of his vape before standing. "In your house? That's a problem. Come on." He headed out the door, not waiting for her to follow.

"Great," she groaned. She hopped from the couch and trotted after him, down the hall and toward the blue curtain. "Laguerre. I know that name. It's not the same family as the old Laguerre house just out of town, is it?"

The Laguerre house was a regular on the gossip circuit among younger witches. During Samhain, the older girls would dare the younger ones to steal a goat or leave a hex on the old hoodoo house.

"There's only one Luguerre family." He pulled the curtain back, holding it for her to walk through.

Inside the small room, braided herbs and painted crystals hung from the corners and wooden shelves covered every inch of wall space. Painted masks hung on the ridges of the shelves that were filled with bulbous jars of murky liquid, rows of cloth sacks, and hand-carved boxes of different shapes ranging between almost hexagons to lopsided ovals.

"You're letting me into the super secret hoodoo cave?" Vianna immediately moved to the closest row of shelves, perusing. A middle shelf displayed a brick with tiny bottles of dust in all shades of red surrounding it. Brick dust. She hadn't realized there was more than one flavor of brick.

Tuck gave a short snort of a laugh. "Super secret hoodoo cave? That's dramatic. No secrets. Just old-school methods of healing. There's a reason you were pulled in this direction, besides catching up with an old friend."

She raised a brow but kept quiet. A demon-bound witch was hardly one to scoff at mystical reasons for things happening. Shuck's energy was a low thrum inside of her chest that felt like non-threatened contentment, and Vianna had always felt more herself and relaxed around Tuck. Who was to say it wasn't for some reason she didn't understand?

Tuck pulled something that looked like a large branch from behind the wooden counter. "New rumors about Csada spawn on the gossip vines every day. His sister went missing a while back. She was a solid practitioner, well-respected, and a lot of suspicion was cast in his direction. She's yet to be found. You do not want to mess with Csada."

She left the shelves and joined him at the counter. "I banished him from the house, but I have a lingering feeling that's not the end of him."

"You may have made yourself more interesting," Tuck said. "I've heard rumors about that house of yours, and if Csada heard the same rumors, I'd say you'll see him again."

She leaned on the counter, looking at the branch that had dried palms tied to the bottom like a make-shift broom. "What kind of rumors?"

"Of the demon kind." Tuck didn't play games. It was refreshing.

They had history, good history, and that was rare for Vianna. She'd give him the same honesty he'd given her. "The Roots house is the family familiar." She swallowed. "My familiar."

Those words smacked her in the chest. *Her familiar.*

Tuck arched his brow and nodded. "The rumor was more along

the lines of demon orgies giving the Roots witches their power. I suppose a demon-possessed house is more practical."

Vianna barked out a laugh, and just like that, they were little kids again: Vianna whispering that she could see ghosts and Tuck asking if they picked their noses. Little-Vie had laughed then too.

Tuck motioned to the broom. "Vianna, meet your new broom. Now, it's not the same as that bippity-boppity shit you do."

She huffed with a grin. Bippity-boppity. *Funny.*

"But brooms have been clearing out the unwanted since the beginning. You have unwanted attention. You need a broom."

"You've got to be kidding me." She tilted her head. "You're giving a witch a magic broom?"

He laughed. "I guess so. I've been working on this one for a while. It was meant to be a wedding gift for my sister, but you're in more need. Everyone will give her a special broom of some sort. She'll have a zillion of them." He pulled a small blade with a simple black hilt from beneath the counter.

She hesitated, twirling the infinity ring on her finger.

"Nervous?" A grin tugged at the corner of his mouth.

She shrugged. "Of course."

"Nah." He motioned for her hand. "Hoodoo isn't meant to harm. Not when it's authentic. Your blood will connect you to the broom. We just need a drop."

Shuck wasn't alarmed. She held out her hand, and he gave a quick jab to the tip of her thumb, then pressed the open wound onto the wood of the broom. The air became heavy with excess humidity, but there were no bursting flames, demonic grumbling, or sparks of light hanging in the air. Just an unseen weight that pressed against her skin.

Vianna raised a brow. "That's it?" She put her thumb in her mouth to clean off the wound, then wrapped it with the purple Band-Aid Tuck offered.

He gave a large white smile. "That's it."

"So I just sweep the house?"

"Pretty much." He chuckled and picked it up, handing it over to her. "Always store it bristles up, never sweep anything out the front door, and use it whenever you feel the urge. It should clean out your house of negative energy and spiritual infection, which is interesting since your house is a literal demon. I'm not sure how that's gonna get along. You'll have to play it by ear."

Vianna held the broom in front of her with both hands, careful not to move it. A magical broom with rules. She stared at it. It looked like a forgotten relic of the past.

"Carry it under your arm." Tuck nodded at the broom. "It will protect you—or it should. If it chooses to."

"Chooses to?" She tucked the broom under her arm as instructed.

"Magic isn't finicky for you? She's a fickle beast for me. There are never any guarantees." Tuck leaned against the counter and pulled his vape from his pocket, inhaling from it.

She looked at him, unsure of what to say. *Thank you* seemed hollow. "You didn't have to do this."

"Nope. I didn't." He shrugged. "But I did. You were always good people, despite your blood. Call it an olive branch."

"An olive branch from a practitioner to a witch? You're going to make Salem explode," she teased.

"About time," Tuck said. "Want something to drink?"

"Yeah. I'd love some water." Vianna stuck around for another half hour, catching up on his sister's impending nuptials and how tourism hadn't changed a bit. When they finished, she promised to stop by again before she left for Boston, and Tuck slipped back into his gaming room, mentioning something about some campaign or another. Vianna gave a nod to the girl at the counter and couldn't help but wonder if she was stalking some poor ex on her phone.

Outside the shop, music drifted from farther down the street. It was the same band she'd heard from Charles's balcony on their first date. The out-of-key trumpet was a dead giveaway. For a moment she wondered if the high-pitched belch was the last thing the ghost-hooker heard in her final moments. The thought made her jittery, and she squeezed the broom more tightly under her arm. Shuck gave a small nudge of a rumble, but she wasn't sure what it meant.

The rest of the walk home was more tiring than refreshing, and most of the same ghosts haunted the same doorsteps and street corners. The old man in his baggy nightshirt still stared out the window of 128 Essex with half his skull smashed in. Dark clouds rolled in, but thankfully, no rain fell. Oak and red maple trees lined the streets as she turned onto Heritage Way. The Roots home was nestled into the middle of the street, and the familiar bird squabbling greeted her.

"I can see when you steal my Wi-Fi, Vianna Roots." The voice came from the neighboring yard.

Vianna stopped and leaned against the wrought iron post with a smile. "Aww . . . I missed you too, Ophelia."

Ophelia Sixton stood on the bottom stair to her porch with a pinched scowl. She was the mother of the Eclipse Coven, one of the founding covens, who specialized in tarot and planetary orbits. Despite her cranky demeanor, she'd always been one of Vianna's favorites.

"You didn't acknowledge me at your mother's funeral." The old woman's voice was curt, but it always was.

Ophelia was curvy in epic proportions, with a silver streak that ran down the front of her parted black afro. She held something small and furry between her cupped fingers—probably a bat. Ophelia had a thing for them.

Vianna fished out the remaining jellybeans from her pocket while still juggling the broom and frowned when only the yellow remained. "I was a little preoccupied with Mother. You know how she is."

"Good riddance." Ophelia's plump lips didn't hint at a smile. She wasn't the joking type.

The constant bickering between the Roots and Sixton families was legendary. What had started the feud was unknown, but Vianna suspected the racial slurs her mother and distant grandmother used had a lot to do with it. For a full year in grade school, bats hung from the front porch, covering it with crap. Vianna had never seen her mother's neck turn quite that shade of scarlet. From that point on, the chore of nightly bat-shooing was delegated to Vianna. Her mother couldn't kill the creatures because one was Ophelia's familiar, but she didn't know which. Harming a witch's familiar was an unspeakable sin.

"No argument from me. I won't miss the evil hag."

"Vianna Roots! It's not proper to speak poorly of your elders, especially your own mother."

Vianna rolled her eyes. The older witches lived by different rules than the rest and expected utmost respect from those younger. Ophelia's age and status earned her the right to say whatever she pleased.

"Is that why you're gallivanting around with the Barton boy? To upset your dead mother?" Ophelia stepped onto the lawn and toward Vianna.

She hadn't thought of how dating Charles would upset Mother. That should have brought some solace or even a smirk, but instead, Vianna felt as though Mother was whispering from the grave. *I told you so.*

"Tempting," Vianna admitted. "But no. No more dates with the Barton boy. That was, well, not good."

"Hmm. All right, then." Ophelia's attention glanced down to the broom, then away. "Make sure to bring some of your moon flowers this fall. You always have the best luck with those." Ophelia headed back toward her house.

"Oh," Vianna called after her. "I'm not staying. I'm selling the house and leaving as soon as possible."

Ophelia hesitated and turned back with a small grin. "Make sure to bring those flowers, dear. It's nice to see you home."

Ophelia went inside, and Vianna turned toward her own yard, knowing better than to argue with her neighbor. The wisteria blooms were fragrant, and she paused to look over the looming house. It had good bones. Just like Salem. But the past was just too much. Shaking her head, she walked up the stairs with her brand-new hoodoo broom, and the front door slid open.

14

Hexed

Vianna wiggled into a more comfortable position in bed. A rolling fog of sleep blissfully slid over her awareness, slowing her thoughts and letting her body relax. *Thank the goddess.* There was nothing more magical than sleep.

A lingering scent of burned herbs, almost like sage but sweeter, wafted through the open window. The breeze lifted the white gossamer curtains into the air like outstretched fingers before her eyelids gave in and closed. The warmth of summer hung in the night air. Sweat beaded across her skin, and the sheets stuck to her legs. Leaves rustled above her head.

Leaves? Her eyes fluttered open.

Dark branches stretched across a star-filled sky. How was she outside? She moved to sit up, but her hands were restrained and she fell back down. Leather cuffs bound her wrists and ankles. She yanked harder on the bindings, but they refused to give. Her heart rate spiked.

"Hello?" Her voice was swallowed by the shadows of trees all around her. She looked from side to side. She was on an altar. An icy coldness from the stone beneath her seeped through her thin T-shirt, sending goosebumps down her bare legs.

"Hey!" she hollered.

No, this wasn't happening. She wasn't a goat who'd been led to its slaughter. This was not how she died. She needed to think. Deep breaths and a slow count to ten.

The coven was behind this. Or maybe Csada. Had they abducted her in her sleep? Vianna wanted to roar. She should have put all the garlic back up, the smell be damned. Leaves rustled in the trees, and a lynch rope dropped from an outstretched branch a few feet from the altar. The rope looked as worn and dirt-crusted as the one that permanently hung around Grandma's neck, but this rope swung on its own—no body.

Her eyes widened. She pulled against the bindings again, knowing it wouldn't make a difference. A black-hooded figure strolled between the trees. They couldn't possibly hang her. There was no death more disrespectful in the eyes of a witch.

"Who's there?" Her voice already felt strangled.

"Too weak to be coven-bound. You should have stayed away," a voice whispered in the breeze.

A woman's limp body dropped from the branches, swinging from a rope. Large dung beetles scattered across the branch the rope was attached to. The hem of a black dress caught in the breeze as the woman's head fell limp to the side. She'd worn the same dress when she appeared to Vianna at the funeral.

Grandma Clarice's brown eyes flashed open and wide. "Weak."

More whisperings as another body dropped from a tree branch. Limp legs with black stockings swayed, rustling the beads of a red flapper dress. Another ancestor. With her head limp to the side, lifeless eyes stared at Vianna.

"An embarrassment," the grandma in a red dress croaked.

"Worthless nitwit." Another voice sounded from beside Vianna. The familiarity of that voice stabilized Vianna into coherent thought. This wasn't real.

She turned toward the voice. Grandma Susannah's body swung from a tree. Her eyes were open and narrowed. She mouthed two words that Vianna couldn't make out. A low rumble echoed through the forest, and two more bodies dropped from branches. One of them, the girl-ghost with ringlets from the funeral, kicked out her small Mary-Janes before she too went limp. Her body swayed in perfect sequence with the others.

"An embarrassment to the Roots name," said the first voice. It wasn't one of her ancestors, but she recognized it. Tiphonie.

Vianna clenched her jaw.

"You're all alone. Death is the only honorable choice," Tiphonie cooed.

In a blink, she was sitting cross-legged, untied on the slab. She squeezed her fingers around the leather grip of a blade, as wetness dripped across her bare legs. She looked down. Deep gashes in her arms gushed blood that soaked through her shorts. She pressed her arms against her chest in a useless attempt to stop the bleeding. In the distance, the growling grew louder.

"Finish it. Restore honor to your family."

Blood covered the altar and dripped from the edge. The splat of each drop sounded like it had fallen into a deep, dark well. A well of her blood. No. She hadn't cut herself. None of this was real. She was dreaming. A branch moaned from the weight of the swaying body. She locked eyes with Grandma Susannah.

She mouthed the same two words. *Wake up.*

More black hoods moved between the trees, chanting, "Finish it. Finish it." The Ramsey twins.

Her hands trembled as she stared down at the blade pushed against her skin. It could all be over. All the nightmares, the loneliness, the murder. Her death could end it all. But Vianna had never wanted to kill herself. She took a deep breath and steadied her hands. There was no guarantee that what came after death was any better than life, not from what she had seen. No. She might be weak, but Tiphonie would have to work harder than that to scare Vianna away.

A loud crack thundered through the trees, and she jolted upright. The trees were gone, and faded floral wallpaper covered the surrounding walls. Her breaths came in gasps. She looked around her room with wide eyes.

It was a dream.

The curtain was stuck in the now-closed window. She swore the window had been open when she fell asleep. Scooting to the edge of the bed, she stood, then swayed from dizziness. After the room stopped spinning, she crossed to the window and pushed it open. A tabby cat darted from a nearby tree branch to the fence before disappearing.

In the windowsill was a crunched canvas bag with a drawstring that could fit in her palm: a hex bag. She plucked it out, stirring up a whiff of the same sweet sage she'd picked up on earlier. Salvia. The smell was salvia, and mixed with the right helpers, it was a good hallucinogen.

She grabbed a lighter from the nightstand, then held the bag outside the window and burned it. Flames turned from orange to purple before finally consuming the bag. She let go, and the little fireball dropped into the dirt below.

There was an obvious reason why Tiphonie would try such a dangerous hex on Vianna. Charles. If Ophelia had heard of their dinners, then the news had probably made the rounds on the coven gossip circuit. Tiphonie was serious about marking her territory. She could have him.

Vianna lumbered downstairs and into the kitchen for some coffee, then remembered that all she had was the bitter clearance junk. Mint tea would have to work. The sunrise blinded her through the window, and she tilted her head away from the sun's rays as she filled up the iron kettle. Turning back to the sink, she stumbled over the broom that was suddenly leaning, bristles up, against the counter. She caught it before it fell to the ground and held it out in examination.

"That is not where I put you last night." After careful consideration, she'd tucked the broom between shelves in the pantry so it wouldn't fall over or be stumbled upon casually, like she'd just done.

"Do not drag tree branches into the house. You'll get dirt everywhere." Grandma appeared by the fridge, arms crossed over her noose.

Vianna rotated the broom in the air. "Hmm." Holding the handle, she set the bristles to the floor and gave a small sweep. She looked around. Everything seemed the same.

"That does not qualify as a proper broom," Grandma said.

Vianna stepped closer to Grandma and gave a few good sweeps at her feet, but she didn't go away. So, the broom didn't get rid of *all* unwanted things.

With a shrug, Vianna went to the pantry to put the broom back, but Shuck rumbled in her chest. Unsure of what else a broom could be used for, she set the bristles down again and swept a corner by the pantry. The rumbles from Shuck deepened into a thick purr. Vianna straightened in surprise.

Grandma moved closer, in a more effective hovering position. "What are you doing?"

Vianna swept along the baseboards, then through the archway. Shuck gave a rumbly, long purr. She'd never heard him make a sound like that. He liked it. A lot. With a chuckle, she swept her way into the sitting room until her phone went off. Shuck grumbled when she set the broom down, and she smiled. The broom and Shuck were going to get along just fine.

Her cell phone vibrated, buzzing over the counter in the kitchen. The phone number was local, but not saved in her phone. She answered, "Hello."

"Ms. Roots?" a deep voice on the other end asked.

She frowned. That was formal, and formalities rarely accompanied good news. "Depends. Who's this?"

There was shuffling on the other end and the sound of a door clicking shut before he answered. "Grayson. Blue Chevy you hit the other day."

Oh. She cringed, having forgotten entirely about that blooper. Ditching out on paying a bill to a police officer wasn't likely to end well. But she didn't really have a lot of other options.

"Ms. Roots? You still there?"

She drummed her fingers against the counter. "Yeah. I'm here."

There was a beat of silence. "Well, I have a friend who's a mechanic, and I thought we'd go through her instead of insurance since they always jack rates up. She said she could buff it out for a couple hundred."

She sighed. "Okay." Payment was a problem no matter who gave the quote.

"So how do you want to pay? Can you transfer funds, or do you want her to bill you directly?" There was a scribbling sound, like he was taking notes.

She could go along with his plan, tell him to bill her directly, then do a whole song and dance with a lost check in the mail, hoping it bought her enough time to come up with the cash. She could imagine those intelligent eyes narrowing at her, just like the day of the funeral. He didn't seem like the type to be humored with a drawn-out song and dance. "I don't exactly have the funds at this *exact* moment."

Another beat of silence. He was a thinker. Thought before he spoke. "And in what moment do you think you will have the funds?"

"Soon." Her wrist felt hot, and she glanced down to make sure she hadn't rubbed against the kettle. "I'm about to run into some cash, and you're first on my list." After a grocery store splurge.

Her wrist went from warm to hot in all of two seconds, and she sucked in air, frowning as she shook it out.

"It's nothing illegal, I assume. This impending cash flow."

She sucked on her lips, turning her arm over both ways. It was burning hot. Roaring-fire hot. She hissed out, "Nope." Deep breath. "Only legal activities over here."

"Ms. Roots?" He let her last name linger for a moment. "Are you all right?"

"Just super." She yanked the handle on the faucet and shoved her hand under the cold water. It didn't make a difference. "I gotta go. I'll be in touch. Soon. Promise." She hung up the phone and dropped it to the counter at the same time.

Clenching her hand into a fist, she yelled out in pain. The floorboards rumbled as fire spread up and over her arm.

"It's back." Grandma appeared in the kitchen archway, her face scrunched in disgust.

"It?" Vianna walked through Grandma, and not even the chill from a ghost calmed the screaming fire spreading over her skin.

Peeking out the bay windows, Vianna saw Csada standing in the middle of her front yard wearing a hemp-thread Henley and rolled-up khakis. He gripped something in his outstretched hand. Something on fire. Vianna growled from the pain but pressed closer to the window to get a better eyeful. It was a voodoo doll, the arm on fire.

"How do I stop him?" Vianna yelled to Grandma without turning away from the window.

"He can't come in. Wait it out, obviously. It will build your pain tolerance to more respectable levels."

Vianna whipped her head toward Grandma, who had settled on the fainting sofa as though they were waiting for a batch of candles to set.

"My skin is on fire!"

There was no building a tolerance for this type of pain. Letting out another cry, she tried to think, to find a solution, to figure out a plan, but her mind couldn't do anything but scream that she was on *fire*. She'd tackle Csada if she had to. Fight him fist to fist. She'd never hit someone before, but the pain had to stop. Looking around frantically, she grabbed the fire poker hanging on the hearth and charged toward the front door.

When she tried the handle, it wouldn't budge.

"Flesh on fire," she yelled. She whacked the door with the fire poker.

Glass shattered outside, and Vianna paused. The front door flew open, and she burst onto the porch, poker raised and ready to fight. But no one was there.

Her flip-flops crunched against broken glass as she ran down the stairs and toward the small flame in the middle of the yard. She stomped on the doll and stomped some more even after the fire was out, stomping until finally the pain on her arm and shoulder faded. Her chest heaved. She looked at her arm, but there were no marks. Not a blemish.

She did a slow circle, looking for Csada. Sun rays reflected in glass shards stuck in the grass. If he was hiding, she couldn't spot him. A motorcycle roared to life a couple houses down, and she hoped it was him leaving. She grabbed the doll and darted back toward the house for safety. The old lantern-style porch lamp was broken.

Shuck had used the glass to protect them. She hopscotched over the sharp shards and into the house, the door closing behind her.

Her breathing was still heavy as she tried to process what had just happened. She flinched at the scratch on the door and set the fire poker against the wall. "Thank you, Shuck."

A rumble answered in her chest, and she nodded. The hemp doll in her hand had black stitching along the edges and small organs made of stuffed red cotton sewn to the outside. The eyes and mouth were stitched with black *Xs*.

Hex bags and voodoo dolls, and that was from within the safety of her demon-possessed house. What would happen if she tried to go into town? She didn't need an imagination to answer that question. She'd be dead. Her breathing calmed as she made her way toward the conjure room.

Csada would be back. Tiphonie had plenty of more tricks to play. Braided garlic wasn't going to work. Vianna needed a talisman, and there was only one talisman of protection that she'd seen in the grimoire. She was going to have to dig up one of her ancestors if she wanted to survive her time in Salem.

15

Grave Robbers

The sun slipped behind the horizon as if it knew the crazy plan that Vianna had hatched and would have no part in it. Sneaking into a witch cemetery, a *legacy witch* cemetery, to dig up a grave bordered on psychotic. Unfortunately, Vianna didn't have a lot of other options.

She'd bound her mother's ghost, making the passed-down mantle of magic "weak" in some way that she didn't fully understand. Then she'd ignored her instincts to avoid Charles and now had Tiphonie as riled as a hornet's nest. And somehow, on top of all of that, she'd attracted the attention of an outcast hoodoo practitioner who might or might not have made his sister disappear. At this point, she was willing to gamble on a crazy plan.

Distracting herself with more cleaning helped the day pass as she waited for the camouflage of darkness. Clouds of gloom had rolled in, promising rain. With a steady hand, she tossed a shovel into her truck bed and zipped up a black hoodie. A pair of mud-crusted gardening gloves were tucked into her back pocket, because something was better than nothing if she was digging up the dead.

She slipped into her trusted Ford and took almost the same route as the day of the funeral but stopped at a trailhead not too far from the dirt road to the cemetery. She turned off the lights. The hiking trail went through a corner of the forest that had an unmarked trail that veered in the general vicinity of the cemetery.

There were no hikers in sight, no errant police officers with knowing eyes, and no clusters of hooded witches. There was no reason to sit in her Ford, stalling the inevitable. She jumped out of the truck and gathered her supplies. Armed with a shovel over her shoulder, she trekked through the tangled tree roots and broken branches. Theoretically, as a legacy witch, she was the scariest thing in these woods. An owl hooted from deep within the shadows. She hunched her shoulders and pulled up her hood.

Watching where she stepped would be smart, but not in this forest. What hung from the branches was more of a threat than any errant tree root. The dangling crosses of Brigid made of hay were for protection, but the hanging bags with burned symbols from the sigil wheel wouldn't protect anyone who bumped into them. The occasional lost hiker would be deterred, but Vianna wasn't a lost hiker, and she kept her eyes peeled as she pushed deeper into the sacred land.

Hollowed bamboo and wooden spoons cascaded in what looked like wind chimes but were actually a warning system for Mistress Epsler, who lived in these parts. Vianna slowed her steps, making sure not to startle the birds.

She walked through a thicket of birch trees, butted up to the backside of the cemetery.

The outline of the wrought-iron fence surrounding the Legacy Cemetery came into view when a bush rustled a few feet away, and she stilled. Were there guard patrols around the perimeter? Upkeep for the graveyard didn't fall under jurisdiction of the Original Blood Coven, making her fuzzy on the details of exactly what the graveyard security was like.

Making as little movement as possible, she searched the shadows. Another rustle shook the bush, and she hunkered lower. Every old witch tale of various familiars—birds, owls, ferrets, wolves, giant scorpions, or spiders—protecting coven territory flashed through her mind, and suddenly she felt certain a wave of all of them would rush toward her. Instead, a lone reddish-brown coyote darted off in the opposite direction. If he was a familiar, he didn't seem to care much about her. She took a deep breath and used the shovel to help herself back up.

Raindrops fell like some bad omen as she closed the distance to the fence and tossed the shovel over. The loud clank as it bounced off a tombstone made her flinch, and she scanned to see if anyone else heard the noise. There wasn't a living body to be seen, which felt like a small miracle at that point. The fence was pointless, short, and easy to hike a foot up and leap over, but only a fool would think the fence was the deterrent. Legacy witches were the true guardians of this land. A hex that created chronic diarrhea for generations wasn't something to take lightly. There were worse things than death, and witches were not merciful.

As she made her way between the tombstones and flowerbeds, she searched the graves, looking for the right one. Giving her mother's grave a wide berth, she settled on the plot for Grandma Clarice, who died in 1948 and was likely all bones and no flesh. In the picture on the mantel above the fireplace, Clarice wore a pinched scowl, tight bun, and a black collared blouse with a starched ruffle that brushed against her jawline. She'd been there the night of the funeral, leading the procession of ghosts that branded Vianna's collarbone.

The strip of plot for Clarice had a small garden growing over the top with patches of grass, a patch of destroying angel mushrooms, and tall stalks of rhododendron. That was probably where Mother had gotten her flowers. The tip of her shovel broke soil as she jammed the heel of her shoe against metal. She was careful to not cut the roots of the mini garden, setting aside the plants so they could be replanted when she was done.

More raindrops splattered, creating puddles in the thick mud, as Vianna dug scoop after scoop. Digging up a grave took time, and when she wiped her brow with her forearm, it was for her own sweat as much as it was from the rain. The white hem of a ghostly dress floated over the grave.

"Took you long enough," she spoke to the ghost of Helen, a regular in the cemetery who took a keen interest in startling Vianna. Helen's long finger pointed toward the far side of the graveyard. A tall figure, very much not a ghost, moved in the distance. Vianna ducked down. The figure turned and headed in her direction.

She frantically looked side to side for a hiding spot. Anywhere. She should have thought this through. The rumor mill was filled with lost hikers gifted with warts and bleeding orifices in the shape of hemorrhoids after trespassing on this stretch of land. She knew they wouldn't go that easy on a witch who knowingly broke coven rules. There had to be somewhere to hide.

The tombstones were too small to fit behind, even curled into a ball. She'd have to make a run for it. She moved toward the tree line, but her foot slipped into the half-dug-up grave, and she landed in more mud. As the rain poured down, the worst idea ever came to mind.

Taking in the size of the hole she'd dug, the horrible idea was her best option. She lay back in the mud, and with cupped hands, scooped dirt over herself. Faster and faster. When she had a thin layer over her legs, she lay down and scooped a few handfuls over her chest, then went still.

It was then that she realized that her current predicament—half buried in her ancestor's grave and plotting to steal skeletal remains as someone moved in the darkness toward her—was definitely a new low.

Water splashed from boots slopping in puddles. The figure was close. Vianna lay still, holding her breath. As creepy as bonding with the dead was, the promise of pain from the living was worse.

Now that she was lying still, coldness seeped down to her bone marrow. Her lips and arms shivered. She hoped the darkness of night would cover the signs of her grave robbing, or soon-to-be grave robbing. Mud squished from the weight of footsteps right above her head. They'd found her. Potential hexes they could use ran through her mind like a flip card of horror: predictable boils, mundane oozing sores, flesh-eating beetles, or hallucinatory joint snapping. Vianna couldn't bring herself to look up.

"This has to be the most weird-ass hobby I've ever seen."

She looked up at the voice, saw familiar pink boots, then bolted to her feet.

Dee's hand was on her hip, covered by a glittery raincoat. "Are you, like, into dead people?"

Vianna flicked clumps of plastered mud to the ground with a slop. "What? No. It's my distant grandmother's grave." She took a deep breath to slow her racing heart.

Dee raised her hands in mock surrender. "I'm not here to judge. You do you, girl."

Vianna wiped the rain from her eyes. "I'm not looking for . . . whatever you're thinking. I need ancestral bones for a talisman." She reached up for her shovel, still lying on the edge of the grave.

Was Dee cemetery security? Vianna gave a sideways glance, but instead of stopping her from grabbing the shovel or desecrating the grave, Dee pulled out a bag of Skittles and munched. Vianna stared at the grave, waiting to see what would happen. Silence stretched as the rain slowed to a drizzle, and she wondered if she should just keep digging. One way to find out. She shoveled more dirt.

"That's one hell of a talisman if you need ancestral bones." Dee walked around to the other side of the grave and sat in the wet grass.

"You're just gonna sit there and watch me?" An icy breeze whistled through the trees and penetrated her wet clothes, making her shiver.

Dee shrugged. "Didn't seem like you wanted help."

"I'm not asking for help." She rammed the tip of the shovel into mud. "I meant you're not going to stop me? Aren't you supposed to be guarding the cemetery?"

Dee tossed another candy into her mouth. "Nope. They hired me to clean the building, mostly the toilets. It's crazy glamorous." She held out the candy. "Want some?"

"Did you wash your hands?" She shoved the shovel deeper into the soil. "You did just say you clean toilets."

"And you're currently standing in a grave. So let's not get into a who's-cleaner contest," Dee said.

Vianna wiped her brow with her forearm and then her hands against her wet shorts before reaching out a hand. "Thanks." Dee tapped the edge of the bag into Vianna's hand and a few rainbow pebbles tumbled out. "You really have a thing for candy." She tossed them in her mouth, and sugar spread over her tongue.

Dee smirked. "Helps balance the bullshit."

Vianna rubbed the back of her neck. She couldn't argue. Even digging up centuries-old bodies seemed less horrific with a mouthful of sugar.

"So, what do you need the talisman for?" Already drenched from the rain, Dee stretched out in the grass.

"It's Salem." Vianna shoveled another scoop of mud. "Hexes and hoodoo dolls are popping up all around me."

Dee sat up. "Hoodoo? Shut the front door."

Vianna tilted her head. "The front door?"

"Never mind." Dee swatted a hand in the air. "There was a girl a couple grades older than me who woke up and found a hoodoo doll under her pillow. She grew sicker by the hour until finally her mom took her to a healer."

"And her liver was missing." Vianna rolled her eyes. That story had been around forever. She bent lower into the grave, scooping mud with her hands in case she was close to the remains.

"Did you know her?" Dee's voice jumped up an octave when excited.

"It's an urban legend. Just like the big, scary Hunters who can take down whole covens in a single night. They're nothing more than bedtime stories to scare younger witches into behaving."

"Hunters are well-known, de facto knowledge—and probably hot. Real-life crime fighters stoking the fire of evil wenches. Mmmm. I could use some of that."

Vianna looked over the edge of the grave at Dee, who shimmied her shoulders, and they both laughed. She turned back to the grave and noticed a speck of ivory peek through the mud.

She cleared away more soil, exposing an earwig that burrowed deeper down, its backside pinchers the last visual. Pulling her hands back, she paused for a deep breath, then shook out the heebie-jeebies. She cleared the soil away from a series of long bones that led down to a hand. A thin stretch of petrified skin fell away, and she cringed, wishing for the earwig instead.

She turned over Clarice's hand to see if a finger was already broken off. No such luck. With her lips sucked in and several deep breaths through her nose, she wrenched the tip of a finger from the skeleton, flinching at the snap against her hands. She popped up from the grave, quickly putting as much distance between her and the bones as possible.

She raised the finger bone in the air. "Got it. Protection given by the witches before me."

"Ballsy, and way more palatable than what I originally thought you were doing." With the rain mostly stopped, Dee pulled down the hood of her sparkling parka. "A good talisman needs at least two different sources."

Vianna hopped out of the hole and shoveled dirt over the bones. "I've got a ring from a very distant grandmother." Not that she wanted more of Grandma Susannah in her life, but nothing could take down the level of evil in that woman. She was a good monster to have on her side, if you could count her as on her side.

Filling the grave went faster than digging it up, and Vianna leaned against the shovel to catch her breath after the last pat-down of dirt and mud.

Dee stood. "I'm gonna need a lot more candy with you around."

Vianna carefully replanted the mushrooms, flowers, and grass. "Why are you hanging out with a grave robber on a Friday night? Surely you have better things to do. Unless you're working the night shift?"

Dee shrugged and ate another candy pebble. "No, I've been done for a while. Just hanging out."

Odd place to hang out, but Vianna didn't say so. She had her own set of oddities.

"My regular crowd chose my ex in the break-up, the covens decided I don't count when playing gender police, and Salem is too small for much beyond that. Grave robbing is looking pretty sparkle-tastic at this point." Dee handed over more candy.

Not fitting in was something Vianna understood. That detail hadn't gone away even when she'd left Salem for Boston. Most of her nights included doing origami from old magazines her neighbor threw out and watching reruns of old sitcoms.

"People suck." It wasn't poetic, but it was true. Dee nodded.

Vianna drummed her fingers against the shovel's handle. She needed to get going but wasn't exactly sure what the proper protocol was for bailing post grave robbing. "Uh, thanks."

Dee handed her the remaining bag of candy. "For the bullshit. See ya around."

They both turned and walked in opposite directions, but Vianna looked over her shoulder, watching her sparkling raincoat disappear into the darkness. She hoped Dee found a place where she belonged. Living on the fringe of society was lonely.

"Watch out for the coyotes." Dee threw the comment out over her shoulder but kept walking. "They've gotten cozy in the woods."

Vianna nodded, then jumped over the fence.

16

A Talisman

The trek back through the forest was brisk, and thankfully, no rustling bushes this time. On the drive home, she sorted through how to make the talisman and found herself obsessively checking her rearview mirror for a motorcycle. She pulled into the driveway and hopped out, leaving the shovel in the truck. Dried mud flaked off her fingers when she reached into her pocket for the small drawstring sack with the finger bone. The front door opened, then shut behind her on its own.

Grandma stood on the stairs, a hint of a grin on her face. "Finally becoming a witch, I see."

Vianna didn't have time to over analyze whether she'd always been a witch, or what qualifications made a witch, or even what all of this meant in who she was becoming. There were larger problems. She felt fidgety even when inside the house. Gaining two enemies in a few short days wasn't a comforting statistic. Vianna needed to up her game, and she hoped the talisman was enough.

Grandma was hot on her heels the whole way to the conjure

room, making the hair on her neck rise like hackles. The feeling of being watched quickened her pace as she rushed through the doorway.

With the tip of her shoes against the carved summoning circle in the middle of the floor, Vianna took a deep breath and shook out her hands. Her entire childhood had been training for exactly this. She hadn't been allowed into the conjure room, to learn the exact inventory of ingredients or how they were organized. She hadn't been allowed to flip through the pages of the grimoire, or watch as Mother cast spells from its pages. But there was a lot that she did know, things she even excelled at.

Vianna knew the mechanics of spell work; Mother had made sure of that. There was a five-point system to understand how the craft worked, mirroring the five points of a pentagram, and young witches had it pounded into them from the womb.

Walking across the summoning circle, she went to the desk and tapped the secret drawer that held the grimoire. It popped open, and she used both hands to pull the thick book from its hiding place. She found the page with the ancestor talisman for protection and double-checked the ingredients even though she had memorized them, and then she triple-checked. Even with a lifetime of training, self-doubt still tapped on her shoulder.

She crossed the room to the wall covered in drawers and pulled open a middle one. Neatly labeled bundles of incense were easy to sort through, and she found bayberry, frankincense, and patchouli. Focusing the mind in the right direction was the first step. She lit the incense in the four abalone shells set in the corners of the room, aligning with points in the Phoenix constellation that rose during Samhain. All Roots witches were born during the Samhain season.

The next drawer was filled to the brim with feathers that Vianna could identify by sight from years of lessons and memorization. She found an eagle feather and used it to spread the smoke. Next, she went to the drawer with rows of black envelopes. On the outside of each envelope was a sketch in silver ink, each different from the last, and used to label what type of dried blood flakes were within. The heavy cardstock scraped against her fingers as she flicked through the different drawings: a goat, a scorpion, a tarantula, a goose, and a crow. She plucked the last envelope and set it in the middle of the summoning circle carved into the floor. After gathering the rest of the supplies from various drawers, she piled them next to the envelope along with a pestle and mortar.

She opened the small hidden drawer in the desk and pulled out the ring she'd noticed when cataloging the room. A simple metal band held a deep crimson stone that wasn't a ruby, but something else. If it was the ring she thought it was, it would serve as the object owned by an ancestor. The spell would turn the ring into a talisman. It had to be the ring she'd heard stories of.

Her mother wasn't one for bedtime tales of princesses or castles, but occasionally she'd told other stories as she embroidered. One tale mentioned a weevil of a man from Salem who married off his sister for the price of a farm that all three could live on. The sister's new husband, however, was a drunk with a heavy backhand. The sister had no rights and no one to care for her plight, but she found solace among like-minded women suffering from the same testosterone ailment.

One evening in the Salem Woods, they discovered boulders with veins of deep crimson—cinnabar. Shortly after, a sickness swept through the town, affecting a small group of residents that included the brother and husband of the woman. It was said that the Original Blood Coven formed during that plague and the sister became the first coven mother.

"That's mine." Grandma hovered in the doorframe.

The family heirloom was essential for making the talisman, but Vianna hesitated. How exactly would her ancestors protect her?

Would it be specifically Susannah and Clarice since the object and bone linked to them? Vianna didn't want either of them hovering around her wherever she went, but they were better than Csada, she supposed.

Which option was worse was a fun internal debate. A pair of murdering grandmas looming over her shoulder at all times? Or sit around weak and vulnerable as she waited for Csada and Tiphonie to attack again? Murderous grandmas it was.

Vianna sat cross-legged next to her gathered pile, the grimoire in her lap. She combined alder-twig shavings, blood flakes from the envelope, dried ants, Virginia-creeper berries, and rosemary oil into the mortar and ground it into a granular paste. Then she added the finger bone and it easily crushed under the pressure of the pestle and smashed into the paste. She wiped a dollop of goo from the mortar with her finger and traced a symbol on the floor—the same symbol with repeating loops on the page of the grimoire. After wiping off the excess paste onto her shorts, she set the ring in the center of the symbol.

She shimmied her shoulders and took a deep breath, rubbing her hands together to shake out the jitters. A thick pillar candle stood by the symbol and she reached out, swiping her fingers over the wick. Flame jumped to life, and Vianna stared. That would never get old. With a steadying breath, she began.

"Connected and bound by blood, I pull on the threads that bind me." A breeze rustled through her hair despite the window being closed. "Roots that bind through blood and name will help our line remain."

The spindle of smoke from the candle turned from a soft gray to a deep red. Chrysanthemum and jasmine scents saturated the room, and a belabored moan stretched down the hallway to the conjure room. Vianna's eyes scanned the circle she sat in the middle of, making sure it was intact, a barrier of protection from her own consequences.

Wispy figures floated through the doorway, and the same faces from the funeral crowded what little space there was around the circle. Without realizing it, Vianna had reached her hand to the ink on her collarbone. She let her gaze linger, soaking in more details of the women who came before her. The one in the red flapper dress had a broken finger and a gash up her arm, and the one in a long bed-gown had dirt-stained fingertips and toes as though she'd just left the garden. One by one, they faded away until only Clarice and Susannah remained.

There was one last step to finish the spell.

"I call to thee for protection and strength. May the Roots forever remain." Vianna lifted the candle and blew out the flame. Darkness cloaked the room, and her body slumped to the ground.

* * *

Chirping birds sounded through the window, and Vianna cracked an eyelid. Supplies from making the talisman littered the floor, and a small cone of sunlight reflected off the glass bottles on the corner shelves, creating bursts of violet and indigo across her arm. She peeled her face from the floorboards and poked at the indents in her cheek.

Her body had shut down. That happened after so long without sleep. She couldn't pass out at night while in bed. Oh no. That would be too easy. When she moved to get up, a sharp jab of pain sliced through her upper back from being slumped over. Light caught the cinnabar of the ring-turned-talisman on the floor. She picked it up, expecting a ghost to pop up or some magical jolt to race through her body, but nothing happened. Slipping the ring on, she stumbled upright and stretched her back, making it pop.

Once she got her stiff joints moving, she briskly walked down the hallway and into the kitchen for a hot drink and to check her phone. She opened the cupboard and saw a chipped clay mug with a shiny white sheen, and she paused mid-grab.

The morning before she ran, she'd argued with Mother over that exact mug. Mother insisted broken things belonged in the trash, and Vianna felt *trash* was code. She'd felt certain her mother could toss her into the trash as easily as a chipped mug, but there it sat on the shelf, never actually tossed.

The crap clearance coffee was in the pantry, and she poured some into the mug, mixing it with water, then sliding it into the microwave. She drummed her fingers against the kitchen counter as she waited. The grimoire offered no details on what happened after the spell for the talisman, but Vianna had slept nightmare-free. Although, that could have just as easily been coincidence. Looking down at her finger, she twirled the red-stone ring that now sat beside the infinity loop ring. The microwave dinged.

She took a quick sip of coffee without letting it cool and sputtered it back out, spilling some down her shirt. She'd burned her tongue. Pulling her shirt away from her skin so that it didn't burn her, she noticed the state of her clothes. She was still coated in muck from the heist at the cemetery. The squeaky faucet in Nancy's bathroom turned on, pouring water, then turned off. Vianna tightened her grip on the mug, flexing the edges of her mouth downward in a scowl. There was no way she could leave Salem before finding Nancy's hand and putting her to rest. She couldn't exactly herald spirits into some bright light or anything, but she could use the hand to banish her ghost from the house and release Nancy from a horrid death loop.

Grandma appeared at Vianna's side. "The coven mother is coming. Tidy yourself so you look a smidgen less like a homeless vagrant."

Grandma excelled at pointing out the obvious, but Vianna didn't give a goat's ass what Grandma or the coven mother thought about her appearance. It'd been a long night. She'd earned her grime. A knock came at the door.

She waved her hand for Shuck to open the door. "By all means, can't let the coven mother wait."

The front door swung open. Josephine and Tiphonie stood with matching scarves, gloves, and scowls.

Vianna leaned against the archway with her now half-filled coffee in hand. "Oh goodie. You're back."

"I see your manners haven't improved." Josephine's voice drowned out the click of her heels as she approached. One eyebrow arched as she looked over Vianna. "You have mud in your hair."

"Huh. How 'bout that." Vianna blew on her coffee as she turned toward the kitchen.

Josephine spoke at her back. "I came to finalize the purchase of the Root's home."

"You will not sell to this dratted cockroach," Grandma said. "And you're bonded to Shuck. You can't possibly run away *now*." She was working herself into a proper hissy.

Vianna settled into a kitchen chair. Of course she was selling. She rested her elbows on top of the table and ignored the tightening knot in her gut.

"I had a lawyer draw up the paperwork." Josephine pulled a bundle of papers from her over-sized leather purse with one of those stupid fringe tassels hanging from the side.

Legal jargon would take more brain cells than available at the moment. "I'll take a look and be in touch."

A knock came from the open front door.

"Holy goddess," Vianna said. "Who's here now?"

"Hello? Vianna? I came to make good on our deal." Charles's

voice sent a shiver down her spine. The archway to the kitchen creaked like old wood shifting. She checked to see if anyone noticed, but both witches were focused on Charles.

Tiphonie turned a deadly scowl at Vianna but didn't say a word. That talisman was going to get a chance to prove itself tonight. Vianna didn't need this kind of drama. Unfortunately, she couldn't shake the guy for the life of her.

"Vianna?" Charles appeared in the archway. He frowned at her muck-covered state, then took in the others. The well-trained politician took over, and a smile greased his lips. The left dimple appeared, as if reporting for duty. "Josephine, Tiphonie, what a pleasant surprise."

"Charles." Josephine reached out a limp hand. He clasped her fingers, then kissed her knuckles. "What a surprise to see you here. Tiphonie mentioned you hadn't been around because you were under the weather?"

Charles nodded easily. When had he been sick?

"Yes, I'm much better. How kind of you to ask."

He stepped closer to Vianna and slid an arm around her shoulder, making her insides shrivel. She scooted away. What delusional world was Charles living in? Was he purposely riling up Tiph? Explaining how a bad make-out session didn't grant them couple status wasn't something she wanted to do in front of others. Plus, she'd walked home. Did he not remember the fight?

"I came to make sure Vianna's set for the gala tonight," Charles said.

Gala? Vianna focused on the chip in her coffee mug and hoped if she left the three of them to chat among themselves, they'd forget about her entirely.

A tight smile spread across Josephine's lips. "I look forward to seeing you there. Such a shame Nancy won't be able to see all her hard work come to fruition. But so generous of your mother to take over the event after Nancy's disappearance."

Vianna jerked to attention, sitting straight in her chair. "Nancy?"

"None of your business, solitary," Tiphonie snarled.

"Manners," Josephine hissed as she gripped her daughter's shoulder. "Tiphonie's outburst was in haste, but she's right, this is a coven event. You're not entitled to such details."

Charles looked about wistfully, lingering anywhere but at them. Meddling in coven business wasn't a man's role, and it seemed he firmly understood that.

"I'll look over the offer and be in touch—," Vianna said again. If they weren't giving her more information on Nancy, there was no point in prolonging their visit. The conversation was over.

Josephine narrowed her eyes at Vianna as she spoke to Charles. "I'm sure Vianna mentioned she's not staying in Salem."

Charles nodded. "She has. Things can change, though."

Vianna sipped her shitty coffee and resisted rolling her eyes. No, things were not changing. Salem didn't get to change her path or tell her who she was. She was a future boutique owner, not a killer witch tangled in coven business. But she couldn't just clean and flip the house anymore. And she sort of was tangled in coven business until she figured out what had happened to Nancy. She couldn't possibly be staying, but she couldn't just leave. She wouldn't turn her back on Nancy again. And she couldn't just hand over Shuck. Things were . . . complicated.

Regardless, she and Charles would never be an item, and that fact was definitely not changing. She still didn't understand why she'd gotten sloppy all over his face. Josephine turned and left with the crispness of a drill sergeant. Tiphonie clamored after her mother. "I expect to hear from you soon, Vianna," Josephine called from the hallway.

The door slammed shut behind them.

17

Pandora's Box

Being left alone with Charles was the last thing Vianna wanted. She could feel his presence behind her like looming dread. The large crack in her coffee mug offered no deeper answers or sneaky escape routes, but she continued her intense examination regardless. Since she'd returned to Salem, it'd been a constant stream of one thing after another, and she was too exhausted for more right now.

He took all of two seconds to make a move. His fingers brushed beneath her shirt, against the skin of her lower back, and she reacted on instinct, shoving his hand away. "You have some real nerve." She looked up at him. "Last I checked, we didn't exactly end on great terms."

"About that." He sat down in a chair across from her. "I said things I shouldn't have. You have every right to be angry. I acted like a spoiled jerk." He wasn't making eye contact but looking at the table instead.

She didn't need his permission to be angry. "I know."

"I had just gotten a stressful work call and wasn't myself. Of course we can take things slow. I enjoy time with you. I like you—*a lot*. I'll take whatever time I can get." He reached for her hand but stopped short, then looked up with the most convincing kicked-puppy look she'd ever seen. It didn't stop her from feeling annoyed.

A slow sip of lukewarm coffee gave her a moment to think of something nice-ish to say. Time with him wasn't the worst. The food was good, and the flowers were considerate, but something had gone wonky. Really wonky. Just like her dream. Had there been magic at play? That didn't make any sense because he couldn't cast spells.

"This has become too complicated. It's not just friends having dinner and catching up." She gave him a pointed stare.

Charles twined his fingers together on the table. "Not complicated." He smiled. "Yes, I'm attracted to you. I'm sure you're used to that. Regardless, I can do just friends, and as a friend, I told you I'd help you pack since I monopolized your evening. Plus, I brought the gala tickets as an apology for the other night. You mentioned Nancy, and I thought you'd like going to the fundraiser. She organized it before disappearing. The event is to raise funds for kids in the foster system."

That sounded like Nancy, and if she were still alive, Vianna would attend in support of her friend. She should go. She owed her friend that much.

"I'd like to support the cause. But I can't get tangled up in coven drama. We can't be anything more than friends, Charles."

He raised his hands in surrender. "It's a friends-only invitation. And my offer to help you pack is penance for pushing you before. I truly am sorry."

It was hard to stay outraged with someone who was apologetic. "Thank you for the apology." She gave a sigh, letting go of her annoyance in the same breath. "So how come your mom took over the fundraiser?"

"Mom and Nancy had been working together on the event from

the beginning, so it just made sense for Mom to take over." He leaned an elbow on the table. "Nancy had the cause, but Mom was providing the art and even turned the gala into a founding-covens event."

"The founding covens are attending?" It was rare to have all four of the founding covens in attendance at the same event, especially one that didn't revolve around a festival tradition. Covens weren't exactly known for their philanthropy.

He nodded. "It wasn't for sure until recently, but now, with Nancy assumed to be missing permanently, it's become a way of showing honor to the Mabon Coven. They've all confirmed."

Nancy hadn't received a pledge invitation from the Original Blood Coven like Vianna. Instead, she'd received an invitation from the Mabon Coven. Of the four founding covens, they were the least murdery—specializing in a variety of gardening and not just poisons.

Charles rubbed the back of his neck. "The whole situation has hit Mom hard, since Nancy was her personal assistant. Mom is handling things well, though."

Vianna set her mug down. "You didn't mention she was your mother's assistant."

"Are you sure? I thought I mentioned it." He pursed his lips and tilted his head.

She was certain he hadn't. That was an odd detail to leave out.

"It's been a traumatic ordeal, and I feel spotty about it all." He reached across the table and put his hand on Vianna's arm. "I'm grateful to have a *friend* there tonight."

She frowned. He'd gone from not remembering Nancy the other day to now needing support while his family mourned her loss. Vianna definitely wanted into that gala now. None of this was adding up, and she wanted to see firsthand what was going on.

"Just as friends," she clarified. "I mean it." She needed him.

There was no way she was getting into a founding-coven event as a solitary witch.

"I look forward to it." He flashed his practiced smile.

A low rumble from Shuck shook her insides, and she could tell it was the someone-is-here nudge. A knock came at the front door.

"That must be the help I hired." Charles stood and strolled to the front door.

Vianna bolted out of her chair and followed. "Hired? For what?"

He turned back to her with his hand on the doorknob, a wide grin across his face. "I hired help for the cleaning, obviously. You can soak in a bath and get ready for the gala. I'll pick you up tonight, six sharp." He winked, then opened the door.

She gaped at his assumption that he had authority to answer the door, much less hire people to tromp through her house without asking.

"Mr. Barton?" A man with sunspots across his receding hairline appeared in the archway, wringing a faded green baseball cap between his hands. "Where would you like us, sir?"

"Miss Roots is in charge." Charles turned to Vianna and gave her a kiss on the cheek. "See you later, beautiful." He turned and left without waiting for a reply.

Vianna's outrage took too long to form words, because he was gone, leaving her with the ball-cap man, staring down at his feet. She clenched her teeth and pushed down the frustration the man in front of her didn't deserve. It was Charles she wanted to rip a new asshole into. The whole *just friends* thing wasn't going to work. Charles didn't understand boundaries. That was fine. He wanted to push, she'd push back. She was going to that gala.

"He hired us for the day, ma'am." The man kept his eyes downcast.

"Have any boxes?" she asked.

"No, ma'am. Mr. Barton didn't mention needing boxes, but we

can go collect some." He looked up, deep wrinkles highlighting the corners of his eyes.

"If you don't mind," she said.

"Not a problem, ma'am. Shouldn't take long. We'll be back within the hour." He nodded and pulled his hat over his head.

"Call me Vie, and that'd be great. Thanks. I'll have stuff piled and ready to go when you get back. I've got some bags for the dump and some boxes for donation. Plus some furniture." She hadn't planned on gutting the house since the coven was buying it, but the furniture would be worth a few bucks in the antique shops. She'd call ahead and have the crew drop it off.

"Yes, ma'am." The man turned and left.

She shut the door and turned back to the house with a sigh. An hour to add to her already existing piles meant she needed to get moving. She started with the upstairs, making a mental list of things to bag up and furniture to be hauled. As she moved through the hallway, she paused outside the door to her childhood room. It would need to be cataloged, just like the others. Maybe Mother had used the room to store the bodies of her victims. A can of gasoline and a match was how she really wanted to handle it. Practicality rarely matched emotion.

If the bedroom hadn't become a morgue, and if her things were still inside, she knew of a decent dress in the closet she could use for the gala. The night she'd slipped out the window and down the tree had been a few days before her initiation ball. She had planned on wearing a tailored cocktail dress with a black lace bodice and a deep green under slip. It had, if she did say so herself, looked stunning on her. She stared at the door.

Her hand trembled as she reached for the knob, then she pulled it back. She cracked her knuckles, then wrung out her hands. He was just a ghost. Closing her eyes, she counted to five and inhaled a deep breath. She could do this.

She thrust out her hand and twisted the knob, then pushed forward. Ignoring the creaky hinges, she propelled herself inside before her nerves won out entirely. The tobacco-scented air triggered a slow-motion merry-go-round of memory: the scratch of chalk against the floorboards, the splatter of blood against her chest, and the sting of betrayal when yanked to her knees by her hair.

Cobwebs stretched down from the corners to the simple redwood dresser with the matching vanity. In the center of the room, the ghost of her Uncle Jasper was on all fours, wearing his standard black turtleneck pushed up to the elbows and tailored slacks. Chalk in hand, a shell with burning herbs sat beside him. His folded, black-velvet suit jacket lay by a discarded knot rug.

He looked up at her with the warmth that had been her only affection in childhood. "Come, give your uncle some help. Be a good girl."

Vianna sucked in her bottom lip and bit down. She turned her back on Jasper and marched toward the closet. He hummed to himself as chalk continued to scratch against the wooden floors, but she didn't turn around, keeping her focus forward as she opened the closet. Straggler hangers lay in the same position on the floor from the night she yanked clothes into the same duffel, now in shreds. No runaway pack to fill this time.

Mother hadn't touched a thing; she'd simply shut the door on Vianna's existence. Wood scraped against wood behind her, and she knew the source without turning around. The chair from the vanity had been pulled across the floor and jammed under the handle against the door. She squeezed her eyes shut, but memories didn't go away like ghosts when she closed her eyes. She'd helped Uncle Jasper sneak into her room that night, and she'd locked them in together, away from Mother.

She stumbled to the window and yanked it open. The warm

breeze didn't help her breathe easier, and her lungs still felt as though they were shriveling into dried prunes. She placed a hand on each side of the window and filled her lungs to capacity.

Uncle Jasper had consoled her for years, had been her only rational voice in a sea of horror. With each new bully at school, each of Mother's rampages, and each new murder victim-turned-ghost, he'd wiped her tears, braided her hair, and helped her to find solace. And then one day, he'd found a solution to it all. There was a ceremony he could help her perform that would break her link to the witches before her and make her stop seeing the dead. Well, that was what he'd claimed. And she'd believed him.

She stumbled back toward the closet. Her hand trembled as she reached for the lace dress and yanked it from the hanger. Turning back around, she froze. She'd relived these moments in her nightmares every night the first year she'd run and still at least once a month since.

He'd dipped his slender fingers in dark ashes before drawing the summoning circle with her. It hadn't dawned on her to question what they were summoning. With a forceful grip on her arm, he yanked her to her knees. She stared up at him, surprised and motionless. He avoided looking her in the eye, binding her wrists behind her back and her ankles crossed together. Despite the doubt that slid through her thoughts, she'd kept her mouth shut. Ceremonies of power were rarely gentle or peaceful.

Her head jerked back, but only in memory, and he marked her forehead in ash. His humming had stopped, and now he chanted. Reaching behind his back, he pulled out a large, rusted blade. The wrapping of the grip marked it as an athame used for sacrifice in rituals. But there was no animal to sacrifice.

The door to her room reverberated, and the floorboards shook. Uncle Jasper's chanting wavered, then sped up, and Vianna's heartbeat raced. Where was the sacrifice to complete the ceremony? Why was she bound? Tears slid down her cheeks, and she refused to answer her own questions.

Pounding against the door from the other side rattled the frame. Mother bellowed from the hallway to be let in. Vianna's choices rolled out before her more clearly than ever. She'd turned her back on her mother's ways, and now she was nothing more than a goat to the slaughter. Her destiny, if she stayed, was to kill or be killed.

Cold steel pressed against her throat, and more tears slid down her cheeks. The ceremony had never been what he'd told her. Scared of the ghosts that filled her days and too weak to behave as a proper witch, she'd hidden in her uncle's comforting false words. This was her fault.

Wood shards exploded around them, and Vianna flinched away from the explosion. Mother rushed at Jasper, and a glint of metal flashed across his neck. Warm blood splattered across the side of Vianna's face. Jasper's grip on her hair released, and his blade clanked to the floor. He slumped onto his side in front of her, limp. Empty blue-gray eyes stared at her as a pile of blood spread from beneath him.

Mother used the tip of her pointed boot to flick a chunk of what was left of the chair out of her path. It dawned on Vianna now that it must have been Shuck's magic that slammed through the door and shattered the chair. She'd never thought of how the door or chair had broken before.

The past continued to bleed into the present and Mother towered over Vianna in the middle of the room, a paring knife hanging at her side, slick with blood. She frowned down—not at the body of her brother whom she'd just murdered, but at Vianna. The smack of her backhand was an explosion of needles across Vianna's jaw.

"Your actions caused this. You're an embarrassment." The coldness of her voice coated Vianna like frost. Mother walked around the circle, examining it with a wrinkled nose. "A summoning circle with you, a willing sacrifice of familial blood. Legacy blood. With an offering of that importance, he could have called a who-knows-what demon. You could have helped him become one of the possessed. Your stupidity is grotesque." Men couldn't bond with demons and gain familiars, but they could become hosts for demons.

Mother turned and stalked to the door, pausing for a moment but not looking back. "Pour a bottle of tequila over him and dump him on the side of the road. He was a drunk who pissed off a hooker. That's what they'll think." Mother tossed the blade at his feet. "Finish it yourself next time. He sleeps with you until you clean up this mess."

It had taken two days for the fog of shock and terror to lift from Vianna's brain. She'd stayed in her room with Uncle Jasper's ghost, replaying the night as his body decayed. When she finally came to and disposed of the mess, she'd known what to do. The following night, she ran.

Shaking off the past, Vianna stepped over the ghost of Uncle Jasper and shut the door behind her.

18

Field Trip

The polished banister was smooth beneath her fingertips. Outer stimuli helped when the past grew too loud. She hadn't forgotten the moments that drove her to run. In fact, that wasn't even the second, third, or fiftieth time she'd relived the worst moments of her life, but it never got easier.

There was one bright spot in this house, and she moved straight toward it: moonshine, even if it was god-awful shit. She grabbed a jar from the pantry and unscrewed the lid over the kitchen sink, then relished the burning liquid as it slid down her throat. Slowly, her awareness settled back into the present; the view outside of the kitchen window came into focus.

The overgrown mess was once a beautiful garden. Her fingers itched to work in the garden, to hide in the manual labor of pulling weeds and conditioning the soil. But there was no time for hiding. After another good pull of moonshine, she rummaged through the junk drawer and found a paper and pencil to make a list of things that could go. The conjure room was off-limits, but she hadn't looked through the candle den, so she headed down the peony hallway.

The door to the den was ajar, and she pushed it the rest of the way open. She'd expected an herbal array of scents to waft over her, but the room smelled of musty mildew. She wrinkled her nose with a frown. Herbs, wicks, sigil wheels, and oil droplets scattered over the thick oak table that sat in the center of the room.

She walked by the shelves that stretched across the wall, running her finger over the layer of dust covering the candle molds and glass bottles with faded labels. At the far end of the den was a cast-iron wood-burning stove with two plum cauldrons, both empty. She picked at a chunk of wax from the rim of the closest cauldron.

Sunlight poured across the table from the large window, and she crossed the room to bask in the warmth, lingering at the view of the backyard and garden. Flower origami—dried hollyhocks and hibiscus twisted into stars, birds, and trees—were tucked into the windowsill. She chewed on her cheek, caught in the bittersweet memories that laced the room. Not everything had been bad here, but Vianna had run and Nancy was left behind. Vianna plucked out a pelican. It surprised her that Mother hadn't thrown them out.

When Vianna first used oils on the dried petals, molding them into various designs, she'd only been fiddling around to distract herself from unwanted visions of the past. Staring intently at her feet didn't ease her anxiety but keeping her hands busy had helped. She'd discovered a calming pleasure in transforming the shriveled flowers into something new.

Mother had chided her about wasting time until the candles and soaps with pressed flowers sold at a higher dollar. But Nancy had loved the flower shapes from the start, requesting different animals and researching techniques for wet origami so Vianna could make more complex shapes.

A knock came from the front door, and she wedged the pelican into the screen between two other birds. The coven would want everything in this room, just like the conjure room. She'd leave it as it was. Heading into the sitting room, she answered the door.

The same older man from before stood with his eyes downcast as he spoke. "We're all set, Ms. Roots. And we brought a trailer for the furniture."

"Perfect." She stepped back from the door to let him enter. "This way."

She led him through the house, pointing out the bags of bedding and boxes of knick knacks for donation and nodding to the conjure room and candle den as off-limits. They could clear the sitting room of furniture, minus the wingback chairs by the windows. Her old bedroom was to be stripped entirely. After going through it all, she wrote the name of the antique shop where Mother was revered as a goddess of good fortune because of her spending. The shop owner would know the furniture and its worth. Vianna would call while the furniture was being loaded. Whatever the offer, she'd take it.

He nodded. "We'll get it handled, ma'am."

"It's Vianna. This helps a ton, thank you."

The man looked up from the ground. "I'll leave my card in case you need anything. Name's Luke." He tipped his head, then turned and began directing his crew.

They picked up the oversized green canapé à confidante sofa, and Vianna let out a sigh of relief. The monstrosity was as comfortable as a boulder, with the additional bonus of taking up most of the space in the sitting room. Why was she still calling it a sitting room? This was the damn living room. Well, it would be if it had a television. And she was selling the house, so it didn't matter what was in the room or what she called it.

Two men carried down the dresser from her old bedroom, and the corner ground against the wallpaper. The floorboards grumbled beneath her feet, and she tapped her toe to hush the house. She moved into the kitchen to check the time and found the bundle of papers from Josephine on the counter. Her fingers lingered over the twine that bound the bundle. Selling the house could fix everything if she could handle Nancy and Shuck first.

She pulled the twine loose and thumbed through the stack. The first few pages were formalities: names, addresses, the registered business logo of the coven, and various laws within the county. Halfway through the stack, she found the offer and gasped.

They had to be kidding.

The old house needed work, she knew that, but the market and this offer didn't match. The home was a two-story historic landmark in the heart of a coven neighborhood. Minuscule payments were written out in installments, with the first six months away. Vianna closed her eyes and rested her head against the cupboard. This offer helped nothing. Maybe she could counter.

She groaned as she pushed off the counter. There was a gala to prepare for. She could figure out the protocol with counter-offers and real estate agents later. One thing at a time, and right now, she needed to get ready.

After a long shower, which congested the bathroom with lemon-and-lavender-scented steam, she headed toward the bedroom. The room felt larger with the vanity and stacked bags in the corners gone. She felt like an invisible weight had lifted, and her lungs could fill to full capacity. A quick peek out the window showed an empty yard. The workers had cleared the bags and left. They worked fast.

The display on her phone read five thirty. Charles would be there soon. It took a shimmying of her hips to get into the lace dress. Ten years was a long time—Grandma may have been right about a few extra pounds on the hips—but the dress still fit. She left her long wavy hair down, giving it a few flips to add volume, and slipped into some strappy heels she'd found in a dust-covered box in the closet.

The cut on her palm was still healing, and she put on a new

Band-Aid. The last detail was the talisman. Leaving the safety of the house—of Shuck—was dangerous; Csada's issues were still unknown, and attending a gala with witches who'd already tried to hex her wasn't the smartest choice of destinations. But not going to Nancy's fundraiser wasn't a possibility. Vianna needed to understand what had happened, and Nancy's business dealings with Rose Barton felt significant.

The talisman sat on the dresser next to the jar of moonshine. She picked it up and the metal was ice-cold. When she slid the ring on her finger, a shimmer rippled through the garden of the red stone, and the ring warmed.

When she walked by the body-length mirror that hung from the closet door, she paused. The woman staring back at her was different, and it was more than a change of clothes. The strapless dress exposed the branding on her collarbone. She leaned closer to the mirror. The puffiness was lessening, and the redness around the branches was barely noticeable. She took a step back, her posture stiff and straight instead of hunched and hiding. Becoming a proper witch had never been the plan, but she wouldn't slink away. Not this time.

"You belong to us." Grandma appeared behind her in the mirror, her wrinkled hands clasped over her dirt-smudged apron.

Behind Grandma Susannah, generations of Roots witches rippled in a line like an infinity mirror. Vianna's fingertips brushed against the twelve branches on her collarbone as she stared at the women who came before her. After a few moments, she broke away and grabbed the jar of moonshine from her dresser. *Her dresser. Her house. Her familiar.* She took a drink. A low growl echoed down the hall and shook in her sternum, followed by a knock at the front door.

The ghosts of her ancestors sunk into a rolling fog at the bottom of the mirror, but two remained: Grandma Susannah and Grandma Clarice. The ring warmed on her finger and Vianna nodded in acceptance of their presence. The talisman had turned them into a party of three. She turned and headed out of the room to answer the door.

"You must carry on the line. The Barton boy is your best option." Grandma's ghost stomped after Vianna out of the bedroom, across the hall, and down the stairs. "Match your cycle with the moon and drink raspberry and nettle leaf tea. If you do it right, you'll only have to do it once. It must be done. Close your eyes and spread your legs. It is the way."

None of the retorts that came to mind would please Grandma, and Vianna wasn't in the mood for being thrown up on, so she stayed quiet. She gripped the handle to the front door, but it stuck. Grandma clicked her tongue, but the knob wouldn't budge. Apparently, Shuck was as thrilled about the date as she was.

"I'll be fine." She sighed. "I can do this."

The moment stretched, and another knock rapped on the door. She waited. A third knock came, and finally the front door clicked open. Charles stood in a tux, holding a fistful of lilacs.

She paused, then fidgeted with the top of her dress to pull it up farther. "Flowers don't really say 'just friends.'"

His attention roamed her body. "Hmm." He cocked an eyebrow. "I didn't realize flowers spoke."

She crossed her arms over her chest, but they did little to shield her. She wanted into that art gallery, but not at any cost. Faking interest in Charles wasn't happening.

He tossed the bundle onto the porch swing. "No flowers. Got it." He held out an elbow to escort her.

This was a bad idea, but sometimes, bad choices were better than doing nothing. She slipped her hand into the crook of his elbow and let him lead her toward his tiny car.

He leaned toward her as he opened the passenger door. "As a friend, you look stunning."

She slid into the car, regret slithering through her like acid worms.

"Fix your face," Grandma barked.

Vianna jumped, squeezing the armrest on the door. Her eyes flashed up to the rear-view mirror as Charles walked around the front of the car to the driver's side. Grandma Susannah sat in the back seat of the tiny convertible, shoulder to shoulder with Grandma Clarice in her stiff black blouse and tall ruffled collar. So this was how the talisman would work, chaining the ghosts that haunted her to her every movement. *Fantastic.* It was better than being defenseless—barely.

"Your face is shriveled like a forgotten prune left on the branch. It's no way to attract a man." Grandma Susannah turned her face toward the window with a raised nose. "This carriage is cramped and low to the ground. Is it for the poor?" She folded her arms over her noose necklace.

Charles slid into the driver's seat. "How about some music?" He pushed buttons on the steering wheel and a synthesized drum-beat came through the speakers.

Both grandmas pressed their backs into the seat and covered their ears.

"What is that noise?" Grandma shrieked.

Grandma Clarice shot daggers from her narrowed eyes at the back of Charles's head. A trail of beetles charged from beneath the hem of her dress and over the middle console of the car.

Vianna tucked her hands into her lap, away from the encroaching bugs. She looked away from the rearview mirror and the console, focusing forward as Charles put the car in drive and they headed out. "I'm not really in the mood for music."

He changed the song to something slower with a male crooning about wanting to touch some woman. The grandmas lowered their hands but kept the scowls.

"Where is that yowling coming from? He speaks like a yaldson." Grandma was still yelling to be heard over the music that wasn't all that loud.

Vianna wasn't sure what a yaldson was, but she doubted it was a compliment about his voice. Charles turned the car onto a main road and Grandma Susannah leaned over Clarice, pressing closer to the window to see more. Clarice sat ramrod straight, avoiding the view as it sped by.

"You're quiet. Probably nervous," Charles said.

Grandma Susannah gasped at a crowd of tourists. "There's so many people. They all dress as crass as you, a gaggle of land pirates, even the men. The buildings are so close, so many. Where are the crops? The horses?"

Charles's words overlapped Grandma Susannah's. "I know the covens can be a little cliquey, but you're there with me. I'll watch out for you." He nodded to himself as he spoke, approving of his own thoughts.

Grandma clicked her tongue. "He's daft, speaking nonsense on matters which he knows nothing about. A man can not protect you against the covens. His seed is his only value."

Grandma Clarice had nothing to add, and Vianna decided she was the more tolerable company in the car, despite the bugs. Charles was delusional to think he had influence within the coven circles or could offer any type of protection. And Grandma Susannah was delusional to think Charles's seed had any worth to Vianna.

"Everything glows," Grandma said. She hadn't looked away from the window.

Vianna watched as restaurant signs and street lights blurred by. The town was awake and bustling, despite the darkness of night, or maybe even because of it. Salem was always busy, but the night crowds were different. Adorned in costumes of dark layers, heeled boots, and hair purposely styled to hang in their faces, they thought of themselves as hunters seeking the dead. Google witches mingled with the new craze of ghost hunting and camera crews.

It was a mystery to Vianna why anyone wanted to see the dead. They had to know what they were asking for since they researched the most horrific murder sites, then flocked to the locations. Somehow, they wanted more.

There was another crowd of ghost chasers, the ones who'd lost someone and couldn't let go. They were the ones that mingled with the google witches, needing to say last goodbyes or understand some family mystery. Vianna understood that side of things a little more. She needed to understand what had happened with Nancy before she could walk away from her ghost. But sometimes knowing made things worse. She'd do anything to unsee Uncle Jasper's death, to wipe the knowledge of what he'd chosen and done. Ignorance would help her sleep at night.

A whisper of a thought splintered dread through her. Knowing what happened with Nancy might hurt just as much as Uncle Jasper. In her last moments, she'd offered Vianna up to Mother, and that stung.

"Vianna." Charles slid a hand over her thigh. "Everything is going to be fine."

Before she could nudge his hand away, he pulled it back, gripping the steering wheel as he slowed the car to a stop in front of the museum. Light shone from every window of the three-story building, and they'd positioned spotlights within the flowerbeds to shine up the length of the pillars that framed cement stairs.

"The other witches are dressed appropriately," Grandma said. "You look ready to do a goat's jig. Cover up."

A goat's jig meant enthusiastic sex in Grandma code. She was calling Vianna a street walker, again. A man in a red vest and black shirt approached, and Charles got out, handing him the keys.

Charles walked around the front of the car and opened Vianna's door, holding out a hand for her.

She looked up and frowned. "Friends."

He stepped back with a groan. "Now I can't be a gentleman?"

She stepped from the car, deciding not to engage with that comment, and looked at the crowds ascending the stairs as she stood.

The women wore flowing ball gowns and were adorned in glittering jewels. The men all wore tuxes like Charles. Vianna tugged the hem of her dress down. Grandma may have had a point. Vianna's sense of fashion had struck out twice now. She straightened and tucked her purse under her arm. This event was for Nancy. Fashionable or not, Vianna was attending.

19

The Founding Covens

Charles extended a hand for Vianna to go first, and they walked up the stairs to the historic museum. Both grandmas trailed close behind. Every local knew the history of the famous building from history classes in public, private, and witchcraft classes. From the very beginning, the building represented a place for those of wealth to showcase their travels.

The location conveniently sat above the heart of an underground tunnel system laced beneath Salem. Convenient, since the tunnels were used to move the spoils of trade and pillage without paying taxes. Nautical superiority had left a mark on the history of the town and even birthed one of the four original covens: the Tidal Coven.

She gave a sideways glance at Charles as they climbed the stairs. "The art gallery is in the old custom house?"

His chest puffed, and he nodded. As far as statements of wealth and status, it didn't get much grander than permits to operate in one of the original buildings of historic Salem. The amount of hoops and bureaucratic tape to rent and then renovate a building of that status were only plausible for an up-and-coming politician.

Security guards in tight polo shirts with coiled wires sprouting from their ears stood at each door. Hired security from the private sector wasn't uncommon at larger gatherings. It was the easiest solution. Witches didn't trust each other, let alone local law enforcement, to secure an area for a public gathering. Security was paid a handsome fee to confiscate a list of items and not ask questions.

"Purse on the table." A guard motioned to a long wooden slab between the two sets of doors. His trained eyes remained forward. Another guard with bulging biceps stood behind the table with a metal poker.

They weren't looking for guns or knives. No, not in Salem. Vials of blood, dead animal parts, hex bags, ceremonial daggers, blood chalk, or anything of suspicious paranormal activity were their target. The city of witches played by its own set of rules. Luckily, she'd only packed a tube of lip gloss and her phone.

She placed her bag on the table, and the guard nodded at Charles. "Mr. Barton."

"They question our intent?" Grandma Susannah snarled as she pressed both hands on the opposite side of the table where the man stood. He probed the small handbag an overly cautious number of times. "If a Roots witch had ill intentions—" She leaned over the table. "—it would take more than an antiquated rogue to snuff out her plan."

After deciding the purse was, in fact, just a purse, they pushed it toward Vianna. Before the guard pulled his hand away, a beetle darted across the table and up his arm. Fast and agile, the bug sped over his shoulder, then across his neck in the blink of an eye. The guard twitched his head to the side but remained in his soldier pose with arms clasped in front. No one reacted. They hadn't seen the beetle, just as they didn't see the grandmas. Vianna tried to be discreet as she looked around for Grandma Clarice. She found her standing in a corner by the right entrance, half-covered by shadows.

Vianna picked up her bag and Charles opened the door that Clarice stood beside. How strong did the talisman make the grandmas? It appeared as though the guard could feel the beetle, the *ghost-beetle*. Would the grandmas be able to touch and move things?

Red carpet led them up a stairwell with the clustered sparkles of chandeliers at the top. Two women in gowns that drooped down the steps behind them lingered on the staircase. They batted their eyes in Charles's direction as he ascended with Vianna. She, unsurprisingly, received only glares. Whether their contempt was over her stealing the arm of the most wanted bachelor, or because she was a solitary witch, was debatable. A good mixture of both was her guess. The grandmas flanked her; Susannah jutted her chin and scowled right back, and Clarice advanced with her entourage of ghost-beetles.

Several archways to a variety of museum exhibits were roped off, but a few artifacts remained in display cases along the walls: a model of an old pirate ship, a china dish, and a statue of George Washington's head with a nautical map printed over it. Charles led them into the main ballroom, where a rainbow of color and texture exploded from guests and art alike.

Paintings in hues of violet, crimson, and sunburst hung on walls, lounged on stands, and swayed from gold chains attached to the ceiling. The people were just as colorful and plentiful. Chiffon draped over shoulders, champagne flutes dangled from manicured fingertips, and gems adorned every female chest and earlobe.

The talisman on her finger warmed in warning, and she snorted to herself. The grandmas crowded in closer, one on each side. She was in a room of blood witches who despised her for turning down some great sisterhood of demon worshiping. She half suspected a bucket of goat's blood was going to splash over her head at any second.

Chattering witches mingled among the paintings, clumped in groups. Vianna's neighbor, Ophelia, stood closest to the door with her Eclipse Coven witches huddled around her in sleek dresses the same shades of the moon. Her afro was twisted into loops, and sparkling gems dangled along her hairline. They nodded in acknowledgment of each other.

Grandma clicked her tongue at Vianna. "It's one thing to allow slaves their own coven, but to let them into a formal event is uncouth." Grandma turned her back on Ophelia. "Stick to your own kind."

Vianna cringed. She was grateful no one else could see or hear Grandma.

"Keep your valuables close. The ship rats washed ashore." Grandma Susannah glared across the room at Alex Hall, the mother of the Tidal Coven.

Alex stood with her shoulders pushed back, chin held high, and feet shoulder-length apart as a witch whispered in her ear. It was easy to picture her standing on a ship deck despite her older age. Her crew surrounded her; all of them had sun-kissed brown skin, long curls or braids with bits of knotted ribbon, and wore dresses with flowing layers that cascaded to the floor.

Alex reached for a champagne flute from a passing tray, and her gaze flicked to Vianna, then away. Memorizing legacy lines was part of traditional witch education, and Vianna knew the basics about the Hall witches. They were the only legacy name to have birthed their coven and maintained the mother status to this day. The Hall women were infamous for their ruthlessness.

Charles stepped closer to Vianna and whispered into her ear, "Relax."

She would be an idiot to relax in this crowd. His closeness

drew glances from around them, and she knew she'd be making the gossip circuit. With a sigh, she reminded herself that she was here for Nancy. Vianna would learn why her friend was in the Roots house, and why she'd been murdered. Someone here had to know something.

Charles stopped a waiter walking by and lifted two flutes from the tray, handing one to Vianna. She took it as she looked around the room. The paintings looked similar to the one in Charles's flat, splattered, thick paint contrasting with brightly colored backgrounds. Grandma Clarice had wandered off, but Grandma Susannah hovered.

A witch with a flower crown braided into her hair walked by, and Grandma's upper lip twitched. "Mabons? They were too weak to last more than three generations. The weak don't endure."

Per usual, Grandma was wrong. The Mabon Coven was the fourth founding coven and was still very active in Salem. They weren't necessarily weak, but their mindset stood out from the others. If there was a coven delusional enough to think it was possible to unite the covens in some big kumbaya, it was the Mabons. They were easy to spot among the other witches since they used flowers as decoration in everything, from their hair, stockings, and purses to the straps of their dresses; they'd taken flower-power to the extreme.

"Charles, darling." A voice rang from across the room.

Rose Barton was walking toward them, wearing a pink babydoll dress that matched the natural flush of her cheeks. It was eerie how easily a witch could turn into a princess.

"Mother." Charles's eyes lit like a kid in a candy store as his mother sashayed over.

This guy was the ultimate mama's boy. After embracing, they turned their attention to Vianna. She forced a tight smile.

"It's nice to see you in more pleasant circumstances, dear." Rose clasped Vianna's hands and leaned in for a quick peck on the cheek.

"I was delighted to hear you two are spending time together. You were always such a sweet girl. It's wonderful to have you home."

"She *should* be delighted," Grandma said. "She should be groveling at your feet. A Roots witch is an honor."

They were both full of crap. There was no honor happening. And as a child, Vianna had never been sweet. She'd been nothing more than a trembling wallflower who did her best to blend into the background.

Vianna pulled her hands back from Rose. "I wanted to offer my sympathies. Charles mentioned Nancy was your assistant. I can't imagine the trauma this has caused you."

Normally, Vianna wouldn't bother with the formalities of parlor talk, but in this case, playing the game might give her information. Rose's name had dominated the coven logs. She had to know something.

Rose patted Vianna's arm. "The poor dear must have gotten into something over her head. It's an excellent lesson for younger witches."

Grandma gave a snort of a chuckle. For a witch not born into legacy blood, Rose acted the part with perfection. In one breath, she'd welcomed Vianna into Charles's arms, and the next, she gave a veiled threat on her life. Rose was posturing up, making sure Vianna knew who had the higher status of the two. But the pissing contest of hierarchy was debatable. Vianna might not be coven-bound, but she'd been born with the label of legacy. For better or worse, that fact mattered.

"It's a shame that, as an older witch, you didn't notice anything out of the ordinary. I'm sure your experience could've helped if she was over her head." Vianna watched Rose's reaction. These verbal jousts were an old, choreographed dance, but it was the non-verbal communication she was watching for.

"Yes. A shame. I'm afraid Nancy was nothing more than my paint mixer, but she'll be difficult to replace. Her expertise in what petals and herbs make the most vibrant hues was extraordinary."

Vianna clenched her jaw. Replacing her paint mixer—that was the extent of Rose's concern. She didn't give a flying shit about the charity, or if Nancy were missing, or even dead. All this woman cared about was her art and showing it off. "How charming. I'm sure Nancy would love being remembered as the extraordinary paint mixer. We should put it on her gravestone."

Rose's posture stiffened.

"Vianna," Charles hissed.

"Her gravestone? She's missing, dear. Not dead. You seem overly emotional about it all. Perhaps the girl ran away. You'd know more about that than me." Rose batted her eyes in feigned innocence. She was baiting Vianna, distracting her. Rose knew something.

There were no ties between Rose and Nancy besides paint. Whatever Rose was hiding, it wasn't obvious. So Vianna grabbed at something random.

"Do you know if Nancy had a cat?"

The question had been a long shot. But in her death loop, Nancy had mumbled something about a cat.

The veins on Rose's neck bulged. "I'm afraid not." With a smile, she relaxed her muscles. "I must mingle with the other guests. You two enjoy yourselves. Make sure to swing by the twilight series in the back. They're my favorite. And Charles, darling, do watch out for Tiphonie. That girl is on the prowl for you." Rose gave a ta-ta wave before gliding toward a group of witches surrounding the Mabon Coven mother, June Proctor.

"She knows of the cat?" Grandma asked. "That thing is a nuisance and its days are numbered."

Grandma knew more about the cat than she'd let on. Vianna didn't bother to hide her scrunched face as she watched Rose join a group with Josephine, the Original Blood Coven mother, and June Proctor.

Charles jerked Vianna's elbow, jarring her. "What is your problem? Did you just accuse my mother of being involved with Nancy's disappearance? You're acting crazy." He lowered his voice to a whisper-yell. "And in *public*."

"I didn't accuse anyone of anything." Her voice was calm and her body still.

Charles's lips thinned, and after a long glaring moment, he stormed off. She exhaled a breath she hadn't realized she was holding. After a few deep breaths and a small shimmy to shake off her nerves, she refocused on the gala and potential gossip.

20

Splattered Paint

Vianna and Grandma Susannah stood in the middle of the ballroom as gowns swooshed and champagne flutes clanked around them. For once, Grandma was quiet. Her eyes darted between witches in different covens, calculating factors Vianna couldn't even begin to predict. Vianna finished off her champagne and swapped her glass with a full one from a tray passing by.

Getting anyone in attendance to talk with her about Nancy, or anything else, was going to be a challenge. There had to be someone with loose lips who'd drink too much or, if she was really lucky, someone who didn't know who she was.

There was a gaggle of younger Original Blood witches, giggling and chattering in a tight group. Beyond them were a few older Tidal witches who unabashedly stared at Vianna. Neither group seemed ripe with the potential for information sharing.

Heels clicked against marble, and someone cleared their throat. Vianna turned to see Tiphonie with one hand on a hip covered in red lace and a flute dangling from the other. Her red hair was piled on top of her head with black chopsticks. "Charles finally expire of you? You weren't bred to entertain a man of that caliber."

Grandma scoffed. "Parker witches haven't changed a bit. She looks identical to her ancestors. Just as pompous, too."

"'Expire of me'?" Vianna wasn't sure if Tiph's word choice was a dig at Vianna being some type of moldy produce, or if Tiph meant to say tired.

Tiphonie scrunched her face. "Whatever. You should leave. No one wants you here."

"How dare she," Grandma huffed. She leered at Tiphonie, nose to nose. "Want is irrelevant. The coven is weak without the Roots."

The whole point of attending this event was to learn something about Nancy. "Catch me up on the recent gossip, Tiph. That's what you do, right?"

"Solitary witches aren't privy to coven business." Tiphonie rolled her eyes, then raised her drink to her lips.

Grandma flicked the bottom of the flute, and champagne splashed across Tiphonie's chest and dress. She yelped, and the glass shattered against the marble floor. Grandma reeled on Vianna, a deep red spreading over the white of her eyes. The surrounding air went cold.

"You are shaming the family name! Letting a worthless nothing call you that!" She shoved at Vianna's shoulder, making her stumble back a step, before stomping off.

"You better knock it off," Tiphonie hissed at Vianna, then looked around to see if others were watching. The group of younger Original Blood witches had stopped their chattering and stared.

Tiphonie raised her voice. "You don't want to mess with me, Vianna Roots."

"You're right," Vianna said. "You're not worth my time." She turned and walked away in the same direction Grandma had gone.

Tiphonie's voice projected at Vianna's back. "That's what weakness looks like, ladies. Take heed and thank Freya we've chosen you for initiation so you don't end up like *that*."

Vianna ignored her and slipped into the crowd, weaving between art and witches. The talisman felt like a beacon for drama, not protection. Giving Grandma the power to move things was a nightmare. Vianna finished her glass of champagne and set it on a passing tray. Grandma Clarice replaced Susannah, hovering at Vianna's side. She didn't say a word.

The crowds of witches all ignored Vianna as she meandered among them. Instead, they were enraptured by the paint-splattered canvases. Her eavesdropping only revealed chatter about paint color and brushstrokes. The entire scene was bizarre. The four founding covens gathering to support Rose felt like an alternate reality. Rose wasn't even a true legacy. Yet, the strongest among them all gathered for her. No one was hexing other families, sizing up familiars, or even threatening to kill each other. The night was still early, so maybe things would liven up.

A sunburst of yellow dominated the soft lavender on the canvas in front of her. Her eyes glazed over, making the painting blur around the edges. Something was caught in the paint. She leaned closer. Crushed lavender buds had been smeared into the purple paint, which was odd since they didn't bleed the vibrant hues Rose mentioned. They did, however, work for relaxation and even subduing with the right buddy ingredients. Still, it was a pretty painting. Really pretty. She loved lavender; her bedroom in Boston sported the flower in a variety of mediums.

Buying the piece might endear her to the coven, make them like her more and want to give a proper offer on the house. Maybe it would even make Rose happy and calm Charles down. Vianna swayed, feeling lightheaded. But she didn't have a single dollar on her, and the few crumpled bills at home wouldn't be enough to buy a work of art like this. Maybe she could get a loan from someone. Maybe Charles could get her a discount.

A growl reverberated through her sternum, clearing the fog that had slid into her mind. The blurred edges around her vision focused, and a wave of beetles scattered across the canvas. Vianna stiffened and pulled her eyes from the painting. Buy Rose's art? Vianna didn't care for art, let alone the grade-school finger painting on display.

Clarice glided in front of her with a pinched expression. She lifted her hand and gave several hard taps against Vianna's sternum. Grandma Clarice was telling her to listen to Shuck. Vianna tilted her head at the canvas, remembering the same art from Charles's loft, the same nausea-inducing fog, and the same warning growl from Shuck. Her familiar was stronger than the spell. A spell. The paintings. Rose had worked a spell into the paintings. Had Nancy known?

Who else knew? The urge Vianna felt to comfort Charles and how it had swollen into a consuming need. Her willingness to buy smeared paint in order to . . . please the coven. To please Rose. To please Charles. Fuck a goat. It was a spell of pleasing.

Vianna spun on her heel in a circle, soaking in the art plastered everywhere. Suddenly, it felt like an explosion of color she might drown in. Surely it wasn't all spelled. Vianna's attention flicked from one canvas to the next, her shoulders shrinking inward. The most powerful witches were all gathered and potentially enthralled. By Rose Barton. This was delusional. It couldn't be. And if they were all eager to please Rose, and Vianna had just publicly pissed off Rose . . . this was bad.

A gentle voice came from behind. "I'm surprised to see you here."

Vianna startled and spun around. Mistress Layton, the coven librarian and Dee's mom. She wore a white satin blouse with a loose bow that hung from the neck and a black full skirt.

"Mistress Layton," Vianna blurted.

"Did I startle you, dear?" She patted Vianna's arm. "What are you doing in this stuffy place?"

Vianna took a deep breath, letting her heart rate slow. "Developing an urge to buy art?"

Mistress Layton nodded. "Rose's work has that effect. Everyone becomes an art lover after one of her shows. Well, everyone but your mother, I suppose. She never attended the galas. Rumor had it that she refused, making the coven mother livid."

Mother had known. Or, at the very least, she'd listened to Shuck.

Mistress Layton sipped her drink and her eyes turned glassy as she stared at the painting in front of them. Vianna looked from side to side, seeing witches in similar states of fog. It wasn't obvious without knowing what you were looking for, but Vianna could see it now. The long stares, the small smiles.

"Rumor has it you came with Charles Barton." Mistress Layton drew Vianna's attention back. "Careful, Tiphonie has staked claim on that one."

Was that a threat? Had Mistress Layton been sent over? Vianna desperately wanted to turn and run from the building. A server walked by with a tray of champagne flutes, and she declined. She needed to make her exit, to get away from the spelled paintings so she could think without worrying if her thoughts were her own or if there was an incoming attack.

"She can have him. I have no intention of leaving with him or seeing him again." A new anger boiled at the thought of Charles knowing about the spell in the paintings. Did he? Men weren't allowed to be involved with coven business. It was likely he was nothing more than a puppet for his mother.

"Relationships are complicated." Mistress Layton sighed.

"Oh, no. Not a relationship. He's all Tiph's. I was just curious about the gala, so he brought me along." Vianna felt like she was walking on eggshells with every word. There was no line to define friend from foe, only brightly splattered paint.

Mistress Layton smiled. "What were you curious about?"

Was Vianna in danger? She couldn't imagine the old librarian hurting her, even if influenced.

"I was surprised that the covens were hosting a charity, and even more surprised that an Original Blood witch was in business with a Mabon witch." Vianna tracked every movement around them and undoubtedly looked suspicious. She tried to calm down, or at least pretend to.

The more she thought about it, the more evident it became that Nancy had known about the spell. She had to if she'd mixed the paint. She may have even been the one who made it possible. But that didn't track either, because she wouldn't have owned a spell of that magnitude. Neither would Rose, for that matter. Very few grimoires would contain something of that level.

"Nancy spent *all* of her time with Rose before she disappeared." Mistress Layton frowned. "I think Rose wanted to do something nice for the girl. She'd had such a hard upbringing, and Rose hasn't had it so easy either. They bonded."

The room spun. They'd been in it together. Was Nancy a victim, or was she part of some big scheme? Was she both? It had to be why she'd called a few months back. She didn't call to get an update on Vianna's worthless job at a craft store—she'd been in a dangerous situation, about to do something stupid, stupid enough to get her killed. Vianna felt sick. If she had answered the phone, if she'd taken Nancy with her, stayed in touch, if she'd done literally anything, things could have gone so differently.

"I better go mingle so I don't upset the coven mother. Take care of yourself, little Vie." The old librarian gave her a smile and wandered off.

"This place is nothing more than a brothel." Grandma Susannah appeared beside her. "Scandalous wenches who do inappropriate things in darkened corners and don't have a thought in their pea brain beyond their fancy gowns. It is time to leave."

That was ironic coming from someone who thought killing people in darkened corners was acceptable behavior. Vianna was ready to leave, anyway. A quick stop to the ladies' room, and she'd walk home. Salem wasn't that large, even in heels.

The grandmas waited outside the restroom. Vianna walked in and Tiphonie was at the sink, trying to wash the champagne from her bodice. She looked up with tear-streaked cheeks. Once she realized it was Vianna, her face scrunched into a sneer.

"If you're going to walk out on Charles Barton, you're stupider than I thought, and that's saying something." She dabbed at the smeared mascara beneath her eyes with a wet paper towel, then flicked it at the sink. Resting a hand on her cocked hip, she turned to Vianna.

She was a rotten brat, and whatever issues she was having were none of Vianna's business. Still, Vianna understood the weight that came with their upbringing. "You can do better than him, Tiph."

"What do you know about anything?" Tiphonie fidgeted with the diamond bracelet that matched her earrings. "There aren't a lot of options in Salem that Mom approves of."

That was how it worked with legacy witches. Carrying on the line was everything. Young girls were bred with men who had money and political power that could further their coven. Whether the guy was a douche was irrelevant. A prick of sympathy swelled in Vianna's chest. Had she stayed in Salem, her mother would have forced her into a similar situation.

"Tiph—" Vianna was interrupted by the bathroom door flinging open.

The Ramsey twins pranced in, then stopped short when they saw

Vianna. They wore matching gowns with necklines that plunged to their navels, one black and the other white.

"Ugh. What is *that* doing here?" the twin in the black dress asked.

"Probably running. Like usual." Tiphonie straightened, her mask back on—but Vianna had seen a crack in the facade, even if only a small one.

Tiphonie's lackeys flanked behind her, making her stand taller and arch her shoulders back. "By the way, how are you sleeping these days?"

Vianna didn't need confirmation that Tiphonie was behind the hex, but Tiphonie seemed determined to make sure she got credit.

"Just peachy. Rejuvenated even. Thanks for asking."

Tiphonie scowled. Had she thought of the self-harm hex herself? Maybe she was just another puppet under Rose's control.

"She's lying. Probably pissed her bed," the white-dressed Ramsey twin said.

Vianna didn't care what they thought. Turning her back on the trio, she pushed through the door and left before the grandmas strolled in and made things worse.

21

Moonshine Party

Vianna hated downtown. And even worse, the museum sat smack in the middle of the congested tourist area. Crowds shuffled behind tour guides with side-strap backpack mics they used to belt out tales of ghosts from the 1600s. Despite the fact that witches were what made the town famous, there were more ghosts of slaves, pirates, and prostitutes than witches that roamed the streets.

Crowds of cameras were pointed at every dark corner as guides encouraged flash photography in order to catch a glimpse of a ghost. They went off like paparazzi, creating a blinding wall of light that left Vianna with her hands outstretched as she made her way through the bodies.

The ghosts roamed the streets, as numerous as the living, and a chill ran through her bones with each ghost she stepped through. Between the cameras, the loud noises, and the dead, a headache began to pulse behind her eyes.

"How can you handle all this noise?" Grandma yelled from right beside Vianna's ear. "There's movement and people everywhere."

Vianna clenched her jaw and surged forward, the grandmothers in tow. Distracted by everything around her, she bumped into a stout man holding his wife's purse as she snapped pictures. He didn't budge, but Vianna nearly toppled over and mumbled her apologies. A car horn blared from the street. She flinched, then looked over her shoulder.

"Vianna!" A familiar face stuck out the driver's window of an orange Jeep. A white daisy was pinned in Dee's updo. "Ma said you needed a ride." She motioned for Vianna to get in.

Bless the goddess. Vianna hurried across the street and slid into white fur seats that smelled of lotus oil. She rubbed at her temples. "Freya's cock, your timing is perfect."

Dee tilted her head. She wore a cotton sundress with printed daisies. "Goddesses have cocks?"

Vianna shrugged, and Dee laughed. Vianna settled into the seat, listening to the club music blasting from the speakers.

"It's louder in this horrid carriage than on the street," Grandma Susannah yelled from the back seat, where she sat scrunched next to Grandma Clarice. Ghost beetles crawled up the side of the Jeep.

Dee found an opening in the traffic, and the crowds slipped into the rearview mirror. The plastic windows were unzipped and fresh air whipped over Vianna's face, taking with it the anxiety of the crowds. Even Grandma Susannah had gone quiet.

"How'd the talisman work out?" Dee drummed her fingers on the steering wheel.

Vianna slipped off her heels and sighed with relief. "Not as I expected. I'm still trying to figure out how it's helpful."

Dee nodded and kept her eyes on the road. "Magic is like that."

Vianna noticed a worn leather belt with straps and pockets for small bottles rolled up in the console. Evidently, Dee dabbled in potions. It was a rigid practice, and there weren't a lot of modern witches who had the patience or the knowledge. *Impressive.*

They pulled up to the Roots family home, and she didn't question how Dee knew the address. Salem was small, even smaller if you counted legacy names.

She grabbed her handbag and heels. "Thanks for the ride."

"Yup." Dee tilted her head and checked out the house through the windshield.

Vianna wondered if the house looked as creepy without ghosts or layers of childhood trauma. The grandmas had vanished from the back seat. Her bare foot dangled from the Jeep in hesitation. She couldn't do anything about Rose and the paintings tonight: it was debatable if she could do anything about it at all. She needed a drink while taking a breather in the safety of her demon home, and drinking alone wasn't ideal.

"My mother stockpiled an obscene amount of moonshine before she died. It tastes like shit." Vianna chewed on her cheek. "Wanna join me?"

Dee lowered her chin and looked at her. "You know I don't do girls, right?"

Vianna barked out a laugh and hopped out. "Just drinks. I'm not looking to get up your skirt."

"It's easier to be up front from the get-go." Dee followed Vianna to the front porch. "People expect weird shit just because I'm trans."

"My only offer is moonshine. It usually makes me feel better, at least for a couple of hours." Depending on the ghost.

The door unlocked and swung open before Vianna even raised her hand, and she pursed her lips. The house needed to work on the whole subtle thing. It wasn't top secret that the Roots family home was possessed, but it didn't need to be advertised.

Dee peeked in as she unwrapped a sucker she'd pulled from her purse. "Kinda empty. And old-fashioned." They walked in, and Dee whistled as she appraised the empty sitting room. Even with most of the furniture gone, there was still the merlot-striped wallpaper, heavy dark drapes, and a few straggler antiques. It was a little old-fashioned. Or *a lot*, really.

"Mom had a thing for antiques." Vianna frowned at the two wingback chairs with a small table by the bay windows. The middle of the room was empty of furniture, but the faded rugs remained. "I had most of it cleared out earlier today."

"There's not a single television or computer in this place, is there?" Dee spoke in hushed tones of horror, as though she could see the body parts hidden in the walls. "No wonder you're so weird. Where's this shitty moonshine?"

"This way." Vianna made a beeline for the kitchen and grabbed two jars from the pantry. "Hold these. I'll get lawn chairs since it's cooler outside than in the house." She thrust the jars at Dee before unlocking the backdoor and strolling outside.

Two rusted, folded-up lawn chairs leaned against the back of the greenhouse, just like when she left. As a kid, she'd set them both out every full moon, in hopes her mother would join her out there. She dragged the chairs across the grass, then gave a hard yank to pry the joints open, sending molded leaves and dead bugs everywhere. Dee stood watching in the grass, her nose scrunched. Vianna shrugged and took her jar, then settled into the plastic-covered, rusty chair.

After an overly dramatic sigh, Dee sat in the chair next to her. "You need new lawn furniture." She twisted open the mason jar and dipped her lolly into the liquid.

"I'm supposed to be selling the house." Vianna took a drink, and liquid fire slid down her throat.

Dee popped the lolly into her mouth, then quickly pulled it out. "Ugh! You weren't kidding. Shit tastes like lighter fluid."

Vianna nodded and took another swig. She held back a cough. The first two drinks were the roughest.

"What do you mean by 'supposed to be selling the house'?" Dee took a deep breath before forcing a gulp down.

"I planned on selling to the coven, but they made a joke of an offer. I was going to counter, but I don't know if dealing with the coven is a good idea right now. Maybe I'll list it online and put a sign out front." She snorted. "Don't mind the demon who steals your crap, or the ghosts that knock stuff over and moan at you, or that on every full moon your neighbors will dance in their yard—naked. Your very elderly and wrinkly neighbors. But the original crown molding is in pristine shape."

Dee chuckled. "I'd lead with the crown molding. It's spectacular."

Vianna snorted. Moonlight spilled over the yard, and crickets and frogs came out in full force. For a moment, Vianna envisioned what the garden had been, what it still could be.

"How are you going to sell the house if it's the host for your familiar?" Dee had the lolly tucked into her cheek as she spoke.

"Oh," Vianna huffed. "So you knew that."

Dee nodded. "The older witches know. Your family is a mystery to the up-and-coming, though."

Vianna opened her mouth to argue that she didn't want any of it, had never asked for any of it, but that wasn't entirely true. She'd asked for the grimoire even though she knew the responsibility that came with it. When making the talisman, she'd pulled on Shuck, welcomed his magic into her. And she didn't want Shuck to end up in another witch's hands, a witch like Rose or, even worse, Tiphonie.

"I was never planning on staying in Salem, but I don't know. I got caught up in something and things are just . . ." She didn't know how to put it all into words.

"Eh. The coven couldn't handle a counter offer, anyway. They probably don't even have the funds for the first offer. They've been broke for some time." Dee took another drink, then popped the lolly back in her mouth.

"How is that possible? The Original Blood Coven has always had more job offers than it can handle." At least, it had for as long as she could remember. Hexing and maiming was a lucrative business.

Dee leaned into her chair. "I don't know the details since I'm not allowed into the financial books or meetings, but it seems to me that the richer Rose gets, the poorer the coven gets. Mom won't hear talk like that, though. The scandal." Dee flashed her eyes wide in mock concern. "She's drinking the crazy Kool-Aid like everyone else."

"You noticed the crazy Kool-Aid effect too?" Vianna dug her toes into the grass and gave a sideways glance at Dee. Did she know about the spelled paintings?

"Every time Ma comes back from one of those galas or a private showing, she's drained the account on another splattered canvas. I can't figure it out. I suppose it's decent art, that's what Ma says." Dee shrugged half-heartedly.

"Or it really is just smeared paint. I didn't feel that way at the gala, though. I wanted to buy a piece." Vianna focused on the empty patch of soil normally ripe with white pumpkins and took another drink. "I have a theory on that."

"Oh?" Dee stretched out her legs and crossed her ankles. Strappy sandals showed off a pedicure that matched the daisies on her dress and in her hair. "Do tell."

Vianna took a deep breath and another drink. Dee wasn't coven-bound, but she came from their world just like Vianna. They were both outsiders, and she needed someone to soundboard with. It was all too much.

"How possible would it be to combine a painting with a spell?" Her fingertips tapped against her jar. "You'd crush the ingredients into the paint, right?"

"What kind of spell?"

Vianna wiggled her toes in the grass for a moment. "A spell of pleasing."

They sat in silence for a few moments. Even the frogs seemed to understand the importance and went quiet.

"You're saying there's a spell of pleasing in the paintings? In the paint?" Dee asked.

"Maybe." Vianna took another drink. "Probably." Definitely.

"A spell of pleasing is big league. It messes with the chemistry of the mind. Only the oldest and strongest legacy families would have a spell like that. And even then, there's, *maybe*, three families in all of Salem." Dee tapped her lolly against the mason jar, her eyes on the trees. "The Halls from the Tidal Coven. Possibly the Epslers from the Original Blood. And the most obvious answer: the Roots."

Vianna stared at the grass, thinking. She knew there wouldn't be too many families that would have that spell, but she hadn't thought to make a list of exactly which families. It couldn't be that short, could it? There were plenty of strong legacy lines, but strong in various ways. This kind of strong, this kind of scary . . . Dee was right. It would only be the worst of the worst.

"The answer was pretty obvious, wasn't it? I just didn't want to see it. Same old Vie, running from the truth." She let her head fall back and looked up at the stars.

"You're being cryptic. What's obvious?" Dee asked.

"The spell. Of course it came from the Roots grimoire. Nancy stole it. She was the only friend who ever made it past the front door, the only witch who knew the house frontwards and backwards. She was perfect for what Rose needed." *Of course.*

Nancy hadn't just been Vianna's friend because she'd liked her. Or maybe she had. Maybe she decided to gain from it after the fact? Vianna sighed. She'd never know.

"Nancy Williams? The missing witch?" Dee asked. "What does she have to do with it?"

"She was working with Rose. She stole the spell and got caught by my mother." Once Vianna said it out loud, it all clicked. Cutting off hands was old-school punishment for a thief. Mother lived by the rules of long ago. An eye for an eye. Just like Earl in the bathroom.

"How do you know that?" Dee asked.

"Because her ghost is haunting the powder room." The moonshine no longer felt like liquid fire, but toasty marshmallows that made everything less dramatic and scary. "I see ghosts."

Dee spit out her drink and coughed on what didn't land on the lawn. "Seriously?"

Vianna nodded. "Yeah." It'd been a long time since she'd said that out loud to another person.

"You're a medium? That explains the shifty eyes! I couldn't tell if you were, like—ya know—not all there, with the way you struggle to make eye contact."

"Gee, thanks."

Dee bounced in her chair with excitement. "There hasn't been a witch medium in Salem for—." She tapped the jar with what was left of the lolly. "I don't know how long. I'll have to check the archives, and that says something because I have a photographic memory. Is it from your father's side?"

Her father's side? That was a sobering thought. Vianna didn't know her father. Mother never spoke of him. Never. Regardless, there wasn't a group of people who specialized in ghost-seeing. Whatever made Vianna see the dead, it seemed to be a special default just for her. "I doubt it."

Dee gave a lazy grin and settled back in her chair as she took another drink. "I'm doubting my ability to drive home."

"You can stay here." Vianna wasn't sure where. "I don't have furniture, but I have plenty of empty rooms and probably some straggler blankets and pillows. I'd offer to share a bed, but you're already suspicious of me getting in your skirt." She laughed at her own joke, loudly, then looked at the jar that was almost half gone. That was gonna hurt in the morning.

"I like privacy. I'll take a bedless room," Dee said. "Obviously with all the pillows and blankets possible."

Vianna nodded. Most of the blankets had been washed. Maybe. "Do you like garlic?"

Dee raised a brow, and Vianna chuckled to herself. It was nice having a roommate, even if for one night.

22

Up In Smoke

Pounding reverberated through Vianna's skull, and she groaned, then kicked at the tangled sheet wrapped around her leg. The movement made the pounding increase, and her foot flopped down, hanging off the bed. She cracked an eyelid open to see Dee leaning against the doorframe, her snarled hair hanging in a side pony and her eyeliner smeared into a point like a failed attempt at an Egyptian eye. Her palm smacked flat against the open door—making the pounding in Vianna's head reverberate all over again.

Vianna threw a pillow at her. "You're loud. Go away."

"Tell that to your guest, who wouldn't stop ringing the doorbell until I opened it. I know your ass heard that damned bell." Her voice echoed down the hall as she walked away.

Water and pain pills were within Vianna's grasp if she could get her hand to the nightstand. She blindly swiped around, knocking the alarm clock to the ground. "Who in Hades is here?" she groaned.

She flopped her hand around the nightstand before she clasped a water jug and pill bottle. *Yes, please, goddess, all of that.* After swallowing a few pills, she lay still, hoping the riot in her stomach and swaying bed would stop. Dee said there was a guest, but there wasn't a single person in all of Salem worth the fight to get vertical.

A voice sang up from downstairs. "Ms. Roots. It's Rose Barton."

Vianna's eyes shot open, and she bolted upright, then instantly gripped her head with both hands in regret. Crawling out of bed and onto the floor was as clos-ish to vertical as she could manage. With her back against the mattress, she chugged more water.

"Ms. Roots?" The edge of annoyance in Rose's tone was easy to catch, even hungover.

"Yeah," Vianna croaked. "One minute."

Her own voice rattled in her head, making her eyes feel as though they'd pop from her skull. After a zombie-crawl to the bathroom sink and a flash of icy water to her face, she lumbered down the stairs. The floor was cold against her bare feet, and she wanted to lie down and smash her face against it. She still wore her too-tight lace dress from the gala, and her hair was in a tangled mess that left no questions about if she was a witch or not.

The entryway and living room were empty, so she followed the voices and aroma of brewed coffee to the kitchen. Dee had magically transformed into a silken robe covered with sunbursts and a match-ing violet hair wrap. Vianna hadn't a clue where she'd gotten them. Dee's back was to her as she poured coffee, and Rose stood behind a kitchen chair, gripping a canvas-sized package in brown paper and twine. Her rigid posture matched her pinched facial expression.

Vianna slumped into a chair and tilted her head at Dee. "I thought I only had instant coffee."

"Mm-hmm." Dee hummed as she turned and placed a steaming mug in front of Vianna. "You did. I, however, have better tastes."

Who traveled with fresh coffee and a satin bathrobe in their vehicle? Clearly that answer was Dee. She shook her head and took a sip of warm nutmeg and silky-smooth coffee. "Wow."

Dee smirked into her mug as she slid into the chair across from her.

"You and Charles didn't leave together last night." Rose took off her gloves.

Vianna sipped her coffee and stayed quiet. Commenting on Rose's stellar observation skills wouldn't help anything.

"Lover's spats are a sign of passion," Rose added.

Vianna choked on her coffee.

Dee spoke over her cup. "That's one option."

Rose narrowed hawk eyes at Dee. "Hello, Samuel."

Dee's lips pinched shut, and her fingers tightened around her mug. Vianna couldn't imagine all Dee had to go through to change her name. Which made it an even bigger slight when people refused to use that name. Rose either couldn't see Dee for who she was, or didn't care. Either way, Vianna didn't give a goat's bleached asshole about Rose.

"Sandeen is welcome here. I can't say the same for you." Vianna rose from her chair and did her best not to cringe at the pounding in her head. "Call her by her real name, or leave."

Rose chuckled but didn't sound the least bit amused. "You're not the brightest girl, so I'll give you a bit of advice. Be careful of the enemies you make, little Vie." Rose punctuated the last two words, then handed over the painting. "Charles's father and I approve of the pairing. Future in-laws deserve respect. Obviously, you'll pledge to the coven before anything progresses further."

Vianna's head felt fuzzy, so it took a moment for her to process all that was wrong in that statement. Who in Hades showed up unannounced this early?

Dee spoke first. "What makes you think she wants to be with Charles?"

"Your tone is unbecoming. I prefer you mind your manners when addressing a proper legacy."

Shuck grumbled through Vianna's chest.

"Yes, ma'am." Dee's face scrunched into a confused tilt.

Rose nodded. "Much better."

Vianna rubbed at her chest. There was a loud creak. The cupboard door swung open, and a mug crashed to the floor.

All three witches jumped. Shuck didn't approve of their visitor. They were on the same page. Dee was the first to react, picking up the porcelain shards.

Vianna got a broom and dustpan from the pantry. "Charles and I are not a couple." She eyed the painting-sized wrapped object as she swept up the remaining shards. "What are you doing here, Rose?"

"I brought a homecoming gift and wanted to let you know how happy your pairing with Charles makes me. I look forward to you pledging to the coven." Rose set the gift on the kitchen table. "You two should get presentable for the day. Talk soon. Ta-ta." Rose waved her fingers and sauntered through the archway into the living room, on a wake of noxious perfume, before leaving.

The front door slammed shut.

Grandma Susannah flickered in the middle of the kitchen archway. "Get it out! Out!"

Vianna stumbled backward and into Dee. The two landed in a sprawled heap on the kitchen tiles. Every cupboard and pantry door in the kitchen flung open and shut over and over as a window slammed with a loud thwack. Vianna stumbled to her hands and knees on rumbling floorboards that suddenly felt like ice as the temperature in the house grew frigid.

"What's happening?" Dee yelled as she used the wall to get to her feet.

"Something is wrong." Vianna stood, covering her ears.

"Obviously! How do we fix it?"

The rumbling increased. Picture frames crashed from the mantel in the other room, and the back patio door flew open. The wrapped canvas that Rose had placed on the kitchen table flung through the open doorway. The package landed in the grass, and everything went silent. Drawers hung open, and debris littered the floor.

"Oh. My. Holy. Hell. It's one thing to hear your house is possessed, it's another to live through it." Dee covered her mouth with her perfect pink manicure.

Vianna nodded. "Pretty much."

"I'm getting a joint." Dee walked out the front door.

The chances of her coming back seemed somewhere around zero. If the roles were reversed, Vianna would run. She closed cabinets and took a few deep breaths. That had gotten loud fast. The front door clicked, and Dee breezed through the kitchen archway with a joint between her fingers and her sunburst kimono fluttering around her.

"You didn't leave?" Vianna blurted.

Dee paused and raised an eyebrow. "Did you want me to?" She held up a lighter and lit her joint.

Vianna shrugged. "No. But I would have left if I were you."

"Hmm." Dee took a drag, then tilted her head as she stood next to Vianna in the open doorway, staring out into the yard. "I actually wanted to get presentable for the day, just like Rose asked. That spell is a whopper."

"Yeah." Vianna nodded, folding her arms around herself. "I can't let her keep doing this." This was bigger than just Nancy.

"Has the house freaked out like that before?" Dee asked.

"No. It was the ghosts, too." Vianna pushed open the back door and stepped into the blaring sunlight.

Grandma Susannah was hot on her heels. "What are you doing standing around? That was a blatant attack on the house. Start setting wards. You must fortify."

As she approached the painting, she cringed at the obnoxious level of noise coming from the birds. They were almost as bad as Grandma Susannah, who was now ranting and pacing in the kitchen. Vianna could hear the bathroom pipes groaning from whatever tantrum Earl and Nancy were having.

Dee followed. "Ghosts as in plural? How many are hanging around?"

"There are four regulars at the moment. And the house itself."

Vianna tore open the wrapping that covered her *gift*, revealing a red and gold canvas with black criss crossed lines. The same urge to please the Bartons slammed into her.

"That's a nasty whopper of a spell," Dee murmured.

Vianna reached her hand back to Dee. "Hand me that lighter."

With one hand gripped on the painting, she flicked the lighter. It only took seconds for the fire to catch. When the flames licked high enough to reach her hand, she tossed the canvas into the old wheelbarrow next to the greenhouse.

Dee handed the joint over. A beer was more Vianna's style, but it had been one hell of a morning . . . and night . . . and week, really. She took a drag and handed it back.

"Do you always carry around a kimono in your Jeep?" Her eyes remained on the fire as she spoke.

"I keep hoping a certain someone will ask me to stay the night." Dee's voice was flat, defeated.

Vianna had minimal experience with romantic relationships, but she could read Dee's expression and tone well enough to understand what she meant. "That sucks."

"Yeah." Dee folded her arms over her chest.

Vianna's phone rang from the kitchen, and she knew it was her landlord from Boston because of the *Jeopardy* tune. Every time she spoke to him, she could hear the show playing in the background, so she'd matched the ringtone. She went back in and grabbed her phone from the charger on the counter. "Hello."

"Hey, Vianna. It's Kevin." The voice of Alex Trebek filled the awkward pause. *Famous Cats in History for three hundred.*

"Look, you've been behind on rent for two months. Plus, the missing month I spotted you at the first of the year."

"Yeah, I know. I've been working on selling my family's home in Salem since my mom died. I should be back soon with cash."

"Look. I think you're a nice girl." *What was the name of the polydactyl companion to Ernest Hemingway?* Vianna squeezed her eyes shut. "But I've leased the property to someone else."

"You've already leased it? All my stuff is still in there!" Her heart thumped faster. She had piles of candle supplies and soap materials. It'd taken her countless shitty shifts at countless shitty jobs to amass the beginnings of her boutique.

"Not anymore. Trash took it away today. I cleaned it out yesterday and kept anything I could sell to pay the debt."

"Trash?" Vianna whispered. "Yesterday?"

"If you harass the new tenants, I'll call the cops." The line went dead.

She slid into the kitchen chair. Her phone hung from her hand in her lap. He had used the death in her family to evict her while she was away. She'd been paying rent under the table, and they didn't have any legal contract. Not having a deposit or decent credit score left her limited in renting options.

"You okay?" Dee pushed through the screen door.

"No." What was she going to do? Everything in Boston was gone. She would never escape this place. Tears threatened, but she used her anger to force them down. She was angry at life, at the unfairness, at herself, at—she didn't know—the air? She was just angry.

Dee leaned against the counter. "Who was *Jeopardy*?"

"My landlord in Boston. Ex-landlord. He evicted me." She dropped her forehead into her palm. Her head still hurt. She couldn't process all of this right now.

"Ouch." Dee stood behind her. "I gotta go home and get ready for work, hon. I'll check on you later." She squeezed Vianna's shoulder and left out the front door.

Vianna went into the backyard. The canvas was smoldering. She flopped onto the grass, then rolled to her back. Birds flew across the sky, and the shadows changed as she let the numbness spread. The sun was annoyingly bright; she hoped it would burn her away, singe her skin until she was billowing smoke like the ruined canvas beside her.

23

Unforgettable

Vianna wiped sweat with her forearm to avoid smearing the dirt from her gloves across her brow. She looked up at the clouds, their edges blood orange from the sunset behind them. Her headache had downgraded to a low pounding, and her muscles ached from a full day in the garden. The external pain somehow made her feel like she had an ounce of control over her life.

Her knuckles turned white as she tightened her grip around the handle of the garden spade and speared the tip into the soil to prepare it for conditioning. Her escape-to-Boston plan had washed away with the phone call from her landlord. She'd lived in her truck on the streets and she wasn't eager to repeat it. She gave a few more stabs at the soil. There was enough mulch and moss in the greenhouse to prep before seed. The house was all she had now. She wasn't giving over Shuck to another witch.

The side gate clicked, and she looked over her shoulder. Charles strolled across the yard wearing a variation of his usual polo with hands in his khakis. Perfect timing. He was the cherry on top of her shit-cupcake of a day. She rolled onto her heels, elbows resting on her dirt-caked knees.

"Vianna." Her name hung in the air like it was a command.

"Look, I don't want to be enemies. It didn't work out between us, even as just friends. Let's just leave it at that. I'm sticking around Salem, and I don't want things more awkward than they need to be." She pulled off her gloves and tucked them in the back pocket of her shorts as she stood.

She hoped he'd agree and just walk away. *Please, Charlie. Just walk away.*

His dimples puckered. "I'm glad you're staying." He stepped closer. "We had a minor spat. Couples fight, and then they make up. My plan was to come over so we could get to the make-up part."

The confidence in his grin made her cringe. She stepped backward. "There's no making up. This is over."

"I don't understand." His jaw flexed. "My mother said she stopped by. Said you guys talked."

Every muscle froze. Did he really know about his mother's paintings? The effect they had? She nodded to the barrel of burned ash, testing the boundaries of the conversation. "Yeah, she stopped by."

His lips thinned, and he walked to the barrel, then turned to her. "You burned my mother's art?"

She shrugged. "Wasn't really my style."

Scarlet blossomed over his neck and ears. Her posture straightened.

"My mother puts a lot of work into her art, Vianna." The curtness in his tone was just like his mother's.

Her chest tightened as she realized he'd expected her to be under the spell now. Charles was using his mother's spells like they were roofies at a house party. How many other women had he done this to? The hooker? The maid? Probably countless.

With her hands on her hips, she looked at the pile of ash, then back at Charles. "Guess she better not gift me any more *art*."

His upper lip curled. "You're being disrespectful."

She didn't answer. She balled her hands into fists as the silence stretched. "I meant what I said. This is done."

His eyes narrowed as he took a step toward her. "Vianna, I forgive you. You didn't know how important the painting was." The predatory stare smoothed into the politician's smile. "Let's get some food into that grumbling stomach of yours. You're covered in dirt and sweat. You shouldn't be doing manual labor like this. It's not very proper. We'll talk over dinner, after you're cleaned up."

She dug her nails into her palms. He'd closed the gap between them. His hand gripped her arm, and he tugged, hard.

"Let go." She tried to jerk her arm free, but his grip tightened. The birds clustered within the trees flocked away in a huddled bunch.

"Stop being so difficult. I just want to spend time with you. Most girls would pay for my attention." His grip loosened, and she pulled away.

Yeah, because you drugged them.

She spoke through gritted teeth. "Keep your hands off me." The creak of old floorboards rumbled from the house.

He leaned in close, and a warm breath spread across her ear. "Don't play hard to get. It's unbecoming."

Vianna suddenly realized how very alone they were. The realization slithered through her like a slow-growth cancer. An aggressive breeze rustled the bottom of her tank top. Silence blanketed the normal croaks and chirps of life throughout the yard.

Charles raised an arm to blanket it over her shoulders, but before he could, she rammed an elbow into his gut and sprinted for the back door to the house. Turning the corner of a hedge, the toe of her shoe caught on a brick, sending her to her knees. She scrambled for purchase to push herself up, but Charles bulldozed over top of her and had her pinned before she could even swing a fist at him. The pressure on her chest and sharp edges of the brick made it hard to breathe.

His face pressed close to hers, and his words were a snarl. "What happened to the timid little mouse from school? You were supposed to be agreeable. You were supposed to go along with what you were told."

She kicked out, but his knee jammed into her thigh, pinning it. His weight pressed against her, and her ribcage felt slick with blood where she'd landed on a rock. She thrust her hip out to buck him off, and he reared back and backhanded her, white spots exploding in her vision. Everything went hazy.

He was up again and pulling her across the lawn by her ankle when her vision cleared. His grip felt like an iron vice. Her vision was still fuzzy, but she flung her hands out, looking for anything to grab a hold of. Upturned pavers and plants left a wake behind them but didn't slow him down. With each new grip she found, more plants were uprooted and added to the trail of chaos.

He gave a hard jerk to her ankle. "You like it rough? Playing nice certainly didn't get your attention."

"Charles. Stop," she choked out. Her voice was a whisper she wasn't sure he could hear.

When he pulled her by the greenhouse, she latched onto the edge of the doorway, and he yanked harder. As he adjusted his grip on her ankle, she kicked out, breaking free. She scrambled upright and barreled toward the shovel leaning against the greenhouse. She wrapped her hands around the handle, turned, and swung with all her strength.

The metal blade of the shovel *thunked* against Charles's skull and vibrated down the handle, through her arms. His body dropped in a slump to the ground.

Vianna let go of the shovel, and it clattered against the pavers. She stood there, motionless.

Had she killed him? Her hands shook, and step by step, she backed away from the still body. Tears tracked down her cheeks. No. She wasn't a murderer. Everything she'd fought not to become, everything she swore she'd never do, none of it mattered. Fate laughed at her pitiful attempt to have free will. She'd never had a choice, not really. She plopped into the dirt. If she didn't check for a pulse, then it wasn't final. With her knees pulled into her body, she rocked back and forth.

No, no, no, no.

She wasn't like *them.* She could see flashes of her uncle's body overlapping Charles's. *Clean up your mess.* Blood spread beneath him, and she shook her head. The blood disappeared along with the vision of her uncle. Her memories and reality had jumbled.

She stumbled into the house and pulled her phone from the charger. Her hands shook as she walked back out and dialed 911. This time would be different. She wouldn't play by their rules.

A baritone voice answered on the other end. "Salem Police Station, is this an emergency?"

"Y-yes. This is Vianna Roots." Her voice broke as she stumbled back into the backyard to the body. "I think I just killed a man. My address is 76 Heritage Way."

The phone dropped from her hand as she slid to the grass. Pulling her knees close, she curled into a ball as she rocked and waited, eyes locked on Charles.

"Welcome to the family, dear." Grandma stood over the body. "I didn't think you were capable. Maybe you'll do more than breed the next heir."

"Shut up," Vianna said.

"You surprised me tonight, *granddaughter.*" Grandma beamed with pride.

Horror spread within Vianna, turning her organs to shriveled and decaying fruit.

"Bodies make good mulch." Grandma nodded at Charles.

Frogs broke the surrounding silence, then crickets joined. What was left of the sun sank below the horizon, and life moved on, leaving the dead in its wake, as it always did. She wasn't sure how much time passed before the side fence clacked and bodies armed with guns surrounded her.

"On your knees. Hands up!" Cones of light blinded her as blurred shadows moved toward her.

None of it mattered. Jail would be better than following in her ancestors' footsteps. Metal bars that trapped her in a cell would stop her from becoming them. It had to. She deserved it.

The edge of a gun barrel pressed between her shoulder blades, nudging her to the ground. She didn't resist. Sharp blades of grass pressed into her face as cold metal looped around her wrists, then clicked tight. Red-and-blue lights flashed against the house.

"He's alive! Someone call an ambulance!"

So many shoes, so many voices.

He couldn't be alive. The sound of the shovel against Charles's head replayed in her memory, the vibration of the handle in her palms, and she closed her eyes as a tear slid over the bridge of her nose.

"Ms. Roots?" A deep voice came from overhead. "You mentioned a dead body? Was it the man on the lawn you called about? Or is there another body?"

"I thought he was dead." She looked up.

Intelligent eyes that she recognized stared down at her. The man whose truck she'd hit. Grayson. He wore a bullet-proof vest over a dark shirt with jeans. "No. He's not dead."

Another tear slid down her cheek. "I thought—I thought I'd killed him. He tackled me. I—I just swung. The shovel hit so hard."

"He tackled you?" Grayson leaned down, elbows on his knees.

He narrowed his eyes at her every injury: her cut lip, the side of her face that was probably swelling, and the wet spot on the side of her shirt that was probably blood. She wasn't weak. A little banged up, but he didn't need to look at her with sad, pity eyes. She wanted the intelligent, assessing eyes back.

More shiny black shoes moved around them. She nodded. Charles wasn't dead. The weight of fear lifted, and she sucked in a deep breath, filling her lungs. The cold metal cuffed around her wrists fell away, and warm hands helped her up. Grayson frowned at her, his eyes softening into pity instead of the intelligent glare he'd given her before. She knew what he was thinking. Victim. Weak. She wasn't.

"I'm fine." She wrapped her arms around herself.

His jaw shifted, but he didn't argue. "Maybe we can sit down on the porch, and you can give me your statement?" He eyed one of the other officers. "Send a paramedic to check her over."

She opened her mouth to protest but stopped when he raised his hands in surrender.

"I know. You're fine. But it's protocol." He motioned toward the porch where she'd moved the rusted lawn chairs earlier, and she followed him.

No one had died, but everything was still a giant mess. She'd called the police on Charles Barton. The line between law enforcement and witches had remained constant through the decades, all the way back to the witch trials. It was a simple line. They didn't interact, ever. She'd publicly gone against a sacred tradition. Denying the coven or running from them was one thing, but calling on the enemy for help? She sank into the chair, and it squeaked in protest.

Grayson squeezed into the foldout chair next to her. He tucked his muscled arms in, attempting to fit them on the armrests. The chair was comically too small for his size, and in any other scenario, Vianna would have laughed.

"Looks like you held your own." He shifted his weight, making the chair wobble.

She nodded toward the weapon on the ground. "Shovel helped."

The corner of his mouth twitched.

A heavyset paramedic with two braids coming out of her ball cap joined them, blinding Vianna with a flashlight in each eye. "How you feeling, hon? Any dizziness or nausea? Any damage in other places I need to know about?" The woman gave a pointed stare.

"No. I'm fine." Vianna looked around the paramedic's shoulder to watch as they loaded Charles onto a stretcher. "He's gonna be fine?"

The paramedic pinched Vianna's chin, pulling her attention back, then tilting her face side to side. "He'll be fine. Probably just a concussion. We'll take him in for tests, and you should come too."

Vianna shook her head. No insurance or money made some choices easy. Besides, she was fine, mostly. The worst of her damage wasn't external. She dabbed at her lip, smearing blood onto her fingers. There was a tear in her shirt as well, but nothing hurt too bad. The paramedic zoned in on the ripped shirt and went to work on the cut beneath. Vianna flinched but swallowed down her whimper as a bandage was adhered to her ribcage.

"Stubborn thing, aren't you?" The paramedic pulled off her gloves. "Put some ice on that lip and take a couple Tylenol. You'll be stiff for a couple days and you should get a proper check up at the hospital by a doctor." She lifted her medic bag and gave a nod to Grayson before leaving.

Grayson cleared his throat. "Ms. Roots, can you tell me what happened? Did you know him?"

Images of Charles's sneer, his breath on her ear, his grip around her arm, and the weight of his body tackling her to the ground replayed in her mind. "Yeah. Charles Barton."

Grayson's eyes flicked up, then back to his notes. He knew the Barton name. Everyone in Salem did. Money worked like that.

"He stopped by, and I told him to go away. He wasn't too pleased." Her eyes averted from the paved walkway. "He tackled me, then dragged me by the ankle." She rubbed her palms over her thighs and let out a long breath. "Which was stupid. I mean, where was he even dragging me to? His car?"

Would her neighbors have done anything? Witches didn't stick their noses in each other's drama, at least not if they couldn't gain something from it. Plus, stepping in for Vianna would mean they thought she was too weak to handle it on her own. "It all happened so fast. I got loose, and the shovel was the first thing I found."

He made more notes on his pad of paper. "Do you want to press charges?"

Her gossiping neighbors would no doubt spread the news of her calling the cops. Filing a report would stoke those flames into a bonfire. She was sick of playing by rules that were generations old and made her the victim. Maybe it was time to make her own rules.

"Yeah. I do."

"All right. We'll get that handled." Grayson wrestled with the chair as he stood. "I'll be right back. Hang tight."

After a few minutes of sitting, watching her yard fill with strangers who darted their eyes at her, then away, she felt antsy. She went inside to the kitchen for both the privacy and protection. Shuck rumbled in her chest when anyone wandered too close to the back door. Vianna watched through the window as several uniforms took pictures and pointed to each other, taking notes. With a huff, she turned and filled the kettle with water, then set it on a burner. A knock at the door almost made her bump the kettle over. Anxious, she had to remind herself that the police were here to help, not excavate generations of secrets that were likely hiding in the garden.

"Come in." She rolled out her neck.

Grayson came through the door. "Your neighbors aren't answering their doors. Do you know of anyone who might have seen anything that would be willing to talk?"

She snorted. This was a neighborhood of witches, legacy witches. He knew that. Not a single one would talk to a uniform. There was a strong possibility that not a single one would talk to her after today either. "You know as well as I do they won't talk to you. Not in this neighborhood."

He folded his arms over his chest. "Protocol. Gotta say we tried."

Grandma appeared in front of Grayson. A low growl came from her. "How dare you let his kind into this house." She snarled as she paced around him. "Probably nothing more than a filthy yaldson."

The officer rubbed his jaw and watched Vianna. She kept her face neutral, eyes on him instead of Grandma's sputtering. Leaning a hip against the counter, she picked at the dried blood on her lip. "What happens next?"

"What you've done will taint the Roots name. You're a blight on our family." Grandma disappeared.

"We'll knock on a few more doors. I'll file a lot of paperwork, and I'll call if you need to come down to the station for more questioning."

He removed a card and wrote something on the back, then set it on the counter. "In case you lost the last one. You can call me anytime." He folded his arms over his chest. "I've never seen a call to this neighborhood, and I don't take that lightly. I mean it. You can call me anytime."

She chewed on the inside of her cheek, nodding. "I'll be in touch. For the damages to your truck. Remember?"

The kettle whistled, and she pulled a mug from the cupboard.

"I remember. You're not all that forgettable." He let himself out and added over his shoulder, "Don't forget to lock up, Ms. Roots."

She set the mug on the counter as she watched him leave. Locks wouldn't make much of a difference in what was coming her way.

24

No More Running

Cleanup from the aftermath of Charles didn't take long, and the only remaining sign of something amiss was the trampled grass. A light breeze cooled her skin and stirred strands of loose hair. Every muscle ached. She wanted nothing more than to soak in a tub of Epsom salts and lavender oil, but the thought of Earl's swaying stare dispelled that fantasy. A quick shower followed by a soft bed would have to work.

Moonlight bathed her garden as she considered the best place to plant a batch of chamomile. *Her garden.* She was right back where she started, stuck in the place she'd spent her adult life trying to forget. She was back at the family home, bonded to the family familiar, and marked by the witches before her, ready to carry the mantle. She wrapped her arms around herself and paced the property. In the end, her mother had won because death was never the last word.

The leaves in the branches overhead rustled, and the soil was rich with the potential for life. Shuck purred inside her chest, and she was finding familiarity with his constant presence. She might be back where she started, but things weren't the same. She wasn't her mother. There was no fighting what was, but she'd do things her way. She would be the next Roots witch to bond with the demon, to live in the house, and to call Salem home, but she wouldn't be a hired assassin for a coven. She was a solitary witch, not a killer.

But that didn't mean she was naive. She knew the entire witch community would be up in arms over her insult against the Bartons. Meetings had probably been called, and the coven caves would be crammed full of witches calling for a vote of action against her. There were no set punishments or precedence for what she'd done. It was unheard of. Almost as unheard of as a legacy witch not bonded to a coven.

After a shower and filling her quota for cursing at Earl, she pulled on a camisole and sweat shorts then sat on the edge of the bed and brushed her hair. God-awful rosebuds covered the bedroom wallpaper instead of the hallway peonies.

She stood and walked to the corner by the window. Using her nail, she scraped at the crease that ran flush with the windowsill, and an edge of the wallpaper pulled back. When she reached to pinch the upturned edge, her fingers shook. With a deep breath, she shook both hands out. The more she relaxed and tried to forget what had happened with Charles, the shakier she became. The flashes of his enraged face wouldn't stop. With a grunt, she reached and gave the paper a hard tug. A large strip ripped down the wall, revealing another layer of wallpaper that was somehow even worse. Birds and flowers were not an elegant design when in micro version with pink and yellow. The house grumbled and rattled the window. If she was staying, the wallpaper was going, all of it.

"You can't like this crap. What demon wants to be covered in tiny flowers?"

She looked around as if the house would reply, but everything was quiet. That seemed as close to an agreement as she was going to get. Nerves raced through her, and she kept moving, wandering downstairs and ending up in the formal sitting room.

She put a hand on her hip. Seeing potential was easier with half the furniture gone. "No more formal sitting room. This is now the living room. We just need a TV and a couch I can sink into with a giant bowl of popcorn." Speaking out loud kept her from listening for the clack of the side gate opening. Charles wasn't coming back, but every noise made her jump.

Her dreams of a couch and TV were a pipe dream. Remodeling required money. That was still a problem, especially with the nagging need to eat. The idea of peddling soul-mate hex bags to tourists for cash wasn't exactly exciting, but she'd done it before.

The front knocker clanked three times, and she flinched with each one. With slow caution, she pulled back the heavy drape. Moonlight highlighted the large bag with bedazzled stars clutched in both of Mistress Layton's hands. Was she here for the coven? The dark of the night was business hours for them. Was Dee okay? Had the coven lashed out at Dee for what Vianna had done? She yanked open the door.

"Mistress Layton. Everything okay?"

The wrinkles in the old woman's face deepened as she frowned. She smoothed a stray hair into her bun with a gloved hand and pulled her shoulders back to straighten her posture. "Hello, dear."

No hug. No smile. No candy. Something was off. Vianna leaned against the doorframe and waited to hear what came next.

"I volunteered to stop by and collect the paperwork to buy the house. It's a smart move, you leaving. I would hate to see something bad happen to you, and . . . I'm worried for you."

"About that." Vianna folded her arms. "I've decided not to sell. I'll be holding onto the family home and staying in Salem."

Mistress Layton shook her head. "Oh, no. It's too late for that. You'll be much safer back in Boston. You must leave. Tonight."

The happy woman who gave her hugs and spoke of wanting her around the library was gone. Mistress Layton sounded scared. Witches didn't scare easily. Running away to Boston held some appeal, just like it had so many years ago, but things were different now. She wasn't leaving Shuck. The house of horrors was hers now, hers to tend and hers to make sure it behaved. There was no apartment waiting for her in Boston, and her dreams of opening an herbal shop were down the drain. In Boston she had a few pots on a deck, but in Salem she had a full garden, a greenhouse, and a conjure room. She didn't have to do harm; she could just as easily do good.

"I'm not going anywhere. For better or worse, Salem is home." As soon as she said the words out loud, it felt real, final. The connection with Shuck shook deep within her bones. "Please inform Josephine I've passed on her offer. The house is no longer on the market." She gave a stiff smile.

Mistress Layton cast her eyes downward. "This isn't just about you anymore, Vianna. Dee is being brought up with your name in discussions, and she already has enough hate flung her way. You can't stay. Please. She's my only family."

Stabbing guilt pierced Vianna's heart. She wasn't leaving Salem, but she wouldn't put others in danger. "I'll tell Dee to stay away."

The words hurt. Vianna really liked Dee.

"She won't listen. Please. Disappear in the middle of the night. Like you did before." The librarian's knuckles went white as she gripped the handles of her bag. Her words weren't a threat; they were a mother's plea.

Twirling the infinity ring on her finger, Vianna looked down, speaking to her feet. "I'm sorry. I can't."

Running hadn't rescued her from the nightmare ten years ago; it wouldn't do so now. Salem, witches, ghosts, and hoodoo would never be easy, but she was done running from them.

"Thank you for stopping by." There was nothing left to say. She closed the door and rested her head against it.

"Vianna, please. You must understand. For Dee." Mistress Layton's voice came from the other side of the door.

Remaining quiet, Vianna clenched her fist and unclenched it, letting the silence stretch until the librarian's heels clicked against the porch as she left.

If she was going to stay, she'd have to fix things, both for herself and for Dee. The problem was Rose. She was behind everything. It rankled Vianna that Rose had one of her family's spells. After everything she and her son had done, they had no right to anything of hers. She went to the conjure room to check the grimoire. With a flick of her wrist, the drawer popped open.

Using both hands, she pulled the old leather-bound book from its cubby and set it on its spine. The pages fell open to a spell for Unmasking the Crone. She flipped through the book and stopped, running her finger down a torn edge where a page was missing.

Rose had done the impossible. She'd stolen a page from the Roots family grimoire. There wasn't a witch who'd mess with Mother, but Rose didn't do things herself. She manipulated others in order to keep her hands clean. That explained why it was Nancy's hand left in the house, but still left out the mysterious cat, if the cat even mattered. And how did Rose get the spell if Nancy never made it out of the house? If Rose was able to get in and out of the house, that was a problem.

Vianna's stomach growled. One problem at a time. Food first, and then she'd figure out the weakness in the house's wards. Her last few dollars would get her food for a day or two until she figured something else out. A small drawer popped out of the desk and clunked into her knee.

"Ow." She frowned down at the open drawer, expecting rabbit eyeballs or cow hooves. Instead, wedged in the compact space, was a thick roll of green bills. She froze.

Her mind went blank. Was she hallucinating? It couldn't be real. She used her index finger to tap the wad and yanked her hand back as if it might bite. It was real.

She pressed both of her hands to her mouth as she half laughed and half cried. "Thank you," she whispered.

Her giggles were stopped short when a knock came at the door and dread sliced through her. What now? She shut the compartment of cash and headed out of the room. The deadbolt clicked as she rounded the corner, and the door swung open on its own.

"Guess the house likes me." Dee held up two plastic bags. "Burritos and avocado fries?"

Vianna held a hand to her chest. "I could worship you."

"After the food." Dee headed to the kitchen.

The smile slipped from Vianna's lips as she recalled the conversation with Mistress Layton. She would have to say goodbye to Dee if she didn't want her getting hurt. They unloaded Styrofoam platters onto the kitchen table in silence. The smell of cumin, garlic, and fries filled the room.

Settling into a chair, Dee spoke around a bite of avocado fry. "You announced your intention to stay with a bang."

Vianna sat down, then pulled over a container with a burrito covered in a green sauce. Selfishly, she wanted to wait until after they ate to say anything. She wanted to pretend, for just a few minutes longer, that she could be normal and have a friend. With a little too much gusto, she sank her fork into the mound of food and pulled a bite with stringy cheese and chicken into her mouth. Her eyes closed, and she moaned. So good.

"Are you eating or having an orgasm?"

Vianna opened her eyes and smiled around her food. "Jury's still out."

Dee chuckled. "You poor thing."

She took another bite. "Your mom stopped by," she said after she swallowed. "She's worried about you." Vianna set her fork down. "I've decided to stay in Salem, and the fallout might be explosive. You could get hurt hanging around me."

Dee finished chewing, then swallowed. She tapped her plastic fork against her enchilada. "You're the only legacy in history to say a word against how things are *supposed* to be. The covens are going bat shit, more so than normal. You're changing things. I want to be a part of that."

Vianna frowned. Living by her own rules didn't mean anyone else had to. "It's not—"

Dee held up a hand. "I'm a grown woman. Let me make my own choices. Besides, you don't look like you have a lot of friends." Dee took a sip from a fountain soda. "And I don't either. So, stop being weird and let me be your friend."

Her heart swelled. She'd take Dee over a hundred rolls of bills. "Fine."

She took a large bite to hide her grin. They ate together and laughed over the town antics that were the same now as they had been ten years ago. Mistress Epsler still talked to her birds instead of humans as she roamed the woods alone, and Mistress Kanker was still the boogeyman with her swarm of scorpions at every witch market. After their dishes were over half empty, they slowed in their eating.

"So, you okay? I heard about the stuff with Charles," Dee said.

Vianna took a drink of soda and then shrugged. "I'm fine." She was overly jumpy and her hands still shook when she sat still for too long. But she'd been through worse. She would eventually be fine.

Dee raised a brow but didn't push further. "I gotta get going. I have a date." She did a little shimmy with her shoulders.

Vianna chuckled. "Then get out of here! He better not be the same one who doesn't invite you to stay over after."

"No judgments. All in good time." Dee gathered her stuff and stood from the table. "I'll call you tomorrow. Try not to start an all-out coven war between now and then."

"Ha," Vianna scoffed. "So funny. Get out of here. I'll clean up."

"See ya, doll." Dee showed herself out.

Vianna cleaned up the kitchen, then made her way upstairs. She sprawled onto the bed. Tomorrow was a new day.

25

The Storm

Dee had left a bag of her fancy coffee from the day before, and Vianna wanted to kiss the woman. She sipped from her chipped mug as she meandered through the backyard again. She still felt fidgety from the shovel escapades, and every noise had her looking over her shoulder. There was a scab on her lower lip, a blue and purple collage along her right side, and matching finger bruises on her arms. All of it would pass.

"That's the fourth time you've paced your property wards." Ophelia's voice carried over the tall wooden fence separating their yards.

Vianna straightened. "Ophelia?"

"Child, mind your manners. I will not put my coven at risk by associating with a traitor witch. Can't an old woman think aloud in her own yard?"

A traitor witch. Ophelia's words weren't all that surprising. The sound of a chair being dragged across a porch was followed by chimes. What was she doing?

"I'm guessing all of the covens have been informed of my treachery?"

"Vianna Roots! I will not associate with you. But if you think aloud in your yard at the same time I do, I can not help that."

Vianna groaned. More games. "Fine. Gee, I wonder if any of the covens plan to retaliate against the traitor witch. My oh my. I'm just talking to the clouds in the sky." She deserved bonus points for rhyming.

Rings of smoke drifted above the fence, and the aroma of mint and coltsfoot seeped into the air. Ophelia had her pipe out. Her voice carried through the fence between puffs. "I had quite the night, called in as a witness to the covens for an emergency meeting. A witch called the cops, and I confirmed as much." Ophelia let out a long puff of smoke. "Never thought I'd see the day. Although I also confirmed that the Barton boy stepped beyond the borders of proper behavior."

Vianna leaned against the fence and slid into a sitting position between the cherry tree and fence post. Her mind raced. This all had gotten out of hand so fast. She'd crossed a line drawn centuries ago. Rose had used the police call to her advantage, despite the fact that the woman should have thanked her. Grandma had wanted Vianna to turn Charles into garden mulch. Ironically, that crime would've carried less punishment.

"Where there any decisions—" Vianna stopped and rephrased. "I wonder if the covens declared any plans of action."

Ophelia took her time replying; the smack of her lips against her pipe was the only sound. Vianna picked at a dandelion while she waited, pinching the base and wiggling to loosen the root.

"The Lunar Coven has declared no action and no enemy. They will, however, raise a brow if said witch continues to pull in outsiders. The Tidal Coven and Mabon Coven agreed with the Lunar

Coven. The Original Blood Coven seems to have a hornet's nest rooted at their base. It's abuzz, and there's no telling what they're going to do."

The dandelion root wouldn't budge without snapping it. Vianna wiggled the base of the weed as Ophelia's words sunk in. All four of the founding covens declaring Vianna an enemy wasn't something she'd considered—the mere thought of it increased her heart rate—but she hadn't crossed that line. That still left her wondering what to do about Rose. Vianna had made her position very clear. She wasn't running anymore. But she also couldn't just ignore a stolen family spell being used to brainwash people.

"I had this crab magoo of a neighbor once," Ophelia said. "She was a stringent, rule-abiding coven witch, to an abrasive extreme. She was a member of the darkest and oldest coven, and her power was immense, as were all the witches of her bloodline. But then she gave birth to the most peculiar daughter."

Vianna rested her back against the fence and drank her coffee as she listened, leaving the dandelion alone.

"The little girl seemed unbreakable in her will. She wouldn't bend to the whims of those before her, despite the monsters that haunted her. And there were more monsters than just that hag of a mother haunting the child. Still, she stood tall."

The mug was smooth beneath her fingers as Vianna drummed on it. "What happened to the little girl?"

"Oh, child." Ophelia sighed. "She grew up to be an unstoppable storm of change."

That wasn't exactly a happily ever after.

Ophelia added, "It would take someone unbreakable to change legacy witches."

Vianna didn't respond. She wasn't unbreakable—more like a pile of walking damage. Fighting to live how she wanted shouldn't be a revolution. Vianna sighed. She couldn't change decades of belief. The best she could do was survive the day.

"I best check on Barnabus. He's been in a tiff lately," Ophelia said.

Vianna asked, "Barnabus?"

"I must be getting old. I keep hearing voices." Shuffling noises came from the other side of the fence, then the back door to Ophelia's house opened and shut. She'd gone inside.

Vianna chuckled into her mug. Barnabas had to be Ophelia's bat familiar. She pushed herself up and headed into the house. Coexisting with Rose while she riled up the coven felt impossible. Maybe survival meant focusing on what she could do instead of the worst that could happen. At least she had the wad of cash in the conjure room. She could feed herself. Had to celebrate the small wins. She couldn't imagine anything better than a splurge at the grocery store, and not just the clearance carts, but a free roam down *every* aisle. And name-brand cereal, several boxes. Anything she wanted. She grabbed the keys and headed out.

The parking lot was only a quarter full, and she parked a few spots from the door. Excitement made her feel light on her feet. Not even a truck ride with the grandmas dimmed her mood. With Rose painting a target on Vianna's back, she couldn't take the ring off. The grandmas were her shadows for the time being.

She was close to skipping as she grabbed a cart instead of the little hand basket. Out of habit, she stopped at the clearance carts and snagged day-old croissants, more mint tea, and off-brand toothpaste. Her cart kept trying to veer right from a stuck wheel, but she ignored it, focusing on the aisles of indulgence.

She took her time as she roamed each aisle and couldn't help but watch the grandmas from her peripheral view. Although Clarice had yet to utter a single word, she used trails of beetles to probe and explore all around her. The errant bug scattering across Vianna's shoe was becoming so common, she'd stopped cringing at them.

Grandma Susannah stood in the middle of the coffee and tea aisle. She narrowed her eyes at a box of chamomile tea that had a dripping honeycomb spoon. "There couldn't possibly be honey in that box. What sort of market is this?" She poked at the display, making it crash to the linoleum.

An elderly woman with grayish-purple hair passed by the aisle, frowning at Vianna. With a sigh, Vianna picked up the boxes. She turned back to the coffee selection, trying to decipher what qualified as good by Dee's standards. Whole bean seemed fancy, but the bag she'd left behind was ground beans, so that seemed safest. A pointed-ear dog wearing sunglasses on a blue bag drew her attention, so it won out. She grabbed two: one for the house and one as a thank-you gift for Dee. It seemed like the friend thing to do.

She saved the cereal aisle for last. Cartoon figures on brightly colored boxes made her inner child squeal. She tapped a finger to her lips as she stood in front of the display that felt like a rainbow of all that was right in the world. She could buy multiple boxes, making the combinations endless.

A hard bump from behind knocked her into a display of leprechauns, and boxes toppled on top of each other. Her hand caught the edge of the metal shelf, saving her from falling. She righted herself and twirled around.

Behind her stood the Ramsey twins. They looked like yoga Barbies with leggings, spandex tops, and blonde curls in high ponytails. Their matching pinched scowls were glossed candy pink.

"That's a lot of groceries for someone leaving town," the one on the right said. Vianna never could keep them straight, not that she had ever put a lot of effort into it.

The grandmas lost interest in the groceries, pressing in close to the twins. A chill washed through the air, and the talisman warmed. Vianna turned back to the colorful display. This didn't need to escalate. She grabbed a peanut-butter-flavored cereal and a chocolate-puff flavor. The Fruity Pebbles were farther down the aisle, but she grabbed a box of Lucky Charms before moving on. She would not let the twins ruin this perfect moment. Her knuckles turned white as she gripped the cart with both hands and moved down the aisle. Confrontation with those two wasn't worth it.

"Poor Charles."

Vianna froze.

"Everyone knows how you assaulted him. You're worse than herpes."

Yeah, she'd assaulted him. And she wasn't above doing it with the Barbies. Instead, she pushed the cart toward the end of the aisle, hoping the grandmas followed. Raising her voice, Vianna turned her head to speak over her shoulder. "I'd take genital herpes over Charles Barton any day."

"Genital herpes?" Grandma appeared at her side.

"Land pirate pox." Vianna wasn't explaining genital warts in the middle of the grocery store to her grandmother from the 1600s.

"Repulsive." Grandma curled her upper lip. "Those girls should be taught proper witch activities instead of spouting gibberish. You should hex them with a bloated tongue. I could help."

Vianna headed toward the refrigerated aisle for some milk, listening for footsteps. When they didn't follow, she let out a breath of relief. One less bit of drama, because Vianna didn't doubt Grandma's offer. The wheel of her full cart made a steady *click-click, click-click* as she put the milk in her cart and walked to the registers. Since it was late morning on a weekday, only one register was open. The twins were already in line. They turned with matching glares when Vianna got in line behind them.

A side display had chocolate bars on sale, and she threw a couple into her basket. The teenage couple in front of the twins took their bags, but the line didn't move. One of the twins stepped forward, but the other blocked the line.

"It's safest if you stay back. Maintain a safe distance so we don't catch whatever you have." She sneered, then turned her back on Vianna.

Grandma closed the distance between her and the twin with a swift march and used the heel of her palm to bop the witch in the back of the head. Evil Barbie's arms flew out in a dramatic swan dive as she fell forward, her face landing on the edge of the register.

"Bitch!" the other twin yelled. She reached for her sister, who had a split lip with blood smeared down her chin.

Vianna cringed and kept her hands on her cart, nice and visible so she didn't seem threatening. "I didn't touch her." But she wasn't blameless either. She'd given Grandma her newfound poltergeist abilities when she made the talisman. That made Vianna responsible for any fight she picked or display of boxes she knocked over.

"Do I need to call management?" the squat man with a receding hairline behind the register asked. His plastic name tag displayed the title store manager.

Vianna kept quiet, her gaze on the twins to see what they would do. Without breaking eye contact, the injured one scooped up their bag of energy drinks and protein bars. "Watch your back, solitary." She wiped her lip with the back of her hand. "That nightmare hex was child's play."

In unison, they turned and strolled off. Vianna let out a breath of relief. Physical fighting wasn't part of the standard curriculum for witches. What was Grandma thinking? The talisman was feeling less like protection and more like a doorway that welcomed even more trouble. Vianna had no one to blame but herself. She'd chosen Grandma Susannah when she chose the ring.

The clerk rang up her loot, and after paying, she pushed the cart toward the exit but stopped by a bulletin board. The automatic doors opened, letting in a rush of hot air, half closed, then opened again. She pulled the cart backward, staring at the picture of a girl on a missing poster. The pale face of the same overdosed prostitute who lingered on Charles's balcony stared back at her.

Betsy Steeple. That was the name on the flyer. She was a mom, and people were looking for her. Nausea crept into Vianna's gut. This had to stop. The Bartons had to be stopped, but she also knew that no one would. She shoved the cart forward and tried to concentrate on being happy about groceries.

Outside, a buzzing filled the air as she approached her truck, but the grandmas blocked her way. She shoved the cart through the ghosts and a chill slid over her fingers—despite the July heat and the broiling sun—slipped up her arms and rippled through her hair. Shaking off the cold, she zoned in on the truck. On the hood was another small canvas bag that looked identical to the self-harm hex from Tiphonie.

Vianna slowed a few feet from the truck, realizing the source of the buzzing sound. Honeybees swarmed her truck. A bee hex? On a witch who loved to garden? The twins weren't the brightest, but they were annoying.

Demon-bound witches stock piled hex bags in the coven caves for situations just like this. The Ramsey twins' mother was still alive, so the mantle or familiar hadn't passed, but they had access to the tools needed to get a job done.

"They make a mockery of the craft," Grandma Susannah growled at her side. "This is pitiful."

Grandma Clarice looked across the parking lot, more interested in a woman walking her German Shepherd. Vianna propped her cart against the tailgate before moving to the hood. With slow and steady movements, she reached through the swarm and pinched the bag, picking it up. She used the lighter from her handbag to light the hex, and it burned in a ball of neon-orange flame before she dropped it to the pavement. A few bees hovered, but most of them left. Vianna shook her head and loaded the groceries. She put the bag with the chocolate up front, opening a bar on the drive home.

"Sugar overcomes bullshit." She nodded to herself. It was her new motto.

She pulled into the driveway and parked. Bags of groceries rested on her hip as she walked up the porch stairs, but the front door didn't open, so she set the bags down.

"I thought we were past this." She sighed with a hand on her hip.

That's when she noticed the white-and-brown clump of fur caught in the window closest to the door. She put her other hand on her hip. That wasn't the normal dead frog or bird clogged in the rain gutter. She leaned closer, then pulled back with her nose scrunched. The animal's head hung on the other side of the window, inside the house, its neck twisted at a weird angle. A long tail hung against the siding of the house. A dead cat.

"House finally caught that damn cat." Grandma appeared on the porch. "Took him long enough."

The window popped open, and the limp body fell to the porch. It'd been caught in the window, probably trying to get into the house. The likelihood of this cat being a stray instead of a familiar wasn't worth taking seriously. Shuck had killed another witch's familiar.

Vianna closed her eyes and let out a lengthy breath. The crimes were just piling up. Calling the cops wasn't enough. Now she was also responsible for the death of another witch's familiar. Well, it had been the house who killed the nosy little demon, but the coven wouldn't care about that detail. An eye for an eye was the only way they saw to right a wrong. That meant some crossed witch would be gunning for Shuck.

Vianna rubbed the back of her neck and paced the porch. Rose was behind all of this. Vianna couldn't run from her problems this time; there had to be some agreement they could come to, some truce between her and the covens, or a promise to stay clear of each other. A steady stream of hexes, attacks, and dead animals wasn't a long-term solution.

26

Gear Up

After staring at the dead cat, pacing the porch, and then staring at the sad lump of fur some more, Vianna made a plan. A sort-of plan. She was going to make Rose face the consequences of her actions. She would show up on her doorstep with the cat.

After shoving the groceries in the fridge, Vianna grabbed a bed-sheet and a pair of gardening gloves. She gently wrapped the limp animal and carried the bundle to the truck. Nestling the body into the footwell of the passenger side felt more respectful than putting it in the back. When she slid into the truck, she wasn't surprised to see the grandmas squished shoulder to shoulder on the bench seat. Grandma Clarice was in the middle with a few ghost-beetles perched on the backrest behind her, and Grandma Susannah pressed close to the window. Ghosts had always been a part of her day; the ghosts being her ancestors didn't seem that much of a stretch from the normal.

Rose didn't live in the same area as most of the legacy witches. Instead, she resided in the neighborhood that had birthed America's first millionaires, those who made fortunes on slaves and foreign trades, calling themselves buccaneers instead of pirates. Vianna drove by the rows of three-story houses, with grand pillars and ornate gates, and pulled her rusted truck into a long driveway lined with solar lights and perfectly pruned shrubs that looked plastic.

Her bravado from earlier had deflated during the drive. Suddenly, confronting Rose on her own turf seemed like the stupidest plan she'd had yet. She slowed, then stopped outside the entrance to the Bartons. The property had a sprawling Victorian house with a mother-in-law residence and a pond separating the two.

She rubbed her palms against her legs, looking down at the sheet-wrapped bundle. Even Grandma Susannah was quiet. Familiars were sacred. As she sat in the truck, calming her nerves, a thought crossed her mind. The cat that Nancy mentioned in her death cycle. This was that cat. And the damned thing had been trying to break back into the house, probably to steal more loot. Ballsy little demon. The cat had to be Nancy's familiar. It made the most sense. Had Nancy been swept up in something with Rose by accident, or had she been no more a victim than Rose herself? Vianna wanted to know. She wanted to see Rose's face when she admitted the cat was Nancy's.

Reaching down, she lifted the light form that was already cold and stiffening. Vianna finally understood what happened. Why Nancy died. How the spell got out of the house. Was that why Nancy had reached out? Vianna blinked away the sting in her eyes and focused on what she could do about any of it.

On a large, wraparound porch, which acted as a barrier to the house, Rose and Josephine rocked on a wicker sofa, each with a glass of lemonade. A groundskeeper paused mid-sheer at Vianna's approach, then briskly turned and walked around the corner of the house. Josephine straightened, but Rose leaned against the armrest with a broad smile, her golden curls shining in the sunrays as though everything was right in the world. An uncomfortable itch crawled up Vianna's spine, and Shuck gave a low growl within her chest.

She looked for a canvas or some trigger for the uncomfortable scratch crawling up her skin but found none. It was paint though, and paint could go anywhere, even under the porch boards for all she knew. It didn't matter. Vianna refocused on the real problem.

Rose was still grinning, enjoying her lemonade, without a single worry in the world. She siphoned wealth, sacred knowledge, and free will from those around her, but the dead left in her wake wouldn't haunt her. She was a knock-off legacy and, yet, somehow more dangerous. If Vianna couldn't steer clear of Rose's destruction, she would be her consequence. Actions deserved consequences.

"You have no respect." Vianna spoke from the bottom of the stairs with the cat cradled in both arms.

Rose sipped her drink through a straw, then crossed her ankles beneath her floor-length summer dress. "Interesting declaration from someone who showed up unannounced."

"You've chosen not to be a part of this world, Vianna," Josephine said. "It's too late to change your mind, unless you've decided to sell the house."

Vianna walked up the steps and placed the dead animal at Rose's feet. Rose tucked a curl behind her ear, uninterested.

"I figured out how you did it, how you stole the spell. Nancy was easy pickings." Vianna rolled out the muscles in her neck, fidgeting against the tears and anger boiling just below the surface. "She knew the Roots home frontward and back. And she had no family, legacy bullshit or not, no family by any definition." Saying that aloud hurt. Vianna could have been her family.

"Nancy wanted to be a part of something and you used that," Vianna said. "You used her as your scapegoat. Her familiar was the last piece. That's how you got the spell. Nancy didn't make it out of the house, but her familiar did. He brought the torn page from the Roots grimoire to you."

"Rose." Josephine straightened. "What is she talking about?"

"Nothing. She's delusional. Nancy didn't even have a familiar." Rose turned with a smirk. "This confused solitary probably scooped up some poor pile of road kill and marched over here expecting to rile me. It won't work."

Vianna pulled the bedsheet back, exposing blood-matted fur, and the awkward twist of the tabby's stretched neck. Rose flicked her eyes toward the animal and froze. That perfect shade of rose drained from her cheeks. Her glass of lemonade shattered against the porch, along with Vianna's understanding of the situation. She took a step back. Rose shrieked and collapsed to her knees beside the lifeless cat. The familiar wasn't Nancy's. It was Rose's. *Flying goat balls.* Somehow, everything kept getting worse.

Josephine's mouth gaped open. Rose scooped the cat from the porch, pressing it to her chest. Through the screen door, a woman in a maid outfit stood wide-eyed.

"You killed him," Rose hissed.

"The cat was dead on my porch when I got home." Vianna held up her hands and noticed blood on them, then tried to rub it off on her shorts. "I didn't kill it."

She was splitting hairs, and she knew it. A witch was responsible for the actions of her familiar. As much as Vianna wanted to argue that it was Rose's fault for sending the damn thing onto her property, now was not the time. She backed down the stairs and toward her truck. Rose whipped her head, tracking Vianna's steps with narrowed focus. Rose stood, and the cat left a red smear down the center of her dress before it thudded on the porch.

Vianna stuttered out a rough exhale.

"Your delivery was received." Rose wiped her palms against each other and flexed her fingers with a cringe when it only smeared the blood. "The laws set before our birth say I have a right to replace what you have taken. Or at the least, to take what was taken from me."

Her words were rhetoric, nothing more than the regurgitation of ink to parchment she'd memorized. Her tears of moments ago were dried, and in their place, greed glistened through her focused stare. Greed for *Shuck*.

Vianna pulled open the door of her truck. "I'm not another one of your puppets, Rose. Everything that happened was your own doing." Vianna hopped inside and backed out of the driveway.

No one chased her down or tried to stop her. Grandma Clarice glared at the porch and Grandma Susannah looked out the passenger window, chin raised, avoiding Vianna. Her vision blurred as she stared at one stoplight after another and finally pulled into the driveway.

Vianna twirled the rings on her right hand as she kept her left on the steering wheel. Every witch jumped at Rose's snapped fingers, every witch but her mother and her. And it had been Shuck who kept them from becoming puppets. All familiars were not equal in power, and whatever was happening in the coven, it was clear he was powerful enough to rise above it. Would it be a constant battle, having witches try to challenge her for him? She thought of Csada and realized it wasn't just witches she had to worry about.

There was no way this didn't end in a bloody mess. The coven would come for the house, and she'd have to stand against them. How in Hades was she going to stand against an entire coven? She was screwed.

The drive home went considerably faster, and she parked the truck, jogged up the porch steps, and grabbed the groceries she'd left earlier. There was no way Rose would rally the coven fast enough to have them on their way already, but Vianna couldn't help but look over her shoulder at every shadow of movement. Once inside, the door closed, and she leaned against it, exhaling a deep breath. She was safer here than anywhere else. So much had changed in just a few days.

Back in the kitchen, Vianna set the bags onto the table. The precious boxes of cereal crunched under her grip as she slammed them onto the pantry shelves. She shoved milk into the fridge and knocked over a crusted bottle of hot sauce. She chucked the bread into the pantry.

She was on borrowed time.

If they were going to take or destroy the house, surely they'd first try to gather the supplies from the conjure room, which meant they might be stupid enough to infiltrate the house. Vianna could only hope. She knew better than anyone the horrors this house was capable of.

Stronger wards at the windows were the first step. The tabby had gotten in too easily. She now understood why Mother had shoved garlic in the windows and everywhere else. She had spelled them as part of her ward, which Vianna had torn down. She could kick herself, but this time she wasn't going with simple garlic. Instead, she'd repay their self-harm hex with one of her own.

In the conjure room, she shifted through drawers, pulling out a falcon feather, dried bundles of salvia, sage twigs, saro oil, flakes of goat's blood, and crushed male black-widow spiders. Gathering ingredients and the grimoire into the carved summoning circle didn't take long. Soon, she was on her hands and knees, drawing symbols in each curved corner. Every grimoire had a self-harm hex, but her intruders would learn that they weren't all equal.

When she was done, she moved from window to window within the house with a mortar full of crushed ingredients that she blew into the windowsills. Then she pricked her finger with an embroidery needle and smudged blood against the frame. At each downstairs window, she whispered, "For any a guest with ill intent, may my blood call forth the fears unrepentant within the depths of their souls."

With the windows guarded, Vianna found herself at the mantle above the fireplace. Her fingers drummed against the shelf holding the black-and-white photos. Black eyes from a different time stared at her as she thought about what the coven would do. If breaking in was too difficult, then what? Her lips thinned. They'd burn the house. An eye for an eye. Familiar for a familiar. Marching to the back door and onto the deck, she grabbed the tangled hose. She yanked on the mess, getting it into a usable state in case the worse happened.

A knock came from the front door, and Vianna jumped, dropping half of the coiled hose around her ankles. She tried to hop out of the mess, but a coil caught her foot, and she landed in a heap in the back doorway. She cringed when the bruise on her ribcage from fighting Charles whacked into the doorframe.

Dee walked into the kitchen in a black jumpsuit and orange cheetah print heels that would break anyone else's ankles. A tote bag dangled from her hand. "Do I wanna ask?"

"How did you get into the house?" Vianna sat up and rubbed at her elbow.

"The front door just opened." Dee sauntered over and held out a hand to help Vianna up. "Your poltergeists are very well-mannered. Is that like a training thing?"

Vianna snorted. "Polite? Poltergeist? I have those too, but the house is more of the demon flavor." Still, she'd never seen it welcome someone in so frequently, or at all. "I think he likes you." She took Dee's outstretched hand and stood.

"Of course he does. I'm fabulous." Dee raised an eyebrow. "But who is *he*?"

Vianna tried to make sense of the tangled knot the hose was in. "The Roots family familiar bonded with the house a long, long time ago."

"Ha! I figured." Dee moved to the kitchen table and set down her tote. "Only the coven mother has access to the records of familiars, but there's always rumors. That's so sick."

Vianna managed to tame the hose and joined Dee at the kitchen table. She'd unloaded teas, more coffee, flavored vodkas, candy, herb bundles, a nail kit, and the same worn leather bundle from the Jeep.

"Quite the spread." Vianna nodded at the piles on the table.

"Your supplies were dismal last time I checked." Dee looked at the pantry and the loaf of bread on the floor that hadn't quite made its mark. "Looks like you finally made a trip to the store."

Vianna moved to the counter and grabbed the bag of coffee she picked out. "I got you something." She held it out, unsure if this was how the whole gift-giving exchange went.

Dee reached for the bag with a bright orange manicure that matched her heels. She cradled the bag with both hands, then looked up at Vianna with a bright grin.

"I don't know much about coffee, but I wanted to say thanks for leaving some. I kinda drank it all. And for . . . everything else."

Dee rushed forward and crushed Vianna inside her arms. She should have figured Dee was a hugger, just like her mother.

"The cartoon dog won you over." Dee pulled back and grinned. She nodded at the table. "Martinis?"

"That might have to wait until the mob threat dies down."

"Mob?" Dee stashed a few vodka bottles in the freezer.

"Yeah, I'm guessing that's what happens when you kill Rose Barton's familiar."

Dee paused, making an *O* with her lips. "Did you? Kill it?"

"No, the house did. It's not safe to be here, Dee." She held up a hand to stop her from arguing. "I know. We had this conversation yesterday, but I've managed to make the situation even worse since then."

Dee moved to the cupboards and rummaged through them. "I'm still staying. Rose brainwashing everyone isn't something I'm just going to sit back and ignore. Especially since it involves my mom. You're the only one going up against her, so this is where I need to be. Now, where are your martini glasses? I need a drink, and then I'll help fortify the house, 'cause—" She motioned to the hose on the floor. "I'm not sure what you got going on with all that, but I think you need some help."

"It's for water." Vianna raised her hands in an *obviously* gesture. "In case they try to burn the house down. And I don't have martini glasses." She finished with the hose and came inside.

"You so need me in your life." Dee pulled down a coffee mug.

She picked up the second hose to screw onto the bathroom faucet when the back door opened and closed on its own. The girls turned and looked at each other. Vianna craned her neck to peek out the window, but no one was in the backyard. The curtains in the living room flung open, then snapped shut.

"Is that the house's way of telling you someone is here?" Dee set down the coffee mug.

"Maybe." Vianna walked into the living room. "We're still figuring things out."

The coven couldn't have gathered that fast. She wasn't ready. She pulled back the heavy curtains just far enough to get a peek. A beat-up cardboard box sat in the middle of the porch.

She shut the curtain and fiddled with the twine tied around her wrist. The coven didn't leave dirty boxes out in the open, and she couldn't imagine Charles touching anything that grimy. That left only one option. Vianna sighed. There was too much going on to add hoodoo into the mix.

27

⚬⚬⚬

War Water

Dee leaned in, pressing against Vianna's shoulder as she looked through the window at the box on the front porch. "Were you expecting a delivery?"

"No." The heavy drape slid from Vianna's fingers, and she moved to the front door. The doorknob stuck, and she groaned. "Shuck, open the door. We have to see what it is."

Dee gave a small snort from behind her, clearly more entertained by the demon's antics than Vianna was. Shuck's broom fell against her, bristles up, from the corner by the door.

"I don't remember that broom being there before," Dee said. "That's not a store-bought broom, is it?"

"No. It was a gift." She tucked the broom handle under her arm. "And Shuck seems to have grown attached to it."

The front door slowly creaked open. Peeking her head out, she looked up and down the porch. The broken light glowed, using magic instead of electricity, growing in brightness until it cast away any shadows that could be used for hiding. No one was on the porch. Just the tattered box with smudges of dirt on the sides.

Vianna and Dee approached the box together. Keeping the bristles close to her, Vianna used the broom handle to poke at the corner. Glass clanked from inside, but nothing rustled or jumped out, so she flipped open a flap. Three mason jars with a yellow-ish liquid sat inside.

"Did you find a supplier for more shitty moonshine?" Dee asked.

Vianna hunched down and used the broom to flip open each flap; the last one had a message written in marker.

War water. Protect my house.

Csada

"War water," Dee said. "That's hoodoo. What does he mean by *his* house?"

"He tried to buy it, and I said no. Hard no. And then I banished him from the house when he started chanting. What's war water?" Vianna looked up at Dee. She had her eyebrows raised, a grin tugged at her mouth, and her eyes widened in excitement.

"You're a junkie for danger," Vianna said. "Aren't you?"

"Danger?" Dee flicked a wrist. "No. Learning new things, however, I'm a full-on addict. I'm from a line of librarians—new books and spells spark-tacular." Dee waggled her fingers for a sparkly effect. "So. War water. I've come across a couple recipes, but every batch I've tried goes wonky. I end up with smelly swamp juice that grows more moss."

"*More* moss?" Vianna stood, looking around the yard for moving shadows.

"War water calls for Spanish moss, rusted nails, and stagnant water. The details beyond that get murky." She reached down and picked up a jar, turning her wrist to examine the floating debris within. "There's a penny at the bottom. It's got something scratched in it." She shook the jar and held it up.

Vianna stepped closer and looked through the bottom of the jar with her. "I see letters." She squinted her eyes. "O.B.C."

Dee squealed and lowered the jar. "Original Blood Coven. He targeted the jars for coven members."

Vianna chuckled. What else could she do? Dee was jubilant over cursing jars aimed at their incoming enemy. Hell, Vianna should be jubilant too. "What do we do with them?"

Dee looked up, tipping her chin to the sky and tapping her nails together as she thought. Or maybe she was rummaging through her vault of photographic memories. With a shake of her head, she refocused on Vianna. "We can either angle them to be knocked over when someone walks by or pour them around the property perimeter."

Vianna considered both options. "I already have wards for the doors and windows. Let's go with the property perimeter. Do we know what it does? Do we trust Csada?"

"I don't know." Dee raised a brow. "You tell me. Do we trust Csada?"

"No." Vianna answered quickly. "But I think he really does want the house, and he needs it standing for that to happen. That puts us temporarily on the same side. See anything about war water hurting the person using it?"

"Don't let it touch you. That seems to be a thing."

Vianna nodded. "Gloves."

She jogged into the house and came back out with her cleaning gloves pulled on. Dee handed over the jar as though it were radioactive. Vianna clasped it with two hands, keeping the murky sloshing liquid far away from her body, and walked across the lawn.

She called over her shoulder, "Any other details I should know about? A special chant or something?"

"Too many variations to say," Dee said. "Just string a few rhymes together. I have a theory that it's really about rhythm, and the rest is just mumbo jumbo." She waved a hand in the air as if that gave answers.

Vianna snorted. She twisted open the lid of the jar, slowly. While pouring the war water along the edge of the lawn, she stumbled around a few words. "A boundary defined by . . ." She cringed. "By rusted nails and moss, will offer something . . . something of a musted guard-boss."

"'Musted guard-boss'? What does that even mean?" Dee's heels clicked against the porch stairs and she came into the yard.

"I don't know. You said it was mumbo jumbo."

"I didn't mean it quite that literally." Dee stopped in the middle of the stone walkway, her hands on her hips. "How about distrusted. Musted isn't a real word. And boss? How about across? Ooo. Maybe cross! Cross with something distrusted."

"I can work with that." Vianna tipped the bottle to keep going, but it was empty.

Dee crossed the lawn and handed over another.

After twisting the lid, Vianna continued. "A border crossed by distrusted foe, decays the will like the rusted moss below."

"Tricky little witch. Decay the will. You're hoping it counters Rose's brainwashing." Dee smiled.

"It's a shot in the dark, but I'll take any form of help at this point."

"Then let's get to work." Dee turned toward the house. "What else we got cookin' in this place?"

Vianna poured the rest of the water and jogged up the walkway. "I've got a demon cookin'. That seems sufficient."

"Not for a coven. The Original Blood Coven." Dee picked up the box of war water and they headed into the house.

Vianna moved through the sitting room and to the linen closet for candles. She handed an armful to Dee, and they covered the surfaces of every shelf and the few tables remaining. Then they lined the hearth of the fireplace, strategically placing candles of clarity and empowerment in axil points.

The talisman on Vianna's finger turned to ice. Grandma Susannah stood in the curtains, looking out the window. "They're coming." Her voice was different, a rough whisper that Vianna had never heard from her.

She went to the window and stood next to Grandma as Dee set out more unlit candles. Coldness seeped from the ring like frost stretching through her veins. There was no snide comment or anti-quated insult as Grandma pressed the tip of her nose to the glass. Thin streaks of frost branched out across the windowpane, tracing the shape of the lone tree in the front yard.

The frost blurred into a fog that settled over the grass and twined around the tree. A crowd of ghosts moved through the ankle-deep white fog, approaching the lawn. The figures weren't as defined as the living, but they didn't glide like the dead, and they weren't caught in their death loops. They moved together, approaching the house, and wore tunics instead of shirts, britches instead of pants, bonnets instead of ponytails. The group had armed themselves with pitchforks and Bibles.

In the blink of an eye, the mob hovered around the edge of the deck. Another blink, and they were dragging an elderly woman down the steps by her hair. Her bonnet slipped from her head, fluttering through the fog and onto the grass. Heavy boots crushed it, smearing mud against the white. The woman kicked, scratched, and spit as they threw her against the tree trunk.

Binding her hands behind her back, they then looped the noose around her neck. A large black dog lunged from the house, teeth bared and claws extended, but the shadows moved faster. A man, dressed in all black with countless pockets and straps, stepped from the group. He raised a pistol with a bulge in the barrel, and a blast exploded; a cloud of purple smoke plumed into the air. The dog dropped to the ground.

"Nooo!" roared the old woman. "I will curse every one of your lines." She surged away from the tree, but the rope yanked her back, thrusting her body up into the air, legs kicking out.

The dog twitched, letting out a broken whimper. Pain sliced across Vianna's collarbone, the brand exploding into pain that made her gasp. She pressed her hand against the frosted window. The dog lay motionless. The old woman's body went limp.

Vianna's hand slid down the window, wiping away the frost, and with it the vision of the past. Grandma Susannah's death loop. When Shuck had lost the dog as a host, he'd jumped to the house.

"You must be stronger than I was." Grandma didn't turn away from the window. "They can't have him. He chose us."

The corners of Vianna's eyes stung. She wasn't stronger than Grandma, but it didn't matter. She wouldn't hand over Shuck. A soft touch landed on her shoulder, and she looked back to see Dee frowning.

"You okay?"

Vianna let out a long sigh. "No, but it doesn't matter. I'm not backing down. This ends tonight."

"Are you sure they'll gather that quickly?" Dee asked.

"Rose wants this too much. She won't wait."

Dee inhaled with a gasp, and Vianna swiveled back to the window. A row of black hoods walked down the street, approaching the property perimeter and the edge of the lawn. The witches in the center of the group held torches. Just a few more feet and they'd cross the line of war water.

Shadows danced over the dozens of cloaks. From inside the house, Vianna could hear the flames snapping; she could smell burned cedar, anise, and pepper from war spells and protection oils that seeped in through the cracked window. Vianna stood beside

Dee, swallowing down the lump in her throat. It was one thing to suspect a mob of brainwashed killer witches were coming to burn down your house—it felt a whole lot different when they actually arrived.

A hooded witch led the rest, charging past the water. She stopped and screamed, dropping to her knees as her voice turned to a high wail before cutting into abrupt silence. A robed figure ran toward the silenced witch, who had her hands around her own throat. The second one froze with her first step across the invisible line of war water. Snakes slithered from beneath her robe and coiled around her legs, torso, and arms, cinching tighter and tighter.

"Their intent," Dee whispered. "The war water sends their intent back on them. The first turned mute, the second is being suffocated by snakes."

Vianna watched with dread. A third witch approached, this one more hesitant, looking in the grass for some sort of clue. When she crossed the line, she dropped like the first two. Her arm yanked above her head like she was a puppet, then snapped the wrong way at the elbow. Her scream shattered the silence. Vianna gasped, covering her mouth. The witch's leg pulled taut from beneath her robes, then snapped similarly at the knee.

"War water is officially on my avoid list," Dee whispered.

A fourth witch stepped forward, but she didn't cross the line. Instead, she tipped her torch to the grass where the three before her had passed. They'd used the first three witches to find the invisible barrier. Fire caught and a wall of flame roared to life across the lawn. Vianna straightened, ready to run for the hose, but the fire didn't spread. It reached higher, deepening in hues of mustard yellow and green that matched the murky water when it was in the jar.

Two witches flung a deep purple robe into the air, its edges rippling out like wings before gracefully falling into the flames. The robes didn't shrivel, but extended out, smothering the flames beneath it. A cloaked figure walked over the robe, fire stretching out on both sides of her. Elegant fingers pulled the hood back to reveal Rose's face. A smile rested on her dainty lips.

"Vie-annn-na." Her voice rang out in a sing-song cheer across the yard.

Witches piled through the opening in the fire behind Rose.

Vianna took a deep breath. This was happening. She would stand against the Original Blood Coven. The point of no return had come and gone some time ago. The only option left was forward.

She opened the front door but stayed within the house. "Rose, what a surprise." She tried to match Rose's smirk, but her lips thinned instead.

"We're here to enact coven law." Josephine removed her hood and stepped beside Rose. "You're accused of killing the familiar of a witch within the Original Blood Coven. Law requires the removal of your familiar in return. This is your only warning. Clear out the conjure room and exit the house."

Torches raised at Josephine's words. Silence strangled every cricket, frog, and rustling leaf. Her neighbors had closed their windows and pulled their drapes firmly shut. Dee stepped beside Vianna, and at her presence, a torch wavered, then lowered. There was no doubting who the shaking hand belonged to: Mistress Layton. Vianna's chest tightened. Dee squeezed her arm. Ghost-beetles trailed between and around their feet, crawling up the doorframe. Grandma Clarice appeared by the window.

"You will not bow to them." Grandma Susannah's voice was a growl at her other side. "Shut the door, little Vianna. We will remind the coven who the Roots witches are."

Vianna put her hand on Dee's elbow, tugging her backward, and the front door slammed shut with a thundering crack. The comment of clearing out the conjure room confirmed how badly they wanted the loot within, and that worked to her advantage because it meant burning down the house was a back-up plan. That bought Vianna time.

"They're splitting up and flanking the house." Dee walked the length of the room, following the movement outside the windows.

The lights flickered, then went out, and darkness blanketed the room. They'd cut the electricity. Orange-and-yellow flames danced in a parade outside the windows as several dozen witches formed a circle around the house.

The deep rumble that connected her to Shuck reverberated in a steady pulse. Raising a hand in the air, Vianna snapped her fingers. Every candle awoke with flame, and the warm glow that bathed the room gave her a glimmer of comfort. They were entering her territory now, her nightmare, her house of horrors, and she was ready for them.

28

Times Up

A sea of lit candles flickered throughout the house. Vianna and Dee stood in the middle of the sitting room, listening for the coven's movements. A click came from the side gate of the house.

"They're in the backyard." Vianna jogged through the kitchen and yanked open the back door.

A circle of hoods was in the far corner of the yard, hands clasped together and chanting. Two figures strolled from the side of the house, trampling through the freshly planted bed of moon flower seeds. Their hoods slipped away, and matching blond ponytails bopped in unison.

A wave of croaks washed over the garden, and Vianna looked around in confusion. The dark soil of the garden beds shifted and turned as the bumpy black backs of toads pushed up through the ground. They sprung free from the soil, hopping over rocks and grass. Dozens turned into hundreds of toads within seconds. Moonlight caught the bright orange of their stomachs as they stumbled and flopped, climbing over one another in a chaotic mess.

"You were told to clear the conjure room. We're here to make sure you actually listen, since it's not really your strong suit." One of the Ramsey twins spoke over the croaking. They moved forward, ending at the edge of the paved walkway.

Vianna's eyes flicked to the huddle of witches in the corner. They were the real threat. The Ramsey twins were a distraction.

"Why are you still standing there?" the twin on the left snarled. "Go clear out your shit, solitary."

"Let her stay," the other twin said. "We've got some games we could play."

Vianna couldn't find it in her to worry over the Barbie twins, her attention consumed by the incoming toads. Trampled grass and vines turned ash gray, then wilted and shriveled in on themselves. Poison. They were going to weaken Shuck by poisoning the house. If they made him weak enough, they thought they might be able to command him to do their bidding. Make him take on a new host? Bond with a new witch? Maybe both. *Not happening.* He wouldn't let harm come to her, and now it was her turn to return the favor.

Toads launched onto the porch from all sides, then jumped against the siding of the house with a series of smacks, piling on top of one another. A loud crack splintered through the air, as if the house were being twisted into pieces. The same ash gray as the grass spread over the side of the house, and Shuck let out a high-pitched whine in Vianna's ear canals. A throbbing ache pulsed through her, and her knees went weak.

With a defiant growl, she ran from the porch and into the house, colliding with Dee. "Oof. We need the moonshine. Hurry!" Vianna yanked open a drawer, making junk clatter to the floor as she searched for the tea light candles.

"We're here waiting, little goat whore," a twin called from across the yard, the god-awful symphony of croaks playing in the background.

With a small candle in her hand, Vianna plucked a jar from the pile in Dee's arms, then rushed to the porch. The gutter fell away from the house, and she ducked as it came down in a sweeping arc, barely missing her head. Piles of toads crowded along the bottom of the house and stretched into pillars along the edges. The ash gray that covered the entire back of the house was hard to make out against the charcoal-gray siding, but it was there, wrapping its poison around to the sides.

The three huddled witches behind the twins tightened closer together, their chanting increasing in speed as the frame around the kitchen window splintered. Vianna gripped the jar of amber liquid, reached back, then chucked it at their feet. Glass shattered against the pavers, and moonshine splattered their cloaks. Jars clanked as Dee ran to Vianna's side with an armful of ammo.

"They're poisoning the house with the toads," Vianna shouted.

She threw a candle into the broken glass, then raised her hand, feeling for the weakening connection to Shuck. His growl was soft, barely a ripple of vibration that came from her collarbone. With her breath held, she snapped her fingers. The candle lit.

Fire rolled out over the moonshine in the garden, flames licked up the bottoms of the cloaks of the huddled witches, and screams filled the air. More witches flooded through the side gate, swatting at the fire that engulfed their sisters.

A tiny fire ball bounced off Vianna's leg, and she hopped back with a yelp. The burning chunk of fabric at her feet turned a bright yellow that smelled of gelsemium and peppercorn. Vianna froze. And not by choice. A numbness burned through her nose and down her throat, spreading down through her chest. She dropped to her knees, mouth open.

"Vie," Dee shouted.

A cold breeze rustled her hair, and Vianna gasped, unable to respond. Feeling came back in jabbing pinpricks throughout her chest. Grandma Susannah snatched at the yellow flame and charged at the twins. With a click of her tongue, she threw their own hex back at them. The twins squealed and ran, but the hex bag pegged one of them in the back, and she froze, just like Vianna. The other twin ran through the side gate.

"Vie!" Dee jumped in front of Vianna to shield her and launched another jar of moonshine, then she turned to help her up. "Holy goddess. Did that flamy-blob-thing just levitate into the air and fling itself at the twins?"

Vianna nodded as she gasped in lungfuls of air. "I'll explain later."

Mobility slid back through her limbs and chest. She pushed herself up and stiffly jogged to the coiled hose by the outside spigot. With one hand, she aimed the nozzle at the siding, and with the other she twisted the handle. Water splashed against the poison with no effect.

"It's not strong enough to break through," Vianna yelled, looking around for Dee, who wasn't on the deck anymore.

Vianna stuck her thumb over the spout to create a stronger stream of pressure, but it only bounced off the film covering the house. Dee burst out from the back door, the worn leather roll of potions in her hands, and she raced to the spigot, dropping to her knees. "I just need a minute." She unscrewed the hose. "Maybe two."

The group of witches began chanting again, and the last of the fire was being swatted. Vianna palmed a tea light candle and tossed it into the shattered glass by the witches. Feeling for the faint connection to Shuck, she tugged on their shared thread of magic and snapped her fingers. More witches burst into flames.

"Hurry, Dee."

Dee tapped a small glass bottle against her palm and blue crystals trickled out. She added a red powder from a test tube bottle, then spit in her palm before dumping the mixture into the hose and reconnecting it. "Try now."

Water gushed through the hose and splashed against the fence. Vianna jumped in surprise, then whipped the nozzle at the house. Caribbean-blue liquid soaked the siding and frogs leaped away in waves, slapping into witches who were no longer on fire and linking arms as they pressed forward. The toxin broke apart and washed down in gray clumps. The connection in her chest hummed stronger. She let out a breath of relief.

The kitchen window slid open, then slammed shut. Vianna lurched toward Dee, and they both hunched down with their arms over their heads as glass shattered. A thump hit the porch. Vianna turned to see a witch collapsed to her knees, her cloak fallen and piled around her. Streams of blood ran down her neck and chest as glass shards stuck out from her skin like knives. The witch roared a scream at the sky. Shuck had thrown glass-daggers.

"You okay?" Vianna asked Dee.

"Yeah. You?"

More screams joined in, and Vianna looked across the yard to see several witches with protruding glass shards.

"Fine. Come on," Vianna said, grabbing the box of moonshine, and she and Dee ran into the house.

The patio door slammed shut behind them. More screaming carried from the backyard, and Vianna looked out the window in the door. Grandma Susannah stood on the deck with a firm stance and hands on her hips, ready for more.

Scraping noises came from the ceiling, making Vianna and Dee look up, then at each other.

"Can they get in upstairs?" Dee asked.

Vianna nodded. They'd probably climbed in through the same tree Vianna had climbed out forever ago. "Come on, Grandma Susannah has the back door."

They rushed into the living room, and Vianna glanced at the windows. The wall of fire had died down to a smoldering campfire that stretched across the lawn. Huddles of chanting witches gathered in the lawn, enforcing the witches within, but none approached the house—yet. They had a ward to break through if they wanted to get through the front door.

Vianna turned and took the stairs two at a time. When they reached the top, a thud came from behind the closed door of her childhood bedroom. Locking the door from the outside, like her mother did to her as a child, crossed her mind. If she could, she'd send the entire room into a dark hell where it belonged. Her hand hesitated at the knob, and she pulled back.

"Everything okay?" Dee asked from over her shoulder.

"Yeah, I just hate this room." That was an understatement.

The talisman flared like a fire on her finger, and despite the pain, it gave her comfort. She wasn't alone. With a quick jerk, she twisted the knob, and the door swung open. Tiphonie was on her hands and knees, drawing a circle in deosil—clockwise—movements. The ghost of Uncle Jasper traced his own circle a few feet away.

With the furniture stripped from the room, nothing remained but the simple white lace curtain that blew outward from the broken windowsill. Large wooden chunks hung from the gaping hole where the window should be. They'd propped the glass panes against the wall. That was one way to break through a ward.

Chalk, herbs, and envelopes scattered around Tiphonie in an unorganized mess. The still-intact window behind her cast a green-yellow glow over the room as she pressed chalk to the floorboards. It snapped in her hand and she gave a high-pitched whine before belatedly noticing their entrance.

"What are *you* doing here?" Tiphonie focused on Dee, her face pinched in a scowl.

Dee rolled her eyes. "Pine branches, mugwort, fern, and hyssop tied with a blue ribbon for fluid change." Dee pointed to a smudging on the wall. "That symbol is for the demon Agares who grants noble titles and teaches languages. A retribution releasing. Can't say we didn't see it coming."

Grandma Clarice glided into the room, hovering close to the half-drawn circle Tiphonie sat in the middle of. Ghost-beetles trailed behind Clarice, then circled around the chalk drawing.

Tiphonie crinkled her too-small nose at Dee. "Boys aren't allowed in coven business."

Ghost-beetles circled from the outside of the chalk and then within. Several reached Tiphonie, scattering up her knees and then up her body. She swatted at one from the side of her face.

"I was feeling sorry for you," Dee said. "But you're a dick." She turned to Vianna. "I'll go watch the front of the house."

Dee headed for the door, and Grandma Clarice stepped beside Vianna, her stance calm and arms relaxed at her sides. She tilted her head and watched with interest as Tiphonie twitched at the beetles she couldn't see racing over her exposed skin. Was Vianna supposed to tackle Tiphonie to make her stop?

A loud thunk made Vianna twirl and race toward the stairs. Dee was sprawled on the hallway rug, motionless. Josephine stood over top of her, a knife gripped in her hand. Vianna dove to the ground, looking for a stab wound, but she couldn't find any blood.

"She's only knocked out," Josephine said. "It's the only warning I'll give tonight."

Vianna checked for a pulse and let out a heavy breath when she found one.

"Come on." Josephine nudged Vianna with the tip of her boot. "Back in the room. Move it."

Vianna flinched away, then stood, shuffling toward the bedroom with Josephine close behind. Tiphonie had stopped drawing the circle, stopped working the spell. Her shoulders hunched inward, and she whimpered. Her head shot up at their entrance, and she jumped up, racing to her mother.

"Mom," she whined. She swatted beetles from her face, and her robes slipped from her arms. Swollen bite marks covered her skin. "There's something on me. They did something."

"Hush." Josephine didn't look away from Vianna as she spoke to her daughter. "There is nothing on you. Finish your duty." She jabbed a finger at the unfinished circle.

"Don't do this, Josephine," Vianna said, trying to feel for the connection to Shuck, the reverberations in her sternum that'd become like a second heartbeat. "Rose has you under her control. Her familiar was snooping in the house, stealing from us. This isn't an eye for an eye. This is just Rose, wanting power for herself. Don't do this."

"You're just like your mother, muttering the same lies. You don't deserve a familiar so powerful." Josephine pointed the tip of her blade at Vianna.

Deserve had nothing to do with it. He had chosen her just as much as she'd chosen him. "He won't accept her, and you know he's too strong for you to force him. Poison won't change that."

"We'll see. Demons love power, and Rose has more than your worthless waste of good blood." Josephine looked down her hooked nose. "Did you think you were strong enough to take on an entire coven? To stop us?"

Clarice stood by the door, chin raised, watching. Uncle Jasper was in the last part of his death cycle. His limp body sprawled on the floor behind them, twitching in his own pool of blood. Ghost-beetles rushed from the hem of Clarice's black dress, and tiny legs scattered across Jasper's blood, leaving crimson tracks that led to Tiphonie kneeling in her half-made circle. More beetles swarmed. Her head twitched to the side, and she grimaced. Her hand shook as she tried to finish drawing the circle but stopped to swat at more beetles.

Stray beetles scattered toward Josephine and up the folds of her robe. She flicked her wrist as a beetle darted into her sleeve. "I'm not afraid of you or this cursed house." She jerked her shoulder as another beetle made its way up. "Take me to the conjure room."

"Mom," Tiph whimpered. "They're all over me." Her fingers scratched beneath her cloak, on her legs, and across her stomach.

Josephine glanced at her daughter. "Finish the spell. I'll handle Vianna." She motioned toward the door with the knife and glared at Vianna. "Move."

With Clarice distracting Tiphonie, maybe it would give Vianna enough time to convince Josephine to call off the coven. If she could prove what Rose had been doing, how she'd been manipulating all of them, maybe they could come to some sort of truce.

Vianna gave a pointed stare to Clarice, then to Dee lying in the hallway. Clarice nodded once, and Vianna had to go with it, hoping they were on the same page. Dee was one of theirs to protect, and she was trusting Clarice to do that.

With a knife jabbed against her spine, Vianna walked down the hall with her chest arched out. The chanting from the front yard grew louder as she walked down the stairs. Loud creaks from the floorboard protested against every step they took. "Rose isn't what you think. She's manipulating the entire coven."

A loud crack thundered from the back of the house and Vianna jumped, worrying half of the house had just blown off, but Josephine pulled her back by her arm. Shuck's grumble was weak in her chest. Josephine pressed the blade harder into Vianna's spine, making her arch her back even more.

"Rose did nothing to you," Josephine hissed. "She supported the coven's offer to buy your house at a fair price. You should have accepted it and run back to whatever hole you crawled out of. I gave you every chance."

They reached the bottom of the stairs, and the talisman on her finger flared with heat. Heels clicked from across the sitting room, and Vianna turned to see Rose approaching from the back door with a pinched look of dismay as she took off her gloves.

Vianna looked behind Rose to the shattered doorframe in the kitchen. They'd broken through the wards. Vianna tried again to feel for Shuck, but his returning growl felt like an echo submerged in water. Distant. She had no idea what to do next.

29

৩৩

Mother

Rose's footsteps were slow, precise; their tempo controlled the surrounding air, shifting time into slow motion. They were the movements of a witch confident that she'd already won. Black coven robes billowed around her, as did her blonde curls, and a serene smile sat on her pink heart-shaped lips. The cloaked witches in the backyard gathered themselves into more huddles, just like in the front yard. Their chanting would give their coven mother—or maybe even Rose—more power, funneling magic from their own familiars. Rose's attention flicked to Vianna for only a moment, then to Josephine.

"You were right, Rose," Josephine rushed out in a stream of words. "The Roots are an infection within the coven, spreading lies and discord. Vianna is just like her mother."

For the first time, that didn't feel like an insult.

"Yes," Rose sighed. "She's turned into quite the disappointment."

Grandma Susannah appeared at Vianna's side. "A legacy disappointment is better than a first-generation disappointment."

Sudden, searing pain made Vianna gasp. Her collarbone felt as though a branding iron pressed against her flesh, directly on top of her legacy ink, and she stumbled, almost dropping to her knees. She hissed through clenched teeth, flinging her hand out and catching herself on the banister. Shuck gave a careening howl that rattled in her skull. The circle. Tiphonie. She'd completed it.

Shiny black beetles spilled across the upstairs hallway then down the stairs. Vianna focused on breathing in and out. They could fix this. Clarice was coming. Grandma Susannah was here. Vianna wasn't alone.

Rose twirled toward her. "I can feel him." Her chest heaved as she sucked in deep breaths of air as though it were magic.

Vianna held back a whimper. She could barely feel Shuck, his grumbles growing more distant as he was pulled from her. But she could feel Rose, like a sour aftertaste seeping into her tongue. Rose strode toward Vianna, and the swarm of beetles scattered, scampering over each other and diving in opposite directions to give Rose space.

Vianna's stomach dropped. The ghost-beetles didn't see Rose as an enemy. Vianna heaved in shallow breaths, struggling to fill her lungs even halfway. The room spun. Clarice stumbled from the bedroom, her hand clutched to her chest as she let out a silent scream. The ring on Vianna's finger didn't warm in warning. Rose had breached more than the house ward. She'd breached the Roots mantle.

This couldn't happen—losing the house, losing Shuck, leaving Dee and Nancy's ghost to Rose—Vianna shook her head. No. This wasn't over. It couldn't be. She couldn't have lost to Rose. As panic sent every nerve in her body into overdrive, one thought settled her.

What would her mother do?

Vianna inched backward, away from Rose, her back bumping into the wall between the front door and the stairs. Her only chance of putting up a fight was in the conjure room, and Rose blocked the path.

"You can feel him? The familiar? Rose! Bless the goddess, it worked! Don't taint your name or the coven's reputation by dealing with this runaway embarrassment. The coven has no need for the Roots name." Josephine used the back of her hand to push a loose strand of red hair from her forehead.

"Taint my name?" Rose straightened with a deep sigh. "My name wasn't written in your precious coven logs before I married. There's nothing to taint." She rolled her eyes. "Legacy witches and their precious lineages."

Vianna slid from being pressed against the wall to inching over the bottom stair, slowly. If they kept talking, maybe she could slip behind Rose and into the conjure room.

Josephine took a step back, her brow furrowed at Rose. "Allowing you to take on a legacy name was an honor. You should be grateful."

"*Grateful?*" Rose pivoted toward Josephine, closing the space between them.

Vianna stepped off the bottom stair and slipped around the banister as Rose backed the coven mother against the door. Vianna kept her focus on the women as she inched further away. Rose's hands wrapped around Josephine's fingers and the hilt of the blade she held. "I've tolerated this long enough. I'm done with you."

Rose lurched forward, turning the blade toward Josephine's gut with a shove. The coven mother gasped, scrambling against Rose and tangling in her robes. Vianna froze, staring, unbelieving of what she saw. She looked behind her, through the kitchen to the broken back door, but the witches were focused on their chants and each other. The curtains were closed at the front. No one saw Rose for who she was, no one but Vianna.

"Dishonorable," Josephine croaked, her arms going limp as resistance slid from her body.

Rose leaned closer, their noses almost touching, and jerked her arm upward. "Honor only matters to those born with titles."

The blade clattered against the floor, and Rose stepped away. Josephine's eyelids drooped, giving a few flutters before her body slumped to the floor.

"Mom!" Tiphonie screamed from the top of the stairwell.

Grandma Susannah appeared in front of Vianna and shoved her backward with both hands. "The conjure room! Go!"

Tiphonie turned and ran toward the bedroom, then slammed the door shut. Another hard shove from Grandma almost sent Vianna to the ground.

Grandma jabbed a wrinkled finger toward the peony hallway. "Move!"

Rearing around, Grandma jabbed the same finger into Rose's shoulder. The smug expression of triumph on Rose's face crumpled into confusion. Vianna scrambled down the hall and into the conjure room. Her thoughts were a tangled mess. Hexes, spells, curses—none of it would stop Rose.

The drawer holding the grimoire flew open, and she yanked the book onto the desk, letting it fall open to the page titled Unmasking the Crone. A thud against the wall from the other room rattled the shelf of poisoned oils. She didn't have much time.

Grandma snarled from the hallway, "First-generation trash."

Shuck's growl shook every board of the house's frame. *Faster, Vianna. Do something.*

Her finger shook as it scrolled down the list of ingredients on the page. As she realized what the spell was for, her stomach dropped. But there was no other choice. She needed help. She had to summon her mother. The spell would pull Mother from the grave and into the circle. After that, Vianna had no idea what would happen to her mother's ghost.

She went into autopilot. Pulling herbs, candles, bones, dried blood, and the horned skull, she piled everything into the center of the room.

"Your little parlor tricks won't work with me." Rose was in the hallway.

Vianna quickly drew symbols within the carved circle. Closing her eyes, she felt for the faint murmur that was Shuck and wrapped her focus around him, hoping there was enough of a connection left, then snapped her fingers.

A trickling burn spread over her fingers and down her arm. Crackles popped, and black sparkles drifted toward the ground, dissipating into the scent of patchouli and mugwort. Grandma Susannah appeared with Vianna in the circle.

Rose strolled through the doorway and into the room, stopping short at the carved arching line, and placed a hand on her hip. "Did you make a circle of protection? How adorable."

Rose began a slow stroll around the circle, each step of her heeled boot clicking like a clock. She stopped at the northern point of the circle and hummed a slow roll of pleasure to herself. "It was quite the gift you gave me—killing my familiar. I had no idea Josephine could force a familiar to bond as retribution."

Vianna hadn't either. "Thou shall not kill another witch's familiar" was not a casual law, and now she understood why. She focused on smashing herbs, blood flakes, oils, and moth wings in the mortar while doing her best not to track Rose's every step. Grandma hovered over Vianna's shoulder, watching each step of the spell.

"And I had no idea a familiar could feel like this." Rose flicked her hand into the air, palm up, and bottles from the corner shelves rose in the air. She twirled her wrist, and the bottles crashed to the floor.

"He's resisting me," Rose pouted. "Clinging to you. I can't quite grasp all of his power."

"He'll never accept you. He's bound to a true legacy line." Vianna paused and looked up. "You have no idea what that means. It's not an entitled label of privilege. Legacies are generations of the persecuted, the hunted—and they finally stopped running. They made a stand and fought back." Her own words caught in her throat as she realized she hadn't understood what a legacy was, either. The Roots women were many things, hard, stubborn, and often cruel; but they also endured, they survived.

Rose gave a fake chuckle. "Yes, poor legacy witches, hunted down, scorned. Nevermind all the killing and behind-the-scenes political maneuvering." She leaned down, close to Vianna, but unable to step or reach beyond the protective circle carved in the floor. "That grimoire will be a nice addition as well."

"I'm going to squeeze her last breath from that worthless mouth." Grandma's voice was unnervingly calm, and she didn't move from hovering over Vianna's shoulder.

Vianna didn't respond to either of them, focusing on the spell.

"I have no choice but to kill you." Rose sighed. "With you gone, he'll have no one but me. Legacy blood or not, it won't matter. Labels are meaningless."

Whether Vianna had chosen this life or not, legacy blood did matter. Rose was wrong. Generations of witches before her meant she was never alone, coven-bound or not. Legacy witches passed down knowledge over time, amassing a power strong enough to create change in everything around them.

"I have things to attend to. I don't have the time, nor interest, to wait you out." She stood and her hungry eyes looked around the treasure-filled shelves and drawers. "I'll have to fashion something to break through your little circle of protection. But if you step out on your own, maybe we can come to some sort of an agreement."

Right, that made sense. Vianna would swipe away her only barrier of protection to let in someone who just vowed to kill her. *Maybe not.*

"Finish this, Vianna." Grandma tapped her shoulder, pointing to the doorway. Ghosts of Roots witches past crammed into the hallway. The little girl with ringlets, the one with red frizzy hair, the one in a flapper dress, and the one in a nightgown with dirt-stained fingers and toes. "They can't help until the mantle is complete. Summon Angeline."

The only way Vianna stood a chance of holding on to Shuck was if she fully connected to her heritage. Every Roots witch had passed the mantle down, all but one. And that was Vianna's fault. She had to make it right.

She added the last of the ingredients to the mortar: flakes of stag's blood, shaved horse's hoof, acacia berries, and copal with cypress oil. Drawers opened and slammed as Rose gathered her own ingredients behind her.

With the tip of an athame, Vianna broke the skin on her index finger, and a red liquid bead formed. She dipped her finger into the paste, then drew the symbol on the skull of the horned bull for Holda, the wife of Wotan, leader of the hunt. Wotan would lead, but Holda controlled where he went. The Wild Hunt would be Mother's passage to the circle.

Rose paced the circle, drawing symbols in chalk at each directional axis as she chanted. She'd stopped trying to distract Vianna with chatter and focused on a spell instead. Time was running out.

With the grimoire in both hands, Vianna faced south on her knees. "Let me tarry awhile and see thy great tower. I call for the rider who flows from thy dark bower. Let the rider lead the crow along the fluid path of my foe. Deliver her to me, as he travels deep below."

Shadows shifted within the room and over Vianna. Invisible

cobwebs stretched around her. The candle fumes turned an inky black that spread through the air and smelled of damp decay. Horse hooves galloped somewhere in the distance, and the echo grew louder as the air grew heavy with the promise of a brewing storm. Rose paused, looking along the four corners of the room. She mumbled something indiscernible to herself.

Tendrils of shadows rolled across the floor, drawn to the circle that had summoned them, and looped around Vianna's ankles. The tendrils hardened into long, pale fingers that clamped hard around her bones as a figure pulled itself up through the floorboards as though rising from the grave.

"Rotten child." The voice scratched across the walls, making the wallpaper peel up at the edges.

"Hello, Mother," Vianna said.

30

A Gift

Angeline Roots rose to her feet with the grace of someone half her age. She pinched a piece of lint off the shoulder of her black satin pajama set. Her ghost had matured, letting go of what her body looked like in the ground and appearing as she did the night she died. Every strand of hair was in its proper place on the short bob she'd worn for all of Vianna's life. With an annoyed huff, her eyes flicked to Vianna.

"You dare call on me?" Each word was a crisp jab. "After what you did." Her upper lip twitched, deepening the wrinkles.

"Angeline," Rose gasped.

Vianna twirled toward Rose, then back to Mother. She'd been summoned. She wasn't just a roaming ghost, and that meant others could see her.

Angeline eyed Rose. "Did you bring me a gift to apologize, child?"

"Gift?" Vianna asked.

"The chance to finish the job." Angeline's voice dropped an octave as she stepped toward Rose. "The little wannabe legacy. I marked you. Your days were numbered. Your death was going to be painful and slow. You deserve nothing less."

Rose stepped away, back straight and chin raised. A slow smile pulled on her lips. "But you died, like the old hag that you are. Alone in your bed, killed by your own weak body. And now I, a first-generation witch, will take everything that matters to you. Your entire line is going to end. Tonight."

Angeline's nostrils flared as she turned toward Vianna. "What have you done?"

"Angeline." Grandma Susannah stepped between Angeline and Vianna. "There's no time for this. Pass on the mantle."

Mother let out a gurgled growl. Rose had dropped to her knees, chanting in inaudible whispers as she drew on the floor with chalk. Vianna's heart pounded against her chest. Once Rose broke the circle, the spell that called the hunt would shatter, and Vianna's chance to save Shuck would be lost.

"Mother," Vianna barked. Angeline snapped her head toward her. "She'll take Shuck and everything in this house. I'm your only option." Just as she was Vianna's. They glared at each other, neither wanting anything to do with the other.

Without warning, Angeline charged. Her jagged nails dug into Vianna's shoulder, scratching at her skin. Vianna yelled and pulled away, but her mother's hand clamped tighter and she leaned her face in close. Vianna bit back a scream, and, instead, steadied her stance and stared into her mother's black eyes.

A bolt of searing fire slashed through her body. A wind rushed through the room and whipped Vianna's hair up and around as her connection to every witch before her snapped into focus. She could feel each one, the pain of their deaths, the things unfinished, the knowledge gained—all of it flooded through her. The last jumbled ball of existence was her mother; the betrayal of Vianna leaving, the urgency to fix the coven, the pressure to measure up, and the possessive loyalty to Shuck. A crack thundered in Vianna's skull as Rose's connection to the mantle snapped. With the mantle complete, bound by generations of blood, Rose had no way in. Glass shattered, and Vianna spun around at the same time as Angeline and Susannah.

Peppercorn fumes puffed in her face, sending Vianna into a fit of sneezes. Rose was on her hands and knees with shards of rainbow glass around her and a pointed piece in her hand. Vianna lunged to stop her, but it was too late. Rose scratched a line through the circle, breaking both the spell of protection and the summoning of Mother. Angeline howled and reached out before being yanked through the floorboards and into a black nothingness. Vianna froze as she stared at the empty space. Mother was gone.

Grandma Susannah shoved Vianna, knocking her to her knees with a painful thud. Rose stood behind her with a knife held out in a jab that she swung toward Vianna. She scrambled backward until her back hit the shelves as Rose followed, slashing at the air.

There was nowhere else to go.

Something poked Vianna in the back, and she reached behind her, fumbling over the ridges of the bull skull. Sinking her fingers into the eye sockets and tightening her grip, she swung the skull in front of her, connecting with Rose's hand, and the blade clattered to the ground. Vianna dove for it.

Rose dove alongside her, and they collided in a mess of thrown elbows and knees, but Vianna came up with the blade. She surged forward at Rose, pinning her to the ground with a knee in her gut and the blade at her throat.

Her chest heaved as she leaned over Rose. "You're done."

Rose arched her neck away from the blade.

Her reign of terror had to end. This was done. But would Rose ever stop? Was killing her the only way to stop the chaos she caused or the deaths she orchestrated? Deaths like Nancy. Vianna's breathing was labored as she stared at the woman. How many had died because of her? How many more would she kill once she found another way in, another loophole or lonely witch to prey on? Killing Rose would save countless lives. The world would be better.

"Finish it." Grandma Susannah stood over them.

Vianna's grip loosened. No. She wasn't one of them, not like that. Anger swelled like a storm. Anger over the past, the coven, Charles, Rose, and Mother. She shoved Rose away and sat in a slump. Vianna knew she was a legacy, a Roots witch, but she would be that on her own terms. No killing.

Rose jolted up and blew another cloud of peppercorn dust, and Vianna threw her hands up, coughing, as Rose lunged with a shard of glass in her fist. Grandma Susannah bulldozed into Rose, and she flew into the desk. Ghost-witches and ghost-beetles filled the room from the hallway, converging around Grandma Susannah and Rose.

This time, the beetles swarmed Rose instead of avoiding her, and she shrieked as pincers latched on to every inch of exposed skin. Grandma Susannah grabbed Rose by the hair and dragged her across the room, then out into the hallway.

Vianna jumped to her feet and jogged after her. "Grandma, enough!"

She didn't acknowledge Vianna, and the ghosts of her ancestors stood between her and Rose. Vianna walked through them and after Grandma Susannah, just as she yanked Rose into the bathroom. The door slammed shut. The house rumbled in Vianna's chest, and, with the mantle completed, she could feel his intent, instead of just hearing his rumbles. He was satisfied with Grandma Susannah's actions. They would enact coven law, taking from Rose all she had taken from others, including her life.

Glass broke, and Rose bellowed a terrified scream.

"Stop it!" Vianna ran to the bathroom door and pounded on it. "Grandma!"

Rose screamed, and Vianna hit the door again, her ring smacking against an indented ridge. The talisman. It was how they had the power to touch. Vianna ripped the ring off her finger, and everything in the bathroom went quiet. She held her breath, listening through the door.

Grandma Susannah walked through the door and Vianna, a deep scowl on her face. She wouldn't look at Vianna, didn't say a word, and vanished. Rose began to sob, and Vianna let out a breath of relief. She let her head rest against the door. Shuck grumbled in her chest.

Vianna flicked at the wall. "Things are changing around here. No more killing."

Vianna grabbed a chair from the kitchen table and wedged it under the bathroom doorknob, securing Rose with Nancy for the time being. A sob from behind her made Vianna spin around, moving toward the stairs. Was Dee okay? She stopped at the sight of Josephine's body on the floor. Tiphonie hovered beside her covered in red welts and staring at a wall.

"Tiph?" Vianna approached. "I'm so sorry."

Tiphonie looked up, blinking in confusion. Her face was a swollen strawberry. She looked back at the wall and rocked herself. Dee first, then she would handle Josephine's body. Vianna raced up the stairs. Dee was already sitting up, head in her hands. Vianna slid to her knees beside her.

Dee groaned. "What'd I miss?"

"Too much. I was worried. Come on." She held out a hand to help Dee up.

The broom that Tuck had gifted Vianna fell across the hallway at her feet.

"That's gonna be a thing, isn't it? That broom just appearing on its own." Dee was still rubbing the back of her head.

With a frown, Vianna picked it up. Brooms were meant to sweep out the unwanted, to clean up. Rose's connection to Shuck and the mantle was broken, but the circle Tiphonie had worked in still needed to be cleaned out. She went into the bedroom and swept the chalk from the floor, using widdershins—counter-clockwise—motions. Shuck gave a low grumble of contentment that shook the wall.

"Did it work?" Dee walked over. "Is Shuck with Rose? Where is Rose?"

Vianna swept the last of the circle away. "Yeah. For a hot minute, Rose was bonded with Shuck. The Roots mantle broke the spell though. It wasn't completed before—the mantle was still open. It's closed now."

Dee rolled out her neck, flinching. "I really did miss a lot. And Rose?"

"She'll live."

"The coven?"

Vianna set the broom bristle-up in the corner and dusted off her hands. "The coven is still out there, and someone needs to tell them Rose killed their leader."

"Oh." Dee nodded, letting that soak in, then linked her arm with Vianna's. "We better get on that."

Her muscles were sluggish as they headed downstairs. Tiphonie was still on the floor, but she'd moved on from staring at the wall and was now sobbing. Dee knelt beside her as Vianna opened the front door. Witches linked hand in hand, chanting to help a battle that had already ended, but no one had told them.

She cleared her throat. "It's over." *No more death. No more blood. Not tonight.* "Your coven mother is dead. This is done."

Tiphonie walked out on the porch, standing beside Vianna. "Rose killed her." A sob shook her chest. "I saw it with my own eyes."

The witches went still. Their torch-lit faces now drawn and confused. Mistress Layton stepped from the crowd. Dee brushed past Vianna and down the porch steps to embrace her mother.

"This isn't over," one of the Ramsey twins snarled. Her robe was burned along the sleeve.

She was probably right. There would always be more problems, blood, and death when it came to witches, but Vianna was too tired to worry about the distant future now. Leaving Tiph to deal with the coven, Vianna went back inside the house.

She walked through the living room where the ghosts of her ancestors lingered. The one with the red-fringed flapper dress leaned against the mantel, the one in a pleated black dress stood by the console table, and the little girl played jacks on the floor in front of the fireplace.

She went into the kitchen and got her cell from the counter where it was charging. For a second time in less than a week, she called the cops.

By the time the flashing red-and-blue lights arrived, the pointed cloaks had slipped into the shadows and disappeared, but not before they shot a few threatening glares in her direction. That was fine. She wasn't her mother, and she wouldn't be disposing of dead bodies or enacting coven law against Rose.

Investigators crawled over her property while she sat on the porch swing, listening to the creaking wood and resting her head against the backrest. She'd already shown the cops Josephine's body and the locked bathroom where Rose was detained. Tiphonie had remained with her mother's body. They'd taken Vianna's statement, and now she waited for them to finish stuff on their end.

The beginnings of a sunrise colored the horizon in a soft pink and orange. She could almost shut out the chaos sputtering around her. A hand jostled her shoulder, and her head jerked up. Had she nodded off? When was the last time she'd slept?

She blinked the blurriness from her vision and recognized intelligent brown eyes and a scowl. She smiled. "Grayson, are you always on duty?"

He huffed. "Do you always call about dead bodies?"

"Nah." She shrugged. "Busy week."

He didn't look amused, but he also wasn't looking at her with the pity eyes anymore. That was an improvement.

"The rest of the statements are handled," Grayson said. "Even your roommate, Sandeen. We're just about wrapped up."

Roommate? Vianna tilted her head. That . . . that could work.

"Wanna tell me what really happened?" He leaned against the railing, watching her every move. His eyes lingered on the scab she'd forgotten about on her lip and the bruises decorating her arms. "Off the record."

She sat up and tucked her feet beneath her, sitting cross-legged. "Rose Barton killed Josephine Parker. I watched it with my own eyes. Tiphonie Parker saw it too. That really is what happened."

"Any idea why?"

"Between you and me, I think it might have something to do with witch business. I don't know, though." Vianna gave a tight-lipped grin. "I try not to get tangled up in that kind of stuff."

"Where is she?" a voice came from the front yard that made her stomach roll. Charles marched up the walkway, followed by several suits. "I brought the family lawyers. You'll have to get through them before you lay a hand on my mother."

Grayson pushed off the pillar and crossed to the top stair of the porch. He folded his arms over his chest and looked down at Charles. "That's not how this works. Her lawyer can be with her, but your mother is being booked downtown."

Charles's neck and cheeks turned a shade of deep scarlet. He spoke through clenched teeth. "Booked for what? You can't honestly take her word." He flung a hand in Vianna's direction. "She's a disgruntled ex who's trying to slander the family name."

Arguing with his delusional lies was a waste of her time. Her head flopped back onto the swing, and she lifted her middle finger at him. He charged the stairs, but Grayson sent him stumbling back with one hand to the center of Charles's polo shirt.

"Now, I know you didn't just charge at a police officer," Grayson said. "Or at a victim whose house you've been caught at before. Someone of your status wouldn't be that . . . challenged."

Charles barked at some lackey to stay by his mother's side.

A gurney with a covered body rolled out the front door. Vianna had never cared for the coven mother, but she hadn't wished her dead. They would release the body to Tiphonie, and she'd go through all the steps to set her mother's soul at peace, as Vianna had with her own mother. Minus the whole binding-her-soul-to-the-grave part. Must be nice not to worry about being haunted by the dead.

With a worker on each side of the gurney, they got it down the stairs. Tiphonie stood on the top stair, watching, and a soft sob made her chest bob every few seconds. Dee stepped onto the porch and pushed a steaming mug into Tiph's hands. Lavender and chamomile wafted in the air.

Dee's focus was still on the open door to the house. "I know you didn't just track mud on those priceless antique rugs." She stomped into the house, but her voice still carried. "I don't care what type of investigator you are. Where are your little booties they wear on TV?" A long pause was followed by, "I saw that look."

Rose was next. They'd cuffed her hands behind her back, and she'd lost her robes at some point, her blonde curls tangled. She wore a diamond-patterned dress, and her arms and chest were covered in red welts. Her focus darted from side to side. "They're everywhere."

Her body jerked away from physical touch. Officers on each side carried her down the stairs. Charles and his team of suits fluttered after.

"She'll likely never see the inside of a court." Grayson stood by the railing. "But the psych ward is better than your doorstep."

"The *psychiatric* ward?" Vianna sat up in the swing.

Grayson nodded. "Danvers. That's where we take criminals who are scratching at their own skin and yelling about ghosts attacking them."

She nodded. Of course. Clearly, seeing ghosts was crazy. He nodded and turned to join a group of blue uniforms. She pushed up from the swing with a groan. Everything hurt. She went into the house where Dee was standing with her arms crossed over her chest and shooting eye daggers at the investigator who was snapping pictures.

"Hey." Dee nodded at Vianna.

"I hear I have a new roommate." Vianna stood beside her, staring at the worker.

"I noticed there was an extra room upstairs." Dee looked over, nibbling on her lower lip. "If you wanted a roommate, ya know, I'd be interested."

Vianna frowned. "After everything that just happened, you want to live here?"

"Are you kidding me?" Dee twirled on Vianna, all but dancing with excitement. "You're the closest to a coven I've ever come."

Vianna's chest tightened. She took a deep breath and hugged her. "Me too."

31

Ghostbusters

A week later, sweat dripped down Vianna's spine as she carried the bazillionth shoe box into the house. "How is it possible to have so many shoes?"

"How is it possible to only have two pairs?" Dee asked from the tangle of cords that hung from the mounted television that Shuck had only minimally grumbled about.

Vianna plopped the tower of boxes on the stairs and joined Dee in the living room. "Are you sure the TV is gonna be ready tonight?"

Dee gasped and pressed a hand to her chest. "You doubt me? I'm offended. Of course it will be ready."

Vianna shook her head with a grin. She picked up the patchwork quilts that'd been used to keep the TV safe during transport, folding them before stacking them in a pile on the oversized couch that Dee had moved in. Vianna was mildly in love with the couch. It was a creamy tan with crazy print pillows, had lounging foot rests on both sides, and best of all, it felt like being consumed by a cloud when she sat down.

"Yes. Movie marathon tonight. I'm thinking *Ghostbusters*, girl version." Dee looked under the TV before plugging in another cord. "It's on theme for an idea I have brewing."

Vianna frowned. "That sounds dangerous. Your movie time just became loaded with ulterior motives."

"My motives are always spectacular, ulterior or not." Dee used a Velcro zip tie to bind the wires together, then stuck it all on the back of the TV. "Have you heard from Csada yet? Cause you know he's gonna want payment for his war water."

"Not yet. Charles's lawyer keeps calling though. Wants a statement to help with their appeal to release Rose from Danvers." Vianna rolled her eyes.

"That whole family is delusional. They should lock up Charles with his mother." Dee plugged the power cord into the wall.

"No argument there." Vianna plopped onto the couch from heaven.

"What about the sexy cop?" Dee stood and turned with a hand on her hip. "Didn't you guys meet up for coffee or something?" She flicked her eyebrows.

"Not coffee. Just settling a debt. I owed him some cash for hitting his truck. Paid him the cash, and we parted ways. That's it." The roll of cash she'd found in the conjure room had helped settle that debt and left her enough to last for a few months, enough time to figure something out for a job. She had plenty of supplies in the house, making her less desperate for a craft-store discount, and she was toying with the idea of an herb shop in Salem.

She shifted on the couch, and something rolled against her leg. She looked down, then jumped from the couch. In the middle of a cushion sat a pile of squirming, rotting grossness. Nancy's hand. Vianna turned away and covered her mouth with the back of her palm.

Dee looked over from the TV and frowned. "Why do you look like you're about to hurl?" She peered around Vianna's shoulder. "What in Freya's cock is that? And why is it on my couch? Seriously?"

Vianna jogged toward the hallway closet for a towel that she brought over. Dee stood over the couch, staring with her hands on her hips. Her expression was more angered than grossed out.

"It's Nancy's." Vianna laid the towel over her hand. "I've been looking for it, actually. So I can banish her ghost. She's trapped in the powder room." Vianna nodded her head in the bathroom's direction.

"And your demon decided to finally deliver. On my couch." Dee twirled in a small circle, hands on her hips. "Don't think I don't see the message. And don't think I haven't noticed that everything teal is missing from my boxes. That is NOT a coincidence. You're not gonna like the payback. You've been warned."

Vianna gently wrapped the towel around Nancy's hand and took it to the bathroom, setting it in the sink.

Dee followed and leaned in the doorway. "Since things go missing in this place so often, maybe we should handle the whole banishing thing now. Plus, the whole water turning on whenever it wants is mildly creepy."

"You noticed that, huh?"

Dee snorted. "Yeah."

"You sure you want to live here? A decaying dead body part just appeared, and I can't guarantee it won't happen again." She hoped it wouldn't. She had every intention of changing the way things were done when it came to Roots witches, but it was going to take some time before the past settled down.

"Well, I'm not super into dead body parts, but I don't think you are either. One thing at a time. Let's start with curing the bathroom of its oddities." Dee nodded toward the hand.

"You are either completely amazing because you can handle all of this, or completely deranged."

Dee nodded in agreement. "Probably both."

After gathering up supplies from the conjure room, they stood outside the bathroom door.

"So she's stuck in her death cycle?" Dee asked. She shifted the bundles of dried herbs, candles, and bottles in her arms.

Vianna nodded.

Dee nodded toward the door. "Right in there?"

Vianna nodded again.

"And we're not going in because . . . "

Vianna closed her eyes. "I knew her. She was my best friend before—." She sighed. "Before I ran."

"Keep going," Dee said.

"And she called me. A few months ago. But I ignored her call." It didn't feel any better to say it out loud. It all hurt. "I think she was being pressured by Rose and needed someone, or something, but I bailed. A whole childhood spent together, and I couldn't be bothered to answer a stupid phone call. I never even tried to call her back." She chewed on the inside of her cheek. "I was too busy hiding." Too scared of Salem, of Mother, of this house, of the ghosts. She opened her eyes and stared at the door. She couldn't face the judgment that might be on Dee's face.

A warm hand gripped her arm. "Vie, no one is perfect. One call shouldn't have that much pressure. One phone call from someone you hadn't spoken to or seen in . . ."

Vianna wiped an errant tear. "Ten years." She shrugged. "Still."

"Ten years is a long-ass time. Nancy was probably in so deep by the time she called, it didn't matter. And even if she wasn't, you can't put her choices on yourself, no matter how many childhood memories you have. At the end of the day, Nancy chose. You can't take on the consequences of her choices, phone call or no." Dee nudged shoulders with her. "Besides, you're making your choice now. You choosing to stay, to free her ghost. You're not a bad person. I have a radar for that kind of thing, and you don't trigger it."

Vianna shrugged. "Maybe I'm not intentionally bad, but I'm a mess."

Dee grinned. "We all are. Come on, let's help your friend."

Vianna walked into the bathroom with Dee right behind her. She set the pestle and mortar on the sink, and Dee lined up supplies in a straight, organized line. The banishment spell in the grimoire would work, with a few tweaks to direct the spell at a ghost instead of a living person. Dee drew a circle on the small space of tiles with ash chalk. Vianna ground measured ingredients into the mortar, and Dee lit incense and spread it with a wren feather for a safe voyage.

Dee hopped up onto the toilet seat, feather still in hand. "I'll watch from here. That circle is tiny, and smudging it or stepping out of it will mess it all up."

Vianna nodded. Using the paste in the mortar, she drew a symbol on the tiles, then set the towel-wrapped hand over top. Maggots stuck to her fingers, and she sucked in her lips to keep from gagging. It seemed disrespectful to gag.

Glancing at the grimoire pages was just to calm her nerves; she knew the words. She gripped an athame from the pile of supplies and pulled the blade across her forearm. A thin red line appeared, and she watched as blood dripped down her arm, splattering against the white tiles of the bathroom floor. Smearing her finger across the cut on her arm, she knelt down and drew symbols in the axil points for north and south. Nancy's reflection flickered in the mirror, unblinking and lips pursed.

Vianna swallowed down the lump in her throat, lifting her chin to look her friend in the eye as she spoke. Splotches of blood flashed in and out: on the counters, in the sink, and across the walls. "By the blood that came before me, the life that feeds the land beneath me, and the birthright bonded to strengthen me, you are banished from this house." Nancy's screams echoed against the walls before turning to sobs. Vianna bent to the hand and unwrapped the towel, drawing an *X* with a circle around it in blood. "I banish you, Nancy Williams, from your death place and from this house."

A wind swirled in the windowless bathroom, and Vianna stood. She wiped the tear from her cheek. The mirror was empty. Her friend was free. She took another deep breath. There was no undoing what had happened. She could only push forward and hope for the best.

Dee stepped down from the toilet and wrapped Vianna in a hug. "It's not your fault. Come on. Let's get this movie party started."

Vianna wrapped her arms around Dee and squeezed. After a long moment, she stepped away and nodded. "I could go for a movie. Popcorn, right?"

"And martinis, obviously." Dee smiled.

Vianna nodded with a shaky laugh.

"You handle all this, and I'll finish up the TV." Dee gave her another squeeze and left for the living room.

After Vianna put everything away in the conjure room, she headed into the kitchen for popcorn. Dee was already there, mixing drinks.

"I have an idea I wanted to talk to you about." Dee took a sip from a martini glass then set it down, adding drops of something from a dropper bottle.

"Uh oh." Vianna unwrapped a popcorn bag and put it in the microwave. She turned to Dee with her arms crossed over her chest.

Grandma Susannah appeared at Dee's side, her brow arched as she watched Dee with the martinis. Grandma had revealed a curiosity toward potions during the last week and had taken to following Dee around, asking her questions that Dee couldn't hear.

Dee waved a manicured hand at Vianna. Her nails were purple with tiny ghosts, and Vianna suspected she'd themed-out for the *Ghostbusters* movie marathon.

"None of that folding your arms and closing off before you even hear my idea." Dee took another sip and nodded with satisfaction before handing a glass to Vianna. "I want you to have an open mind."

Vianna bit back a grin as she took the offered glass. "Spit it out."

"Paranormal investigators! Hold on." Dee raised a hand. "Don't say anything. I just want you to think about it. You've got an ability no one else has, and we just solved a massive mystery with the whole brainwash-all-of-Salem plans Rose had. It would be perfect for us. Obviously, you'll need my help with social media and PR. And you bring the whole seeing-ghosts aspect. So we'll go fifty-fifty."

"No wa—" Vianna stopped at Dee's raised brow and tilted head.

"I said no answer yet. Just think about it. We'd be like the real-life ghostbusters. And the coven pardoned you of any wrongdoing, so we could totally take on witch clients, cop clients, hoodoo clients. You've got all the connections, Vie."

The microwave dinged, and Vianna laughed, pulling out the popcorn and dumping it into an old wooden bowl. "Let's get our priorities straight. First, we need to get you settled in. Maybe organize the kitchen, so you have a martini station."

"Oh, I'll need an entire wall of shelves in the pantry for potions, too." Dee carried the drinks into the living room.

Vianna followed with the popcorn and a happy grin. "Obviously."

April 2023
Cover art by Evelyne Paniez, www.secretdartiste.be

Author's Note

Dear Reader,

Another book about Salem witches. I know, trust me, I know. But I couldn't not.

Although story-telling is a consuming hobby for me, I have dabbled in genealogy for over fifteen years. I'm compelled by my ancestors; the lives they lived and the blood I'm honored to share with them makes me feel a little less insignificant in a giant world.

So it should come as no surprise when I tell you that there was a real flesh and blood Susannah Roots who was, indeed, accused of being a witch during the infamous trials that shook Salem, Massachusetts. And, yes, you guessed it, she's my ancestor.

Legacy Witches is not about the real Susannah Roots. The real Susannah Roots was a widow who owned a farm and had bad blood with her neighbors. Court records show that the Roots shamed their neighbors by accusing them of thievery years before the trials.

When the accusations were at their peak, the neighbors took advantage and accused Susannah Roots of being a witch. She wasn't hung on her property, but shipped off to Boston and imprisoned with countless other elderly. She died a couple months after her release and her property and valuables were awarded to the state.

Legacy Witches is not the real story of Susannah, just like it's not a realistic view of Salem or its inhabitants. It is merely the story that formed in my head when I looked at the names that rippled down my family tree from Susannah Roots. Each of those names spoke to me, and so now, they speak to Vianna.

Thank you for reading this story and I hope you are as excited as I am for book two.

Sincerely,
Cass Kay

Acknowledgements

So this is the part where I mention all the people I'm wildly grateful to for supporting me, right? Okay. *rubs hands together* I've got those. Let's do this.

How far back do I go? Do I mention the high school creative writing teacher who told me I had a passion for learning and my writing was fantastic? Because of her, I indulged my interest in quirky things and it's developed into a collection of encyclopedias that inspires and fortifies all my stories. I had a college professor who told me I could be a writer. I held onto his words as I went through the process of rejections and hard knocks. Teachers have the power to influence and change a person's path, and I'm grateful for the ones who've touched mine.

I'm massively grateful for my family and their patience with the countless hours and days I'm holed away in the 'writing dungeon' to meet some self-imposed deadline, all in pursuit of chasing my dreams. My husband is my pillar, insisting that my art is a priority and I'm grateful that he believes that dreams and passions are the important stuff because I often forget that. My two boys are so patient with their mother, who always has her computer in her lap working on some chapter or another of some book. They're some of my favorite brainstorming buddies and remind to live more outside of my books.

Writing a book is hard. Have I mentioned that? There's so many cogs that make it all function, and it takes persistence and edits. Holy poopsycle, so much editing. I would have never survived the journey without my writing group. Those nine women pick me up when I crash, laugh at my absurd characters, help me fight my inner demons, and share wisdom from all walks of life. They are my writer family and understand a special part of my soul. I love you, ladies.

Immy and Owen, my super fast and efficient proofers, you are amazing. Thank you for dropping everything to accommodate the small slot of time in which I needed a quick read. Your catches and thoughts made this story better. Thank you.

And last, but never least, is my writing soulmate, Poppy Minnix. Imagine if you had a person who cared about your family, cared about your garden, cared about your crazy monster puppy, and shared the same passion for writing so you could talk for *hours on end every day* about that passion? Yeah. That's her. The magic she has to unlock my brain when stuck on a plot hole or the ability to love my characters—quite possibly more than I do—is irreplaceable. To writing all the books, together and individually, Poppy dear. All the books.

About the Author

Cass started her writing career as a journalist in college who moonlighted as an actress. Now at home with her husband, two sons, and two dogs, she's discovered that fiction novel writing combines her love of the written word with her love of creating compelling characters.

When not staring at a computer screen, she can be found planting bulbs in the garden, with her nose in a book, or watching Smallville with her family.

authorcasskay@gmail.com
www.instagram.com/casskaywrites
www.twitter.com/casskaywrites